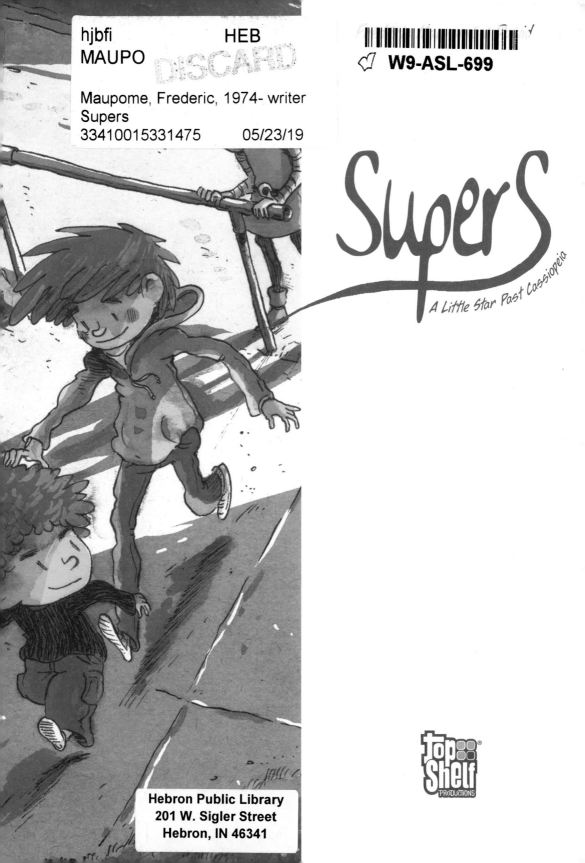

SuperS

A Little Star Past Cassiopeia

Top Shelf PRODUCTIONS

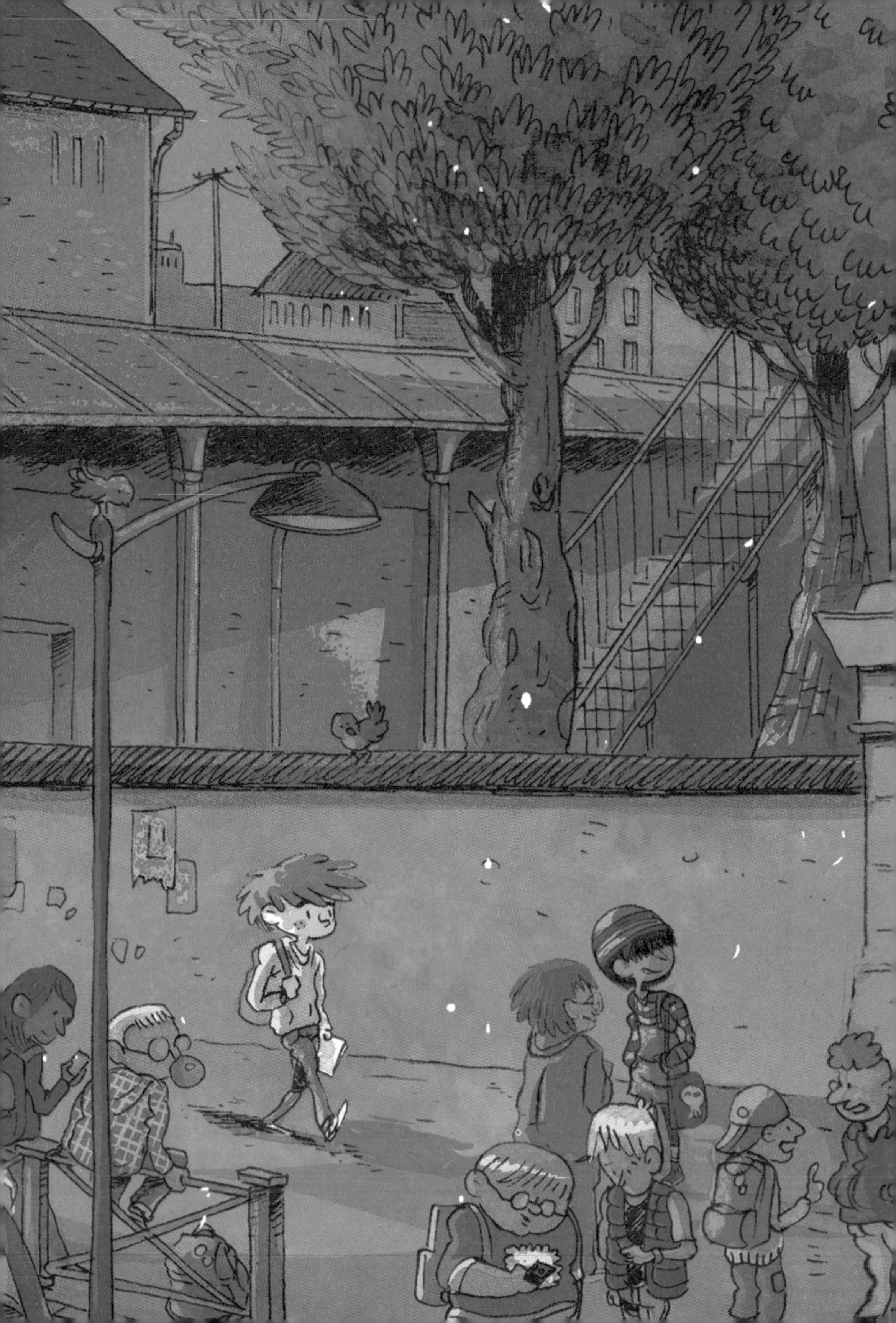

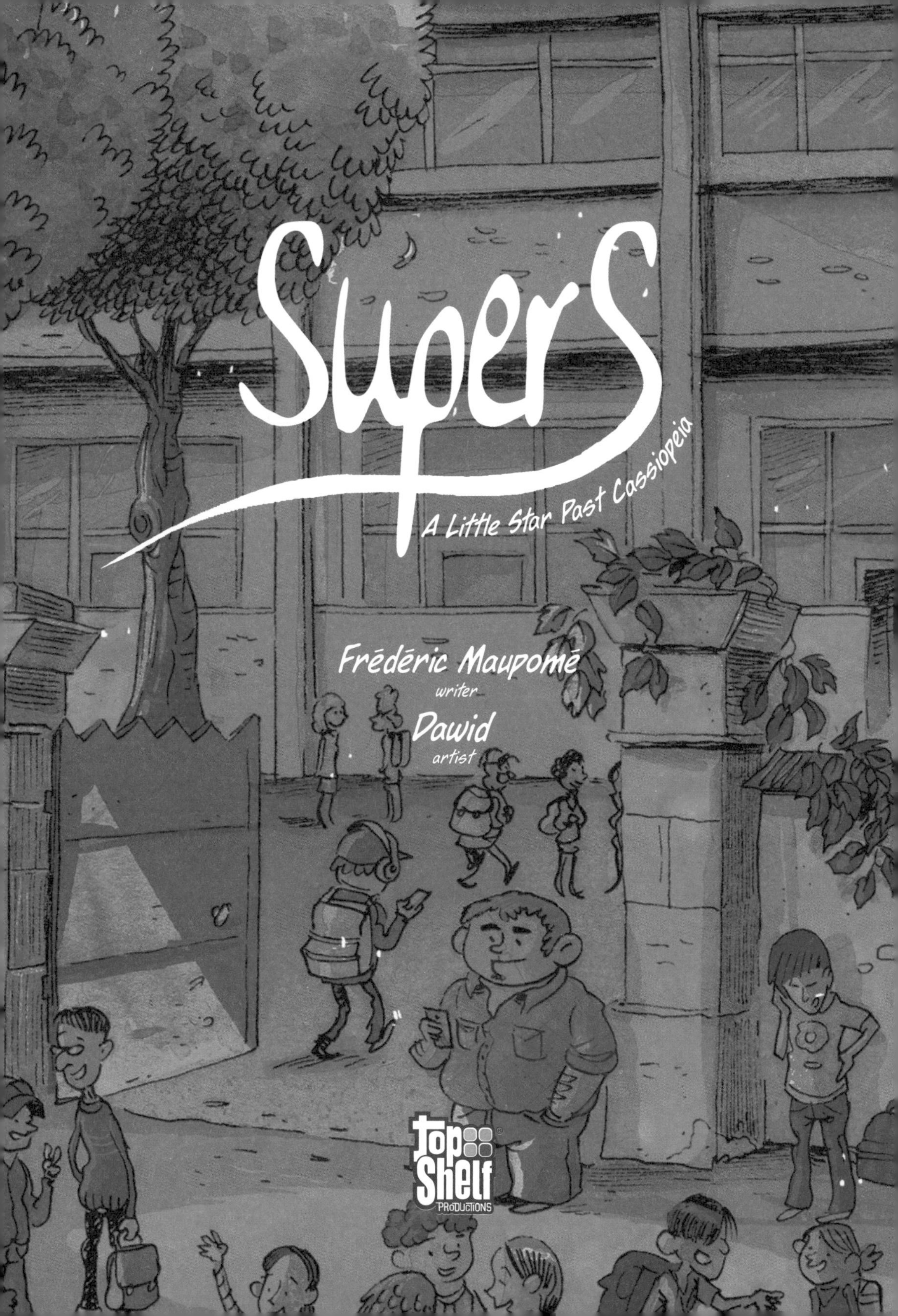

Supers

A Little Star Past Cassiopeia

Frédéric Maupomé
writer
Dawid
artist

Top Shelf Productions

Published by Top Shelf Productions, PO Box 1282, Marietta, GA 30061-1282, USA.
Top Shelf Productions is an imprint of IDW Publishing, a division of Idea and Design
Works, LLC. Offices: 2765 Truxtun Road, San Diego, CA 92106. Top Shelf Productions ®,
the Top Shelf logo, Idea and Design Works ®, and the IDW logo are registered
trademarks of Idea and Design Works, LLC. All Rights Reserved. With the exception
of small excerpts of artwork used for review purposes, none of the contents of
this publication may be reprinted without the permission of IDW Publishing. IDW
Publishing does not read or accept unsolicited submissions of ideas, stories or artwork.

Editor-in-Chief: Chris Staros.

Lettering & Design by Gilberto Lazcano.

Printed in Korea.

ISBN: 978-1-60309-439-9   22 21 20 19 18   5 4 3 2 1

Visit our online catalog at topshelfcomix.com.

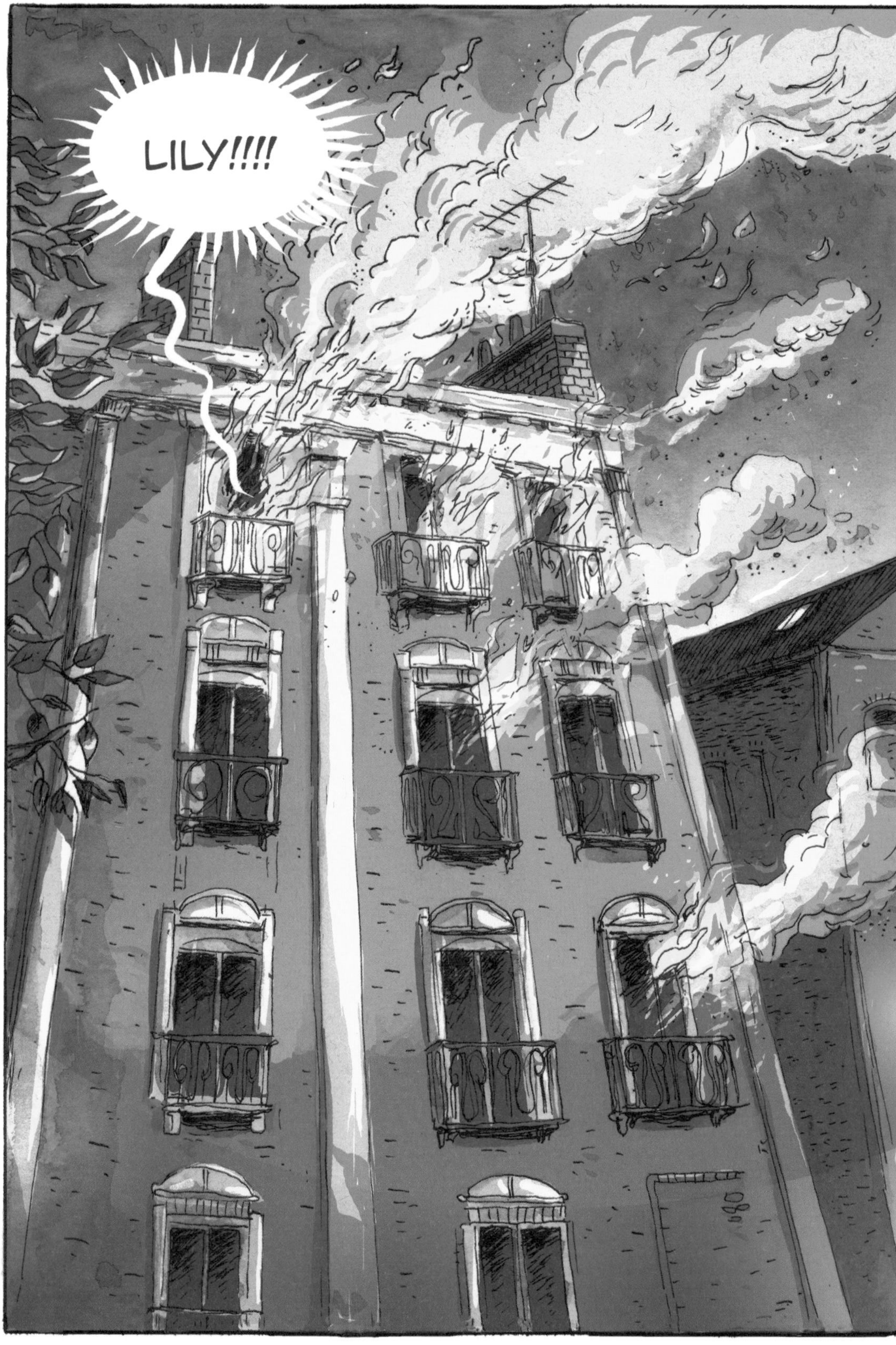
LILY!!!!

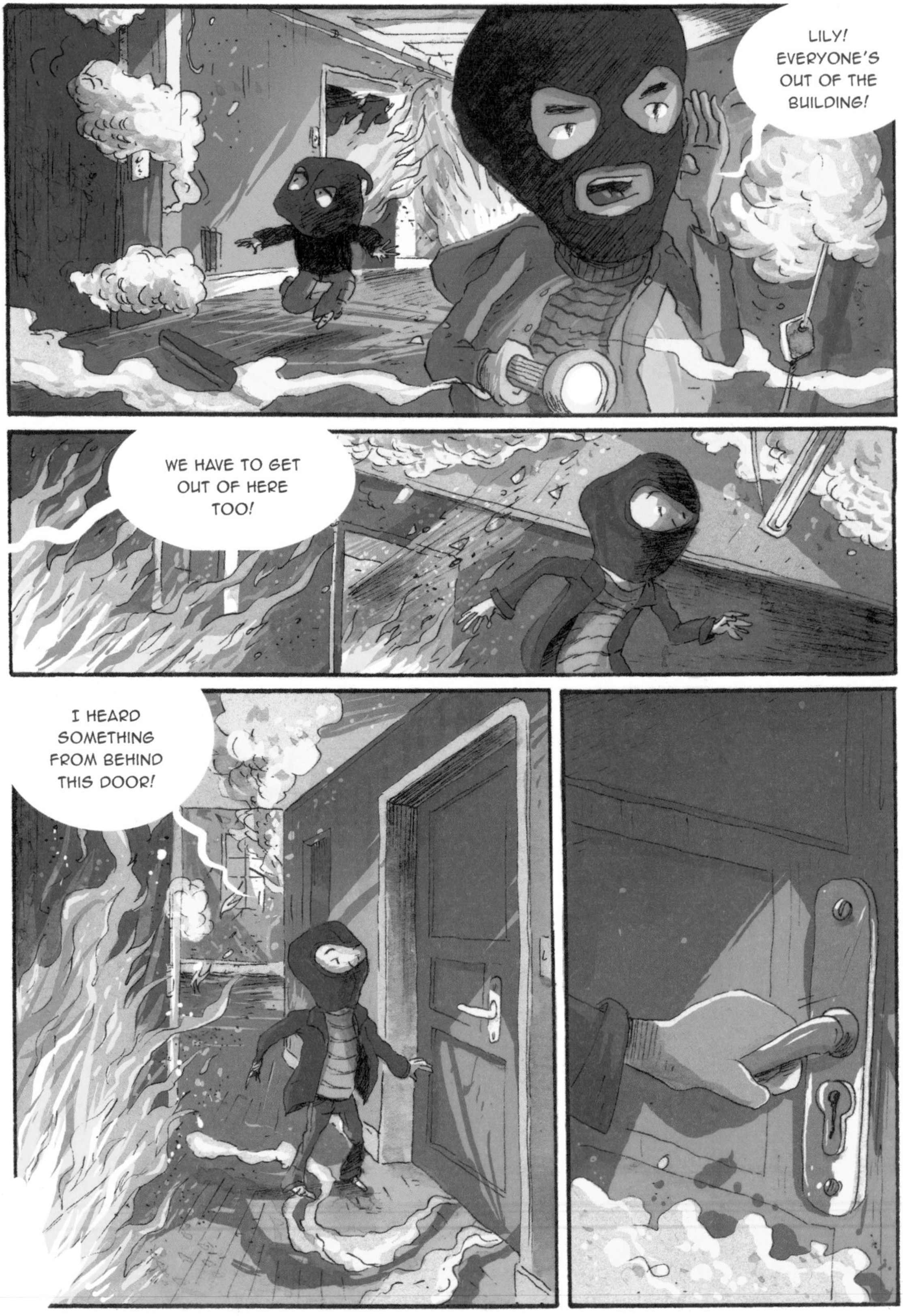
LILY! EVERYONE'S OUT OF THE BUILDING!
WE HAVE TO GET OUT OF HERE TOO!
I HEARD SOMETHING FROM BEHIND THIS DOOR!

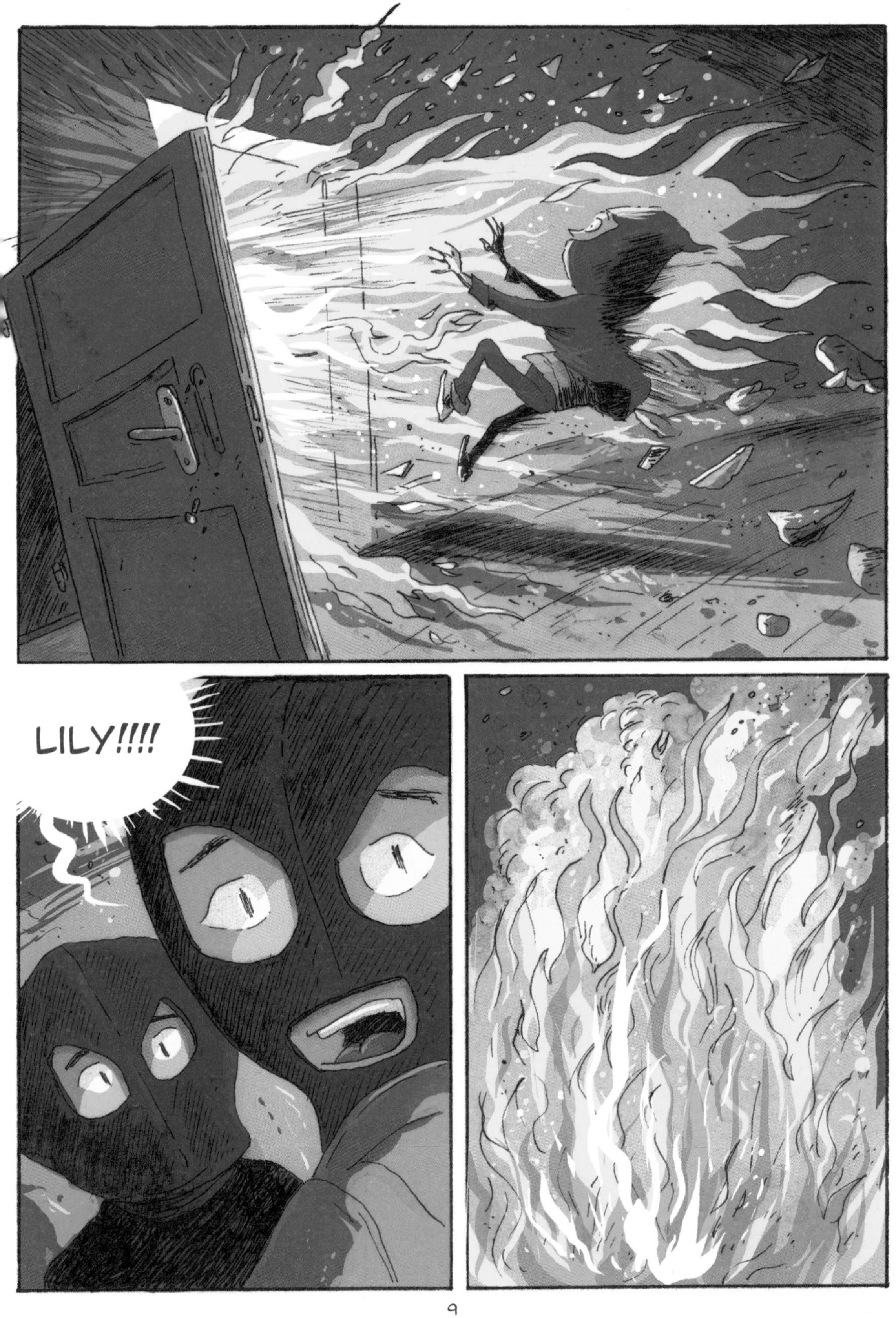
LILY!!!!

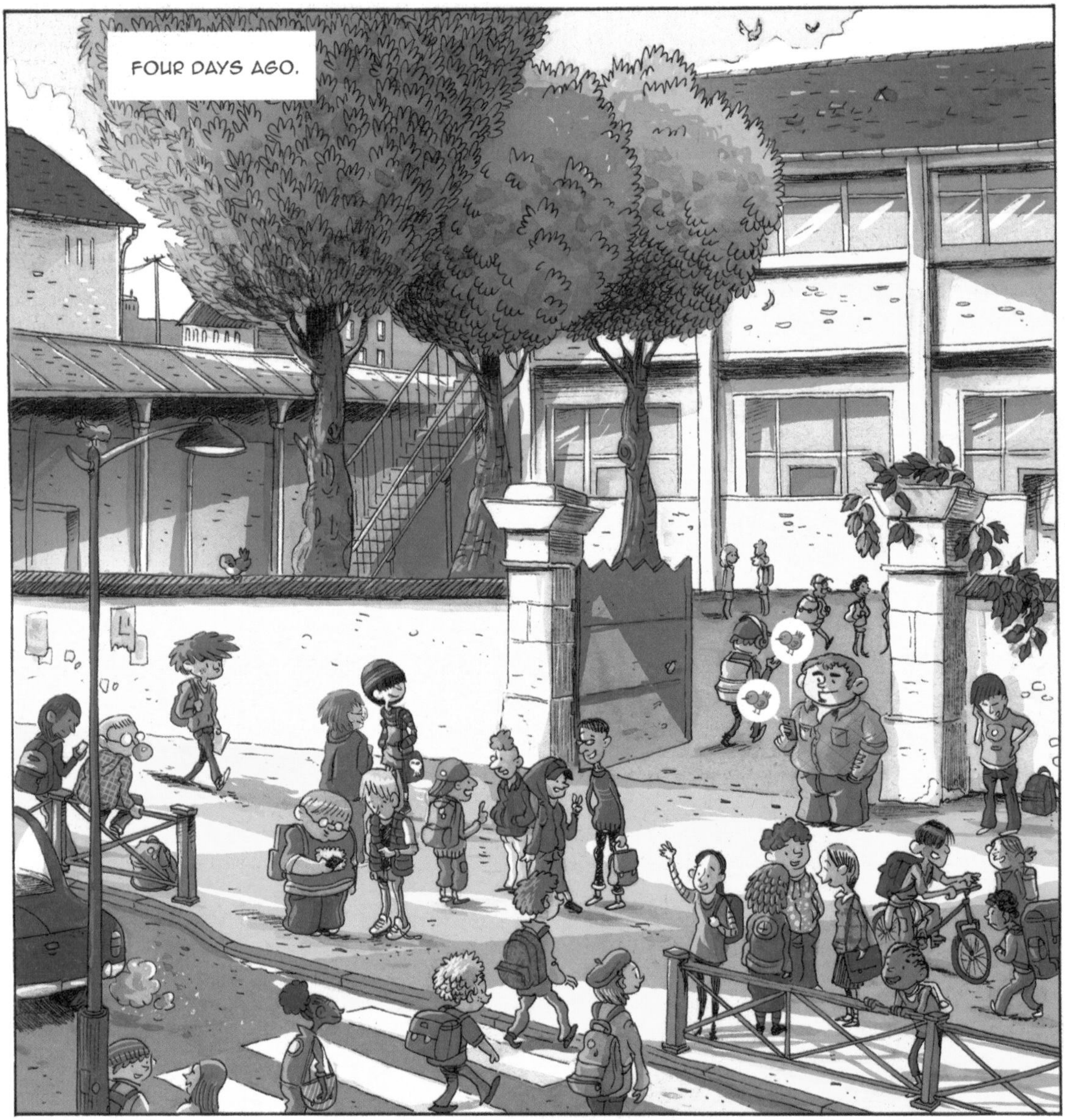
FOUR DAYS AGO.

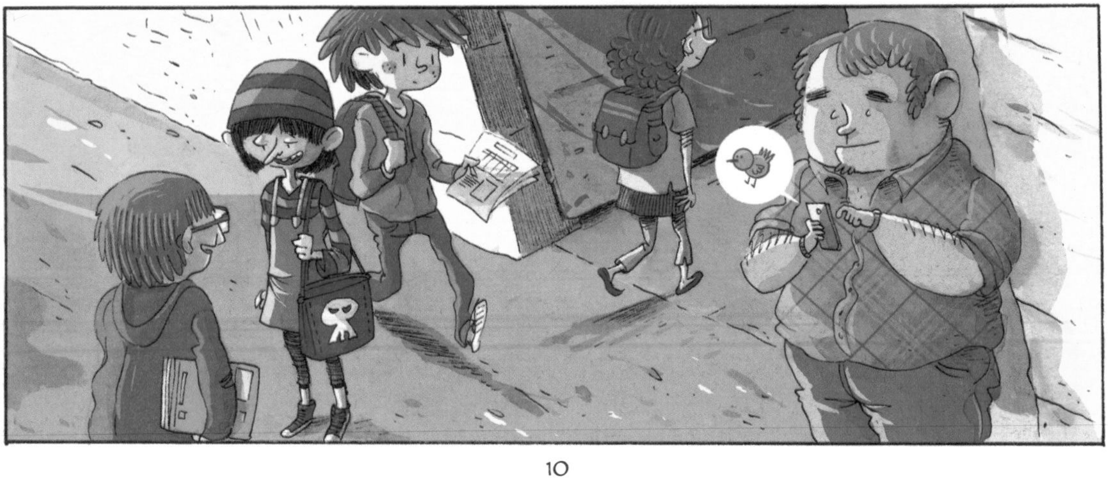

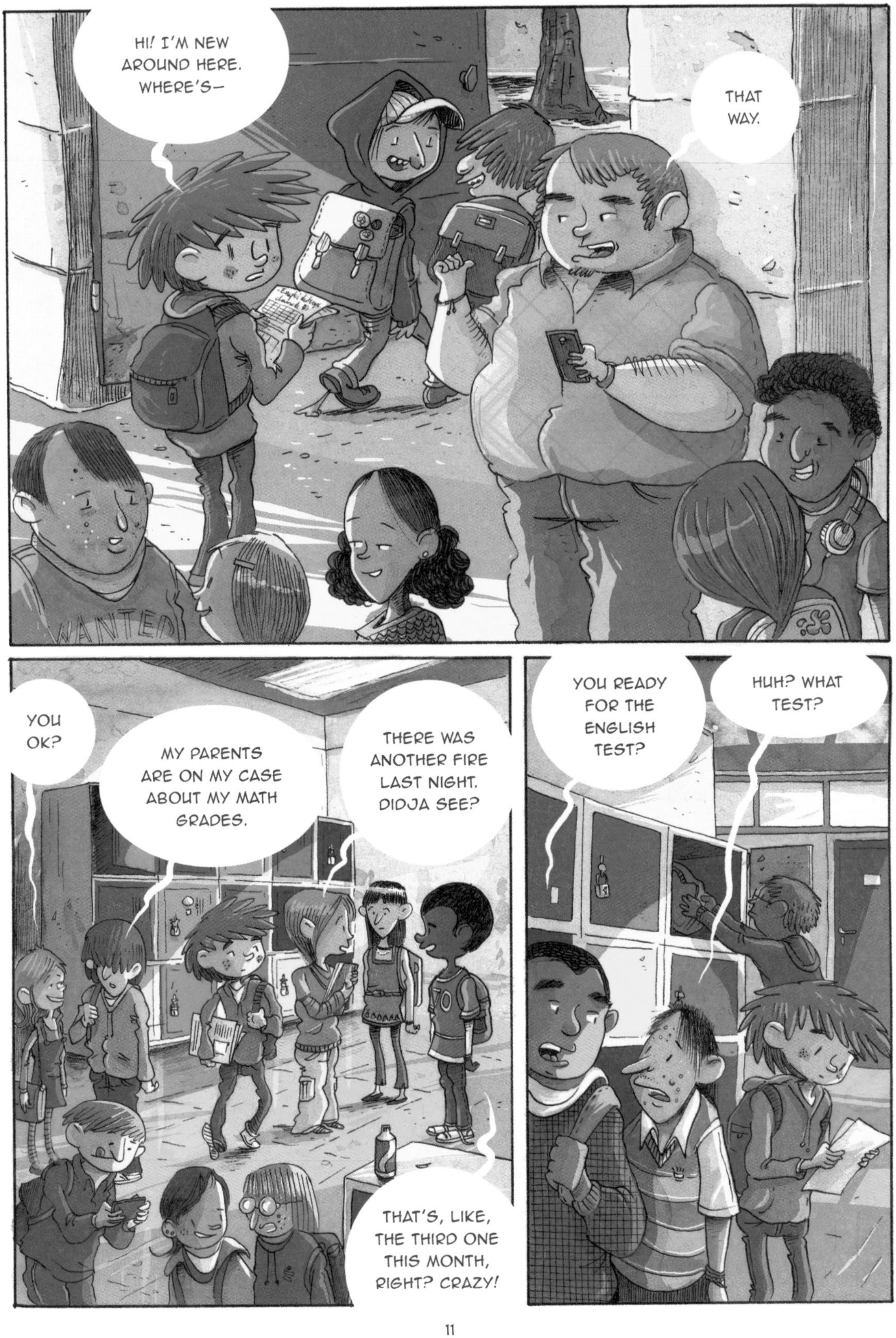
HI! I'M NEW AROUND HERE. WHERE'S—
THAT WAY.
WANTED
YOU OK?
MY PARENTS ARE ON MY CASE ABOUT MY MATH GRADES.
THERE WAS ANOTHER FIRE LAST NIGHT. DIDJA SEE?
70
THAT'S, LIKE, THE THIRD ONE THIS MONTH, RIGHT? CRAZY!
YOU READY FOR THE ENGLISH TEST?
HUH? WHAT TEST?

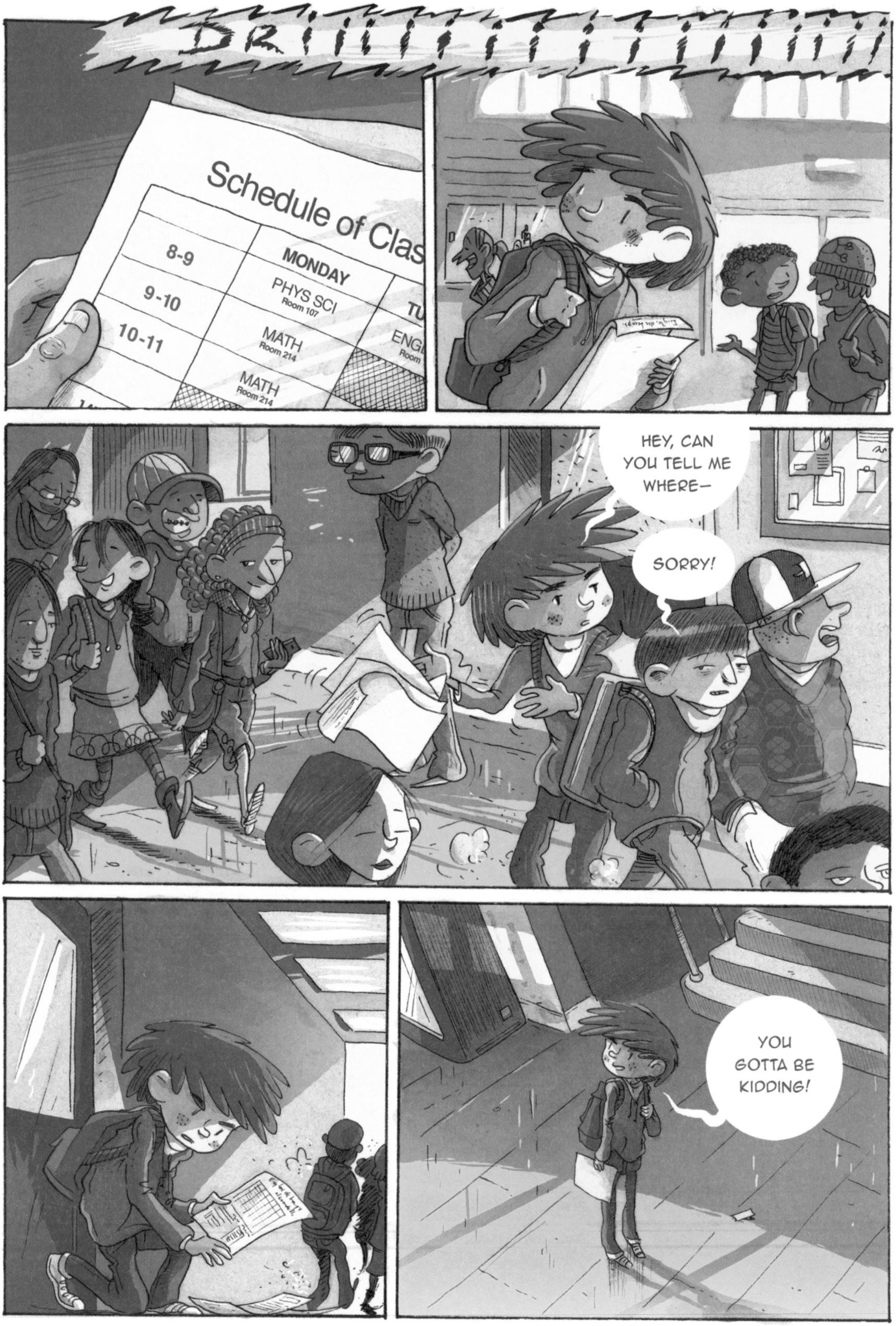
DRIIIIIIIIIIIIIIII
Schedule of Clas
8-9
MONDAY
9-10
PHYS SCI
Room 107
10-11
MATH
Room 214
MATH
Room 214
HEY, CAN YOU TELL ME WHERE—
SORRY!
YOU GOTTA BE KIDDING!

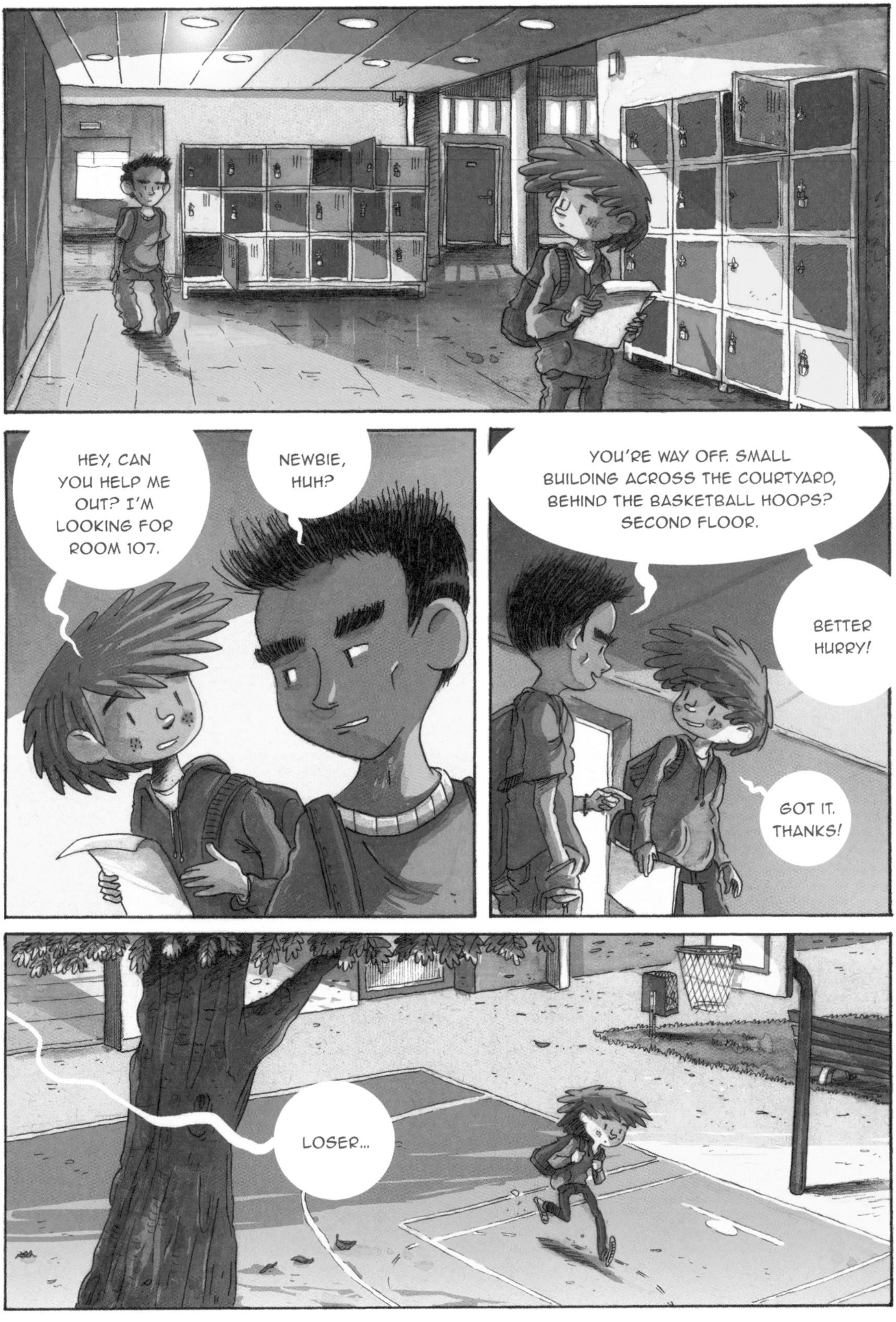
HEY, CAN YOU HELP ME OUT? I'M LOOKING FOR ROOM 107.
NEWBIE, HUH?
YOU'RE WAY OFF. SMALL BUILDING ACROSS THE COURTYARD, BEHIND THE BASKETBALL HOOPS? SECOND FLOOR.
BETTER HURRY!
GOT IT. THANKS!
LOSER...

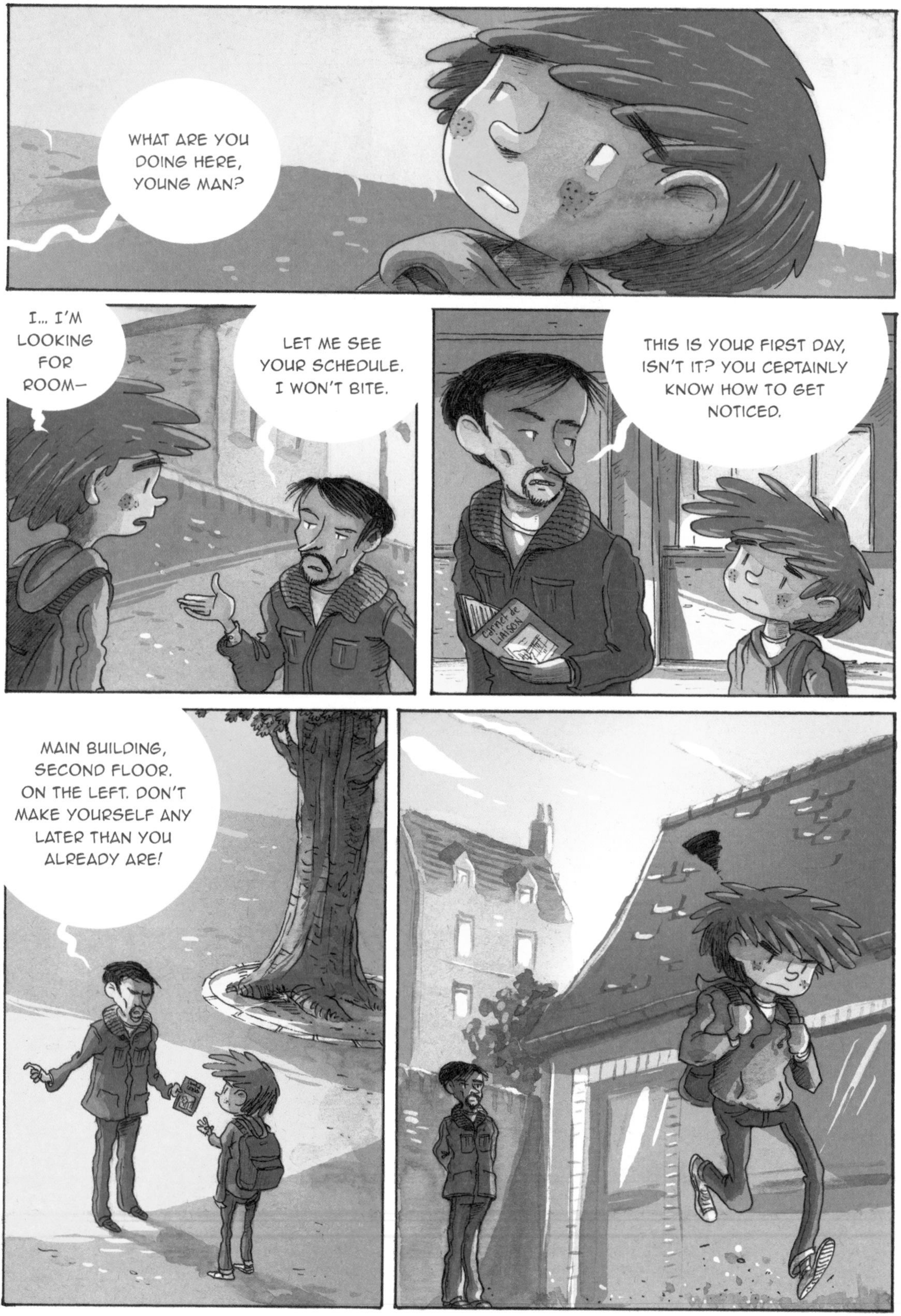
WHAT ARE YOU DOING HERE, YOUNG MAN?
I... I'M LOOKING FOR ROOM—
LET ME SEE YOUR SCHEDULE. I WON'T BITE.
THIS IS YOUR FIRST DAY, ISN'T IT? YOU CERTAINLY KNOW HOW TO GET NOTICED.
MAIN BUILDING, SECOND FLOOR. ON THE LEFT. DON'T MAKE YOURSELF ANY LATER THAN YOU ALREADY ARE!

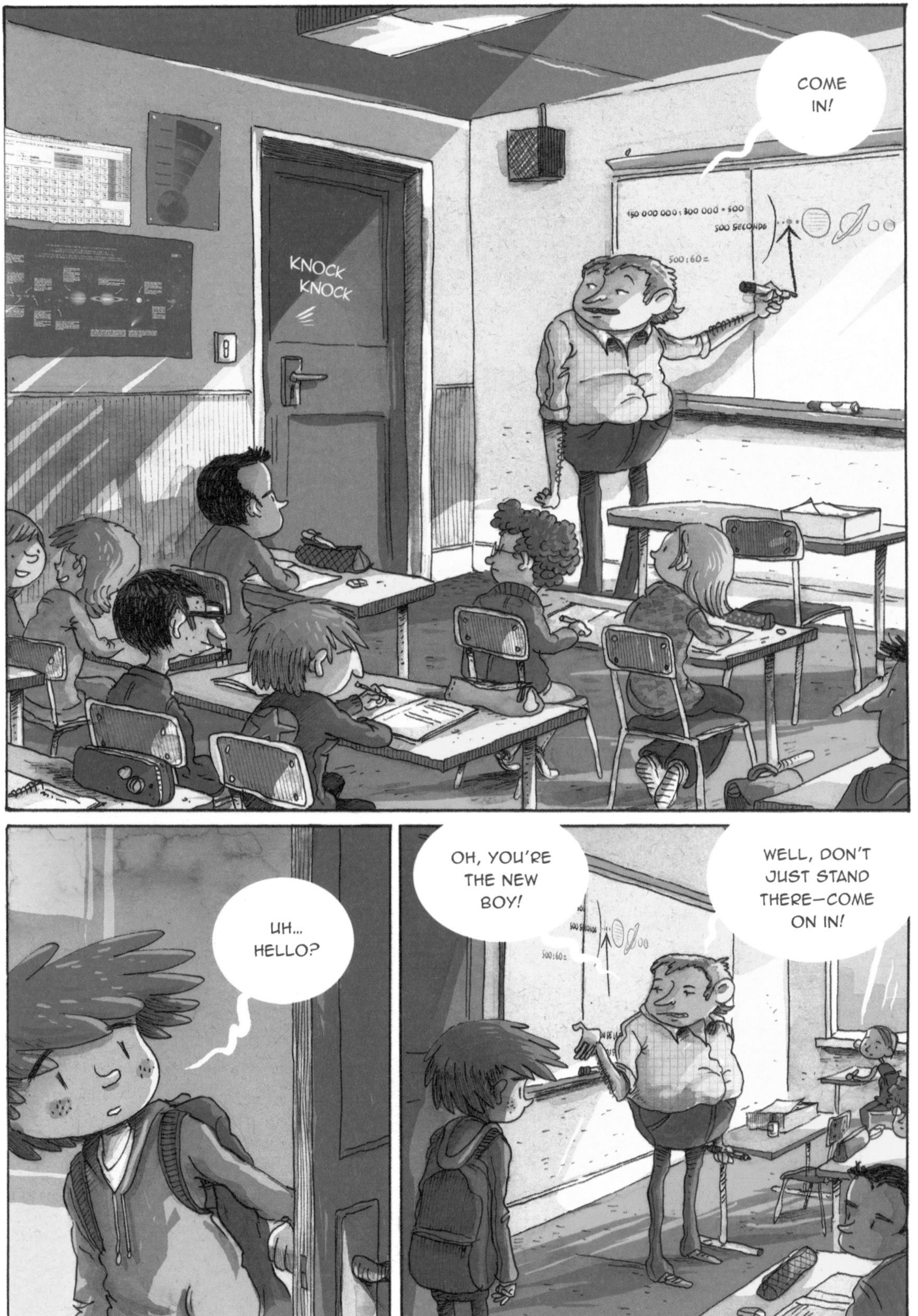
COME IN!
KNOCK KNOCK
150 000 000 : 300 000 = 500
500 SECONDS
500 : 60 =
UH... HELLO?
OH, YOU'RE THE NEW BOY!
WELL, DON'T JUST STAND THERE—COME ON IN!

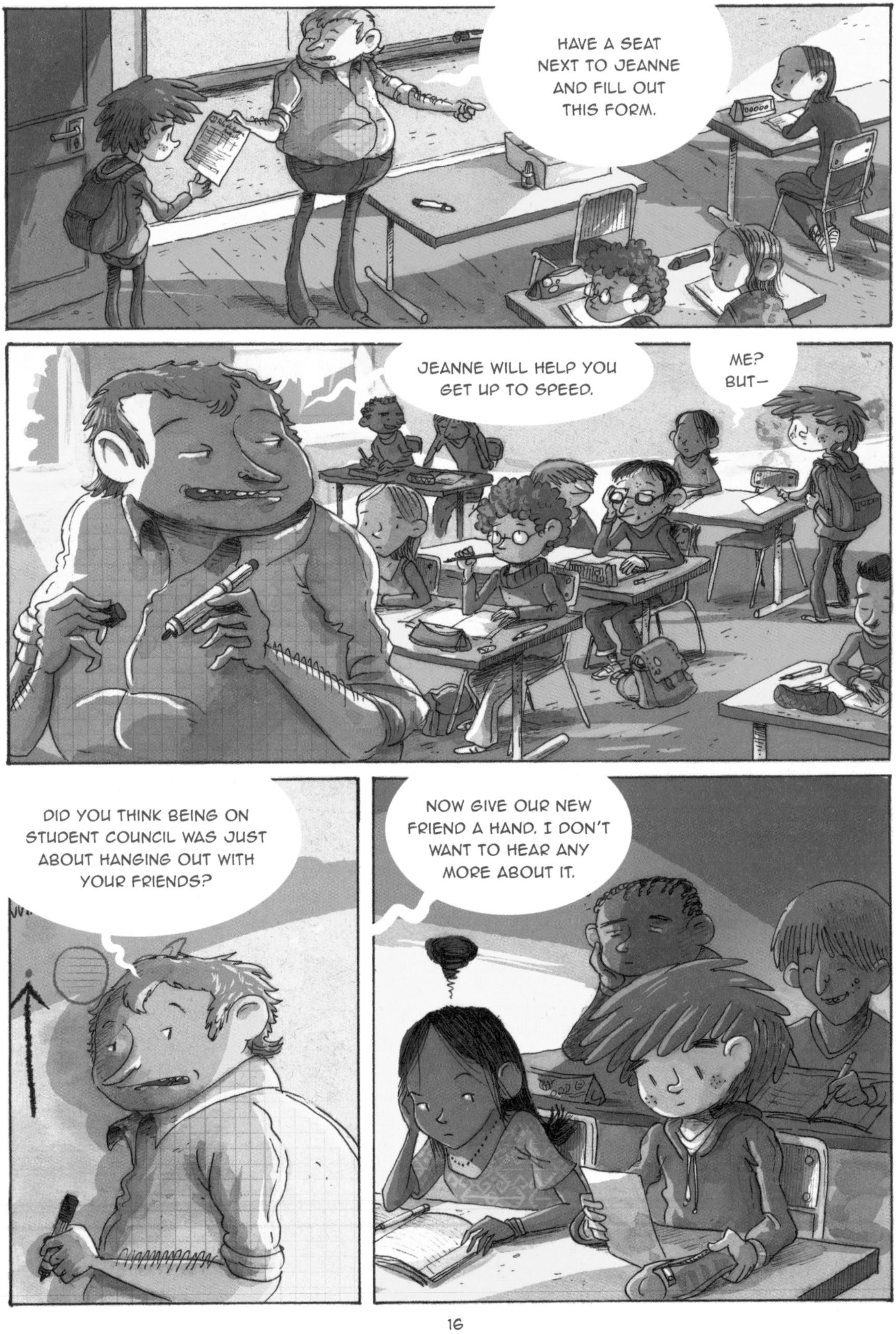
HAVE A SEAT NEXT TO JEANNE AND FILL OUT THIS FORM.
JEANNE WILL HELP YOU GET UP TO SPEED.
ME? BUT—
DID YOU THINK BEING ON STUDENT COUNCIL WAS JUST ABOUT HANGING OUT WITH YOUR FRIENDS?
NOW GIVE OUR NEW FRIEND A HAND. I DON'T WANT TO HEAR ANY MORE ABOUT IT.

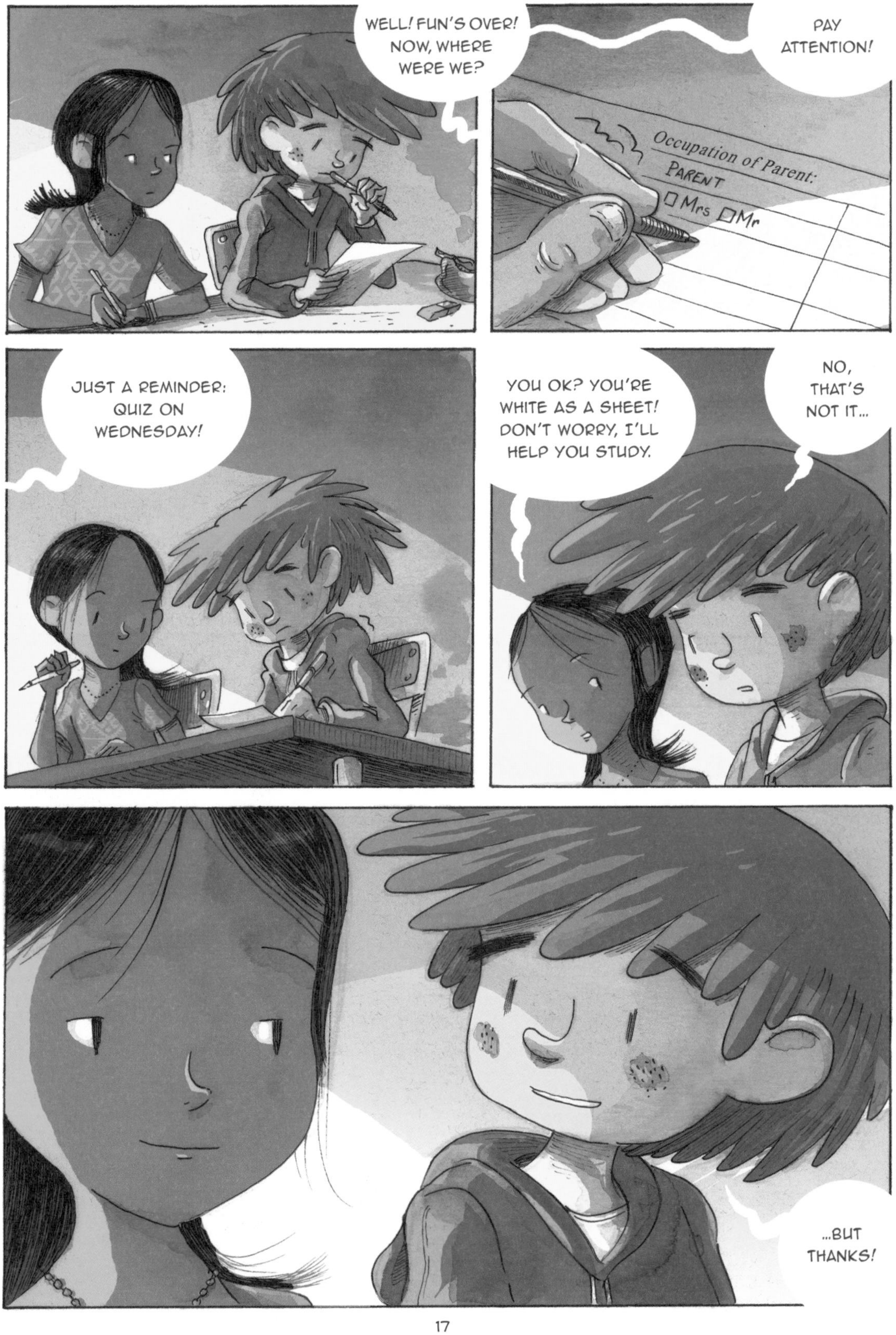
WELL! FUN'S OVER! NOW, WHERE WERE WE?
PAY ATTENTION!
Occupation of Parent:
PARENT
Mrs
Mr
JUST A REMINDER: QUIZ ON WEDNESDAY!
YOU OK? YOU'RE WHITE AS A SHEET! DON'T WORRY, I'LL HELP YOU STUDY.
NO, THAT'S NOT IT...
...BUT THANKS!

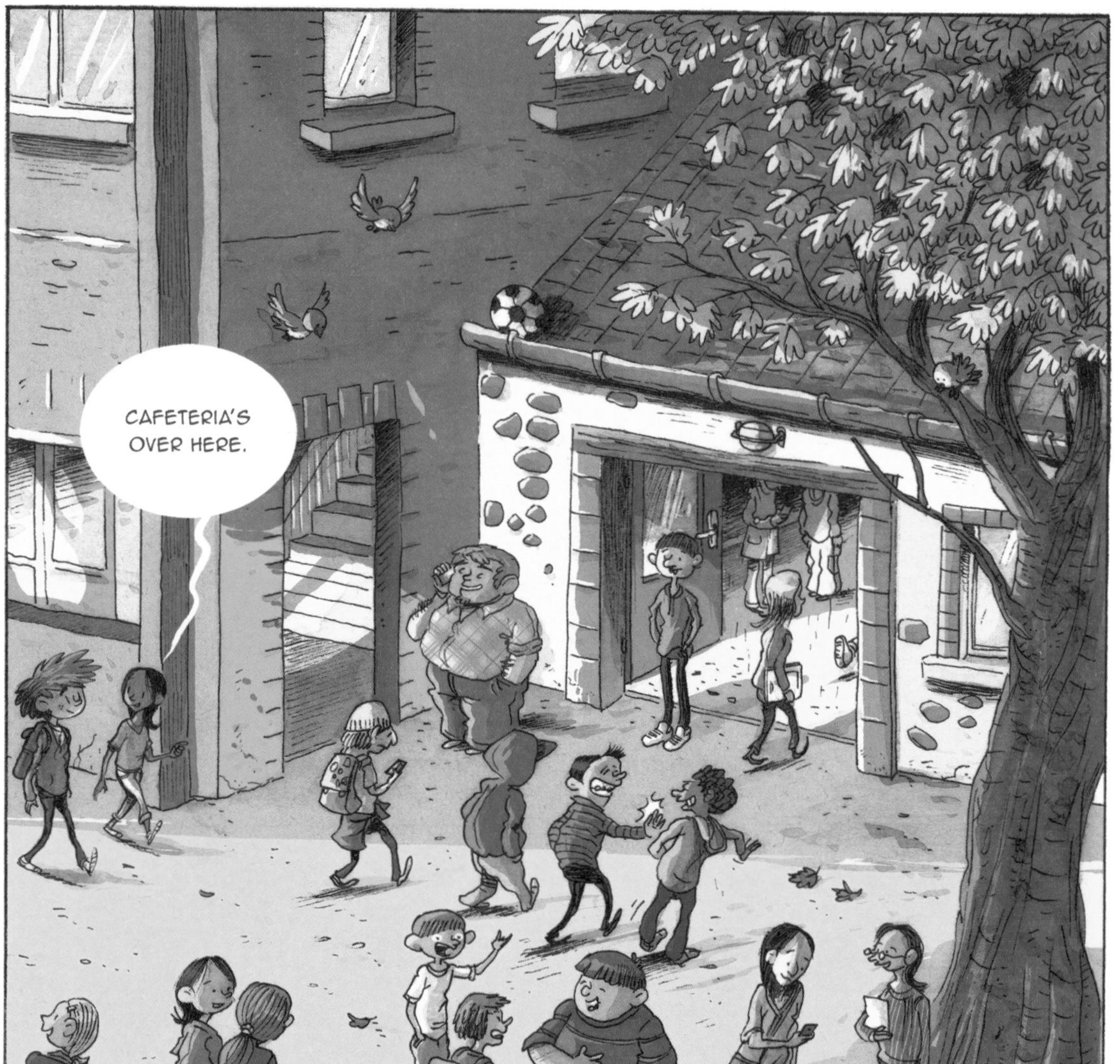
CAFETERIA'S OVER HERE.

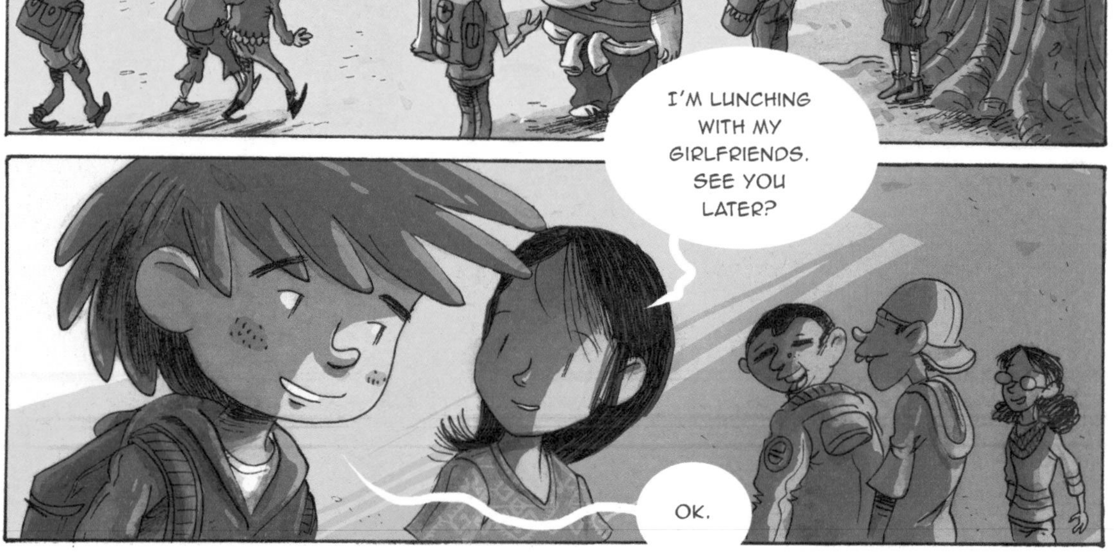
I'M LUNCHING WITH MY GIRLFRIENDS. SEE YOU LATER?
OK.

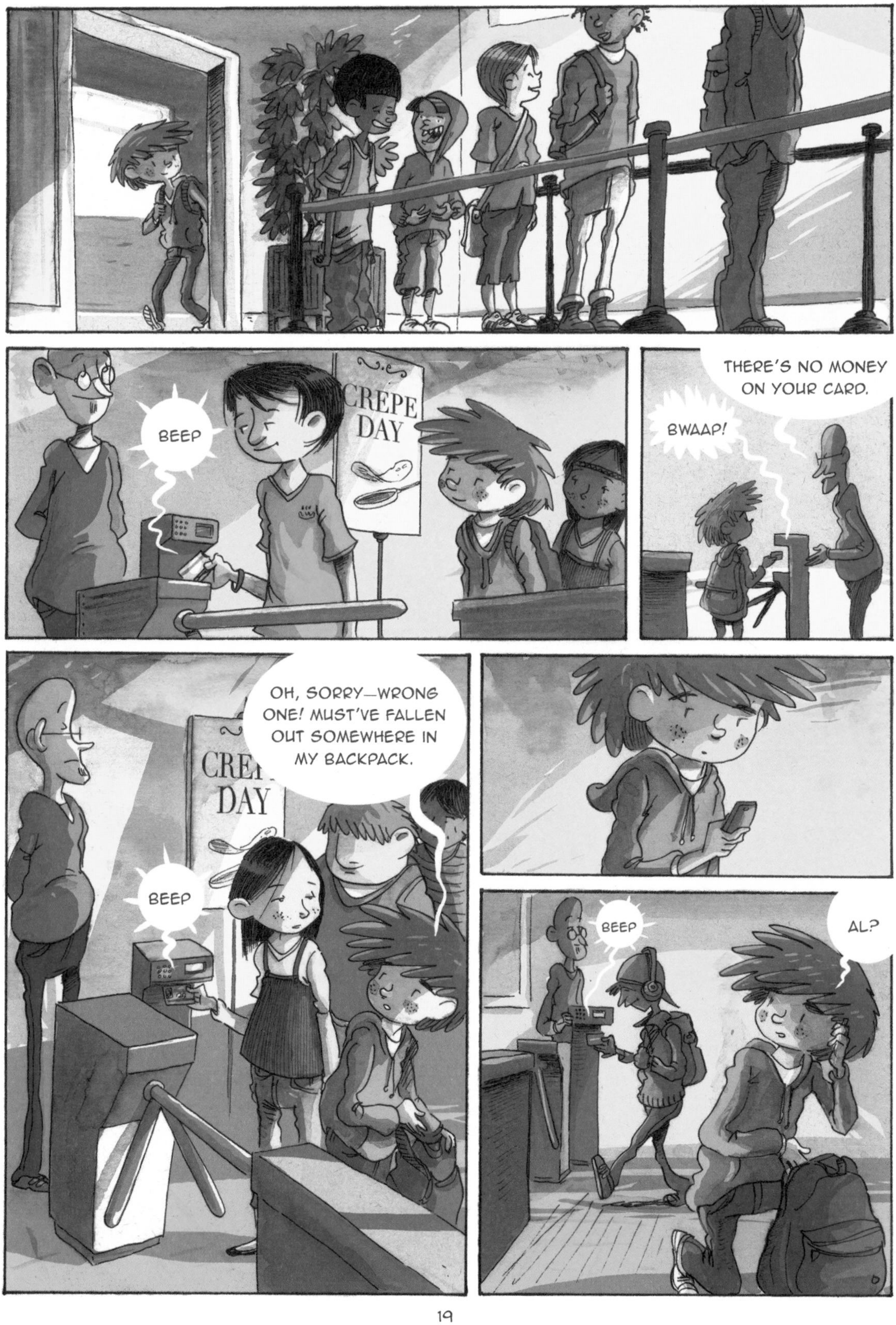
BEEP
BWAAP!
THERE'S NO MONEY ON YOUR CARD.
CREPE DAY
OH, SORRY—WRONG ONE! MUST'VE FALLEN OUT SOMEWHERE IN MY BACKPACK.
BEEP
BEEP
AL?

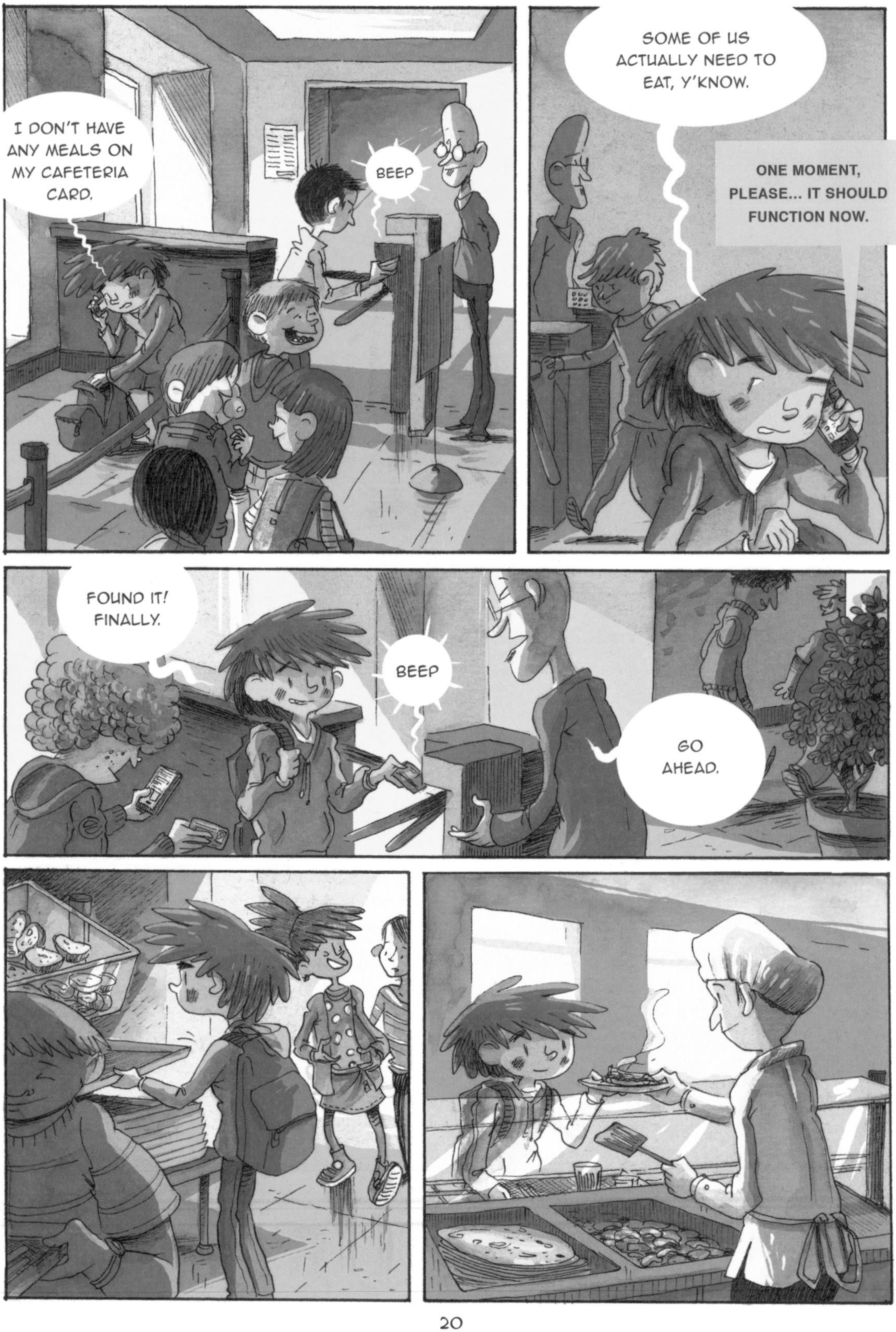
I DON'T HAVE ANY MEALS ON MY CAFETERIA CARD.
BEEP
SOME OF US ACTUALLY NEED TO EAT, Y'KNOW.
ONE MOMENT, PLEASE... IT SHOULD FUNCTION NOW.
FOUND IT! FINALLY.
BEEP
GO AHEAD.

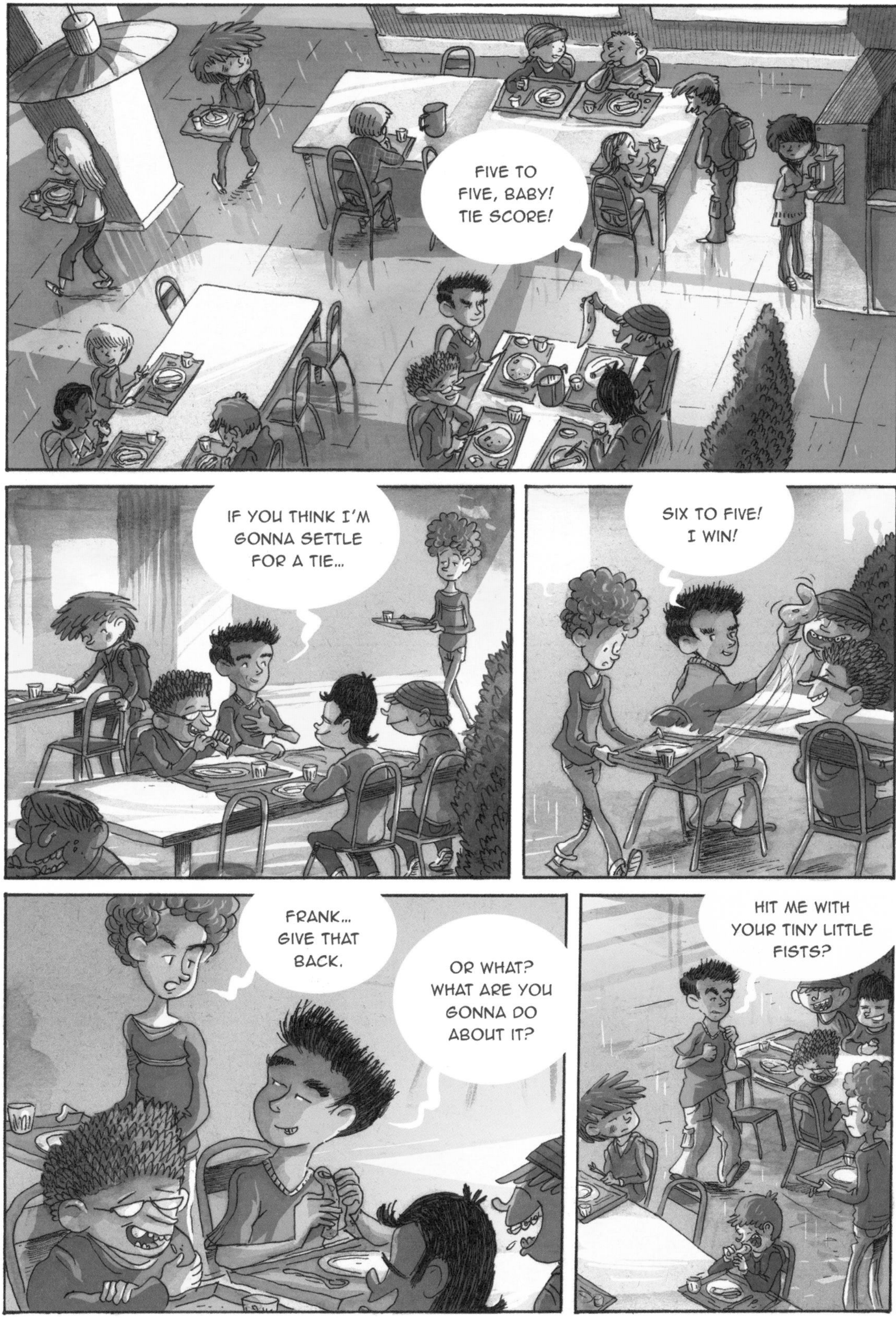
FIVE TO FIVE, BABY! TIE SCORE!
IF YOU THINK I'M GONNA SETTLE FOR A TIE...
SIX TO FIVE! I WIN!
FRANK... GIVE THAT BACK.
OR WHAT? WHAT ARE YOU GONNA DO ABOUT IT?
HIT ME WITH YOUR TINY LITTLE FISTS?

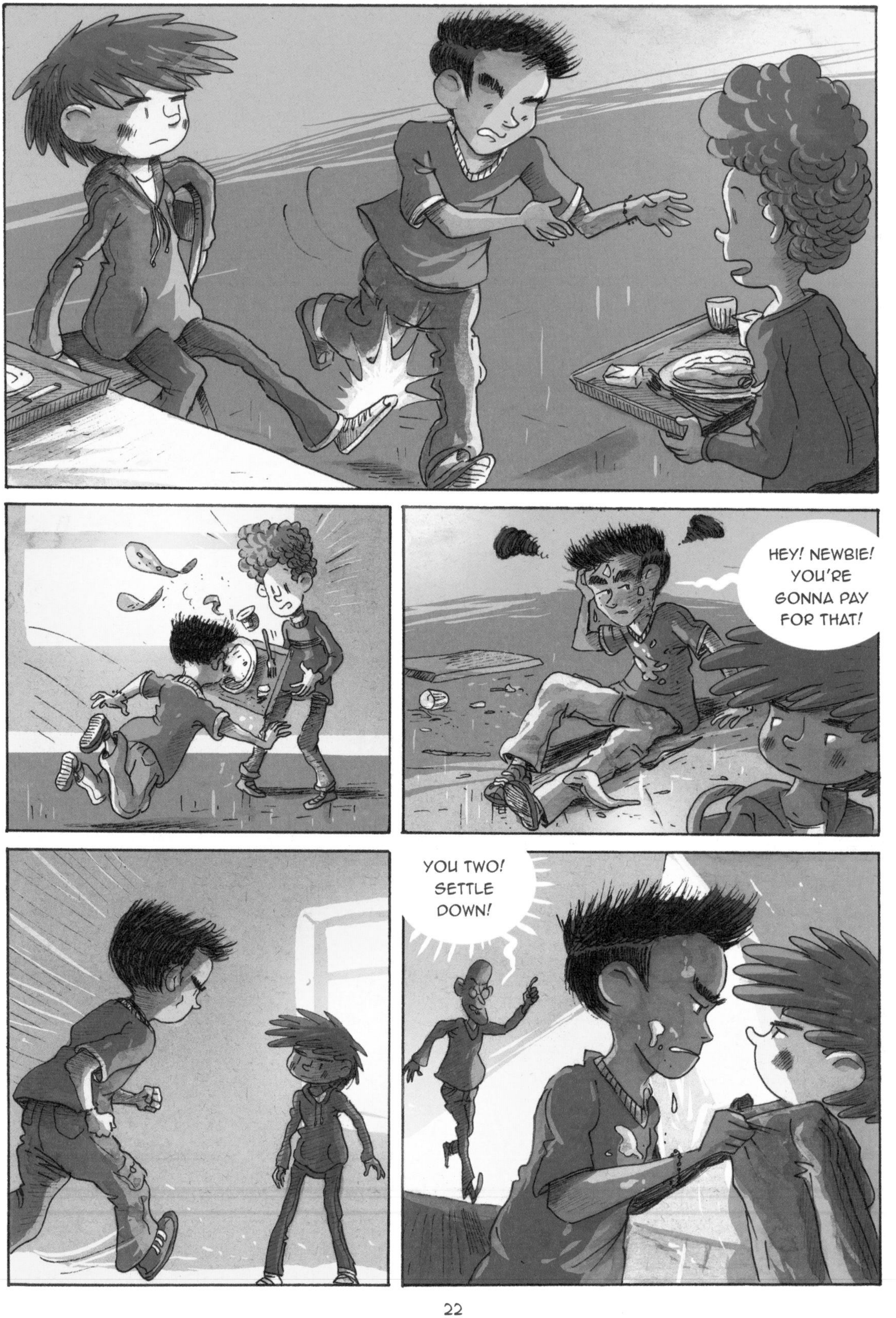
HEY! NEWBIE! YOU'RE GONNA PAY FOR THAT!
YOU TWO! SETTLE DOWN!

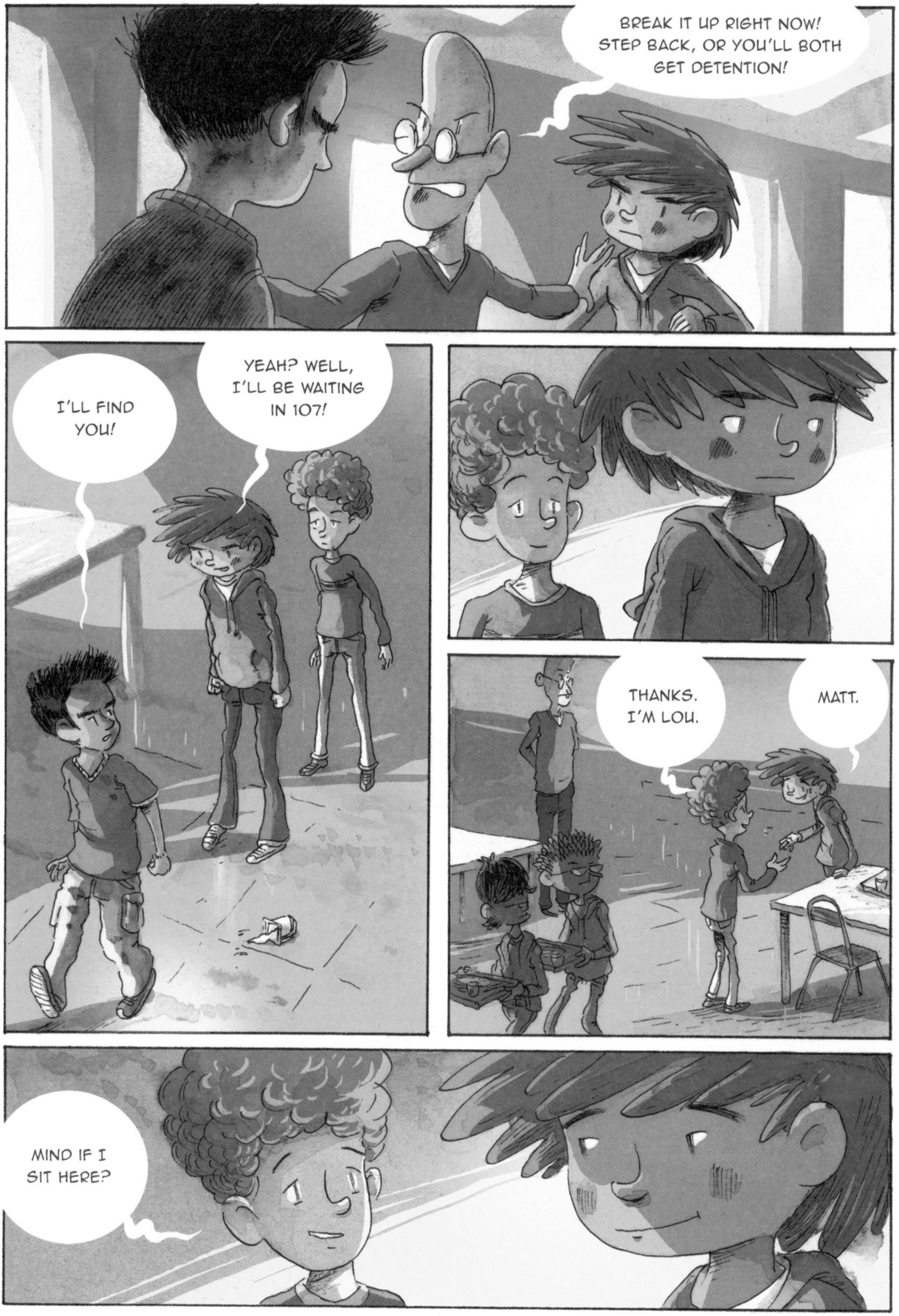
BREAK IT UP RIGHT NOW! STEP BACK, OR YOU'LL BOTH GET DETENTION!
I'LL FIND YOU!
YEAH? WELL, I'LL BE WAITING IN 107!
THANKS. I'M LOU.
MATT.
MIND IF I SIT HERE?

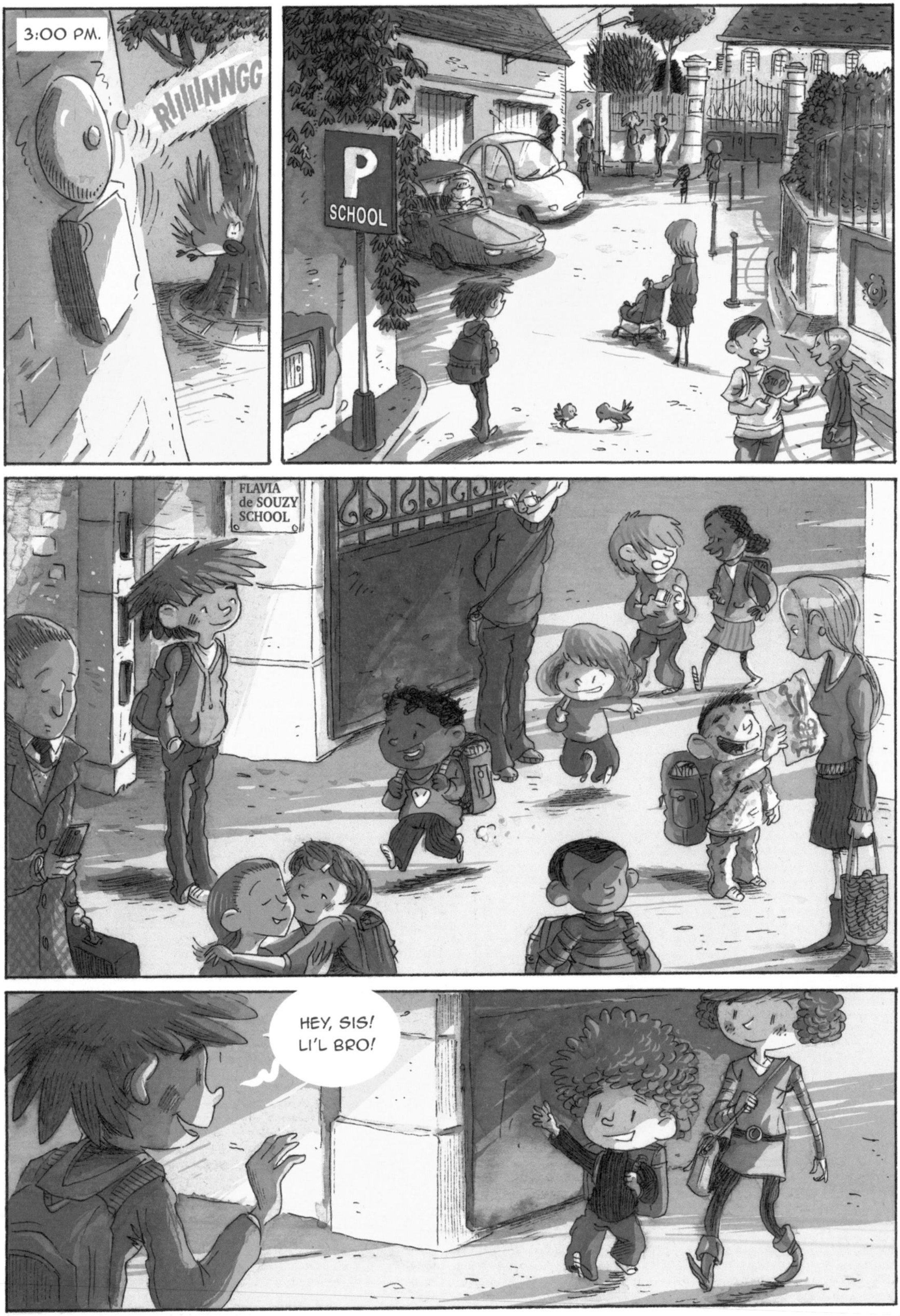
3:00 PM.
RIIIINNGG
P
SCHOOL
STOP
FLAVIA de SOUZY SCHOOL
HEY, SIS! LI'L BRO!

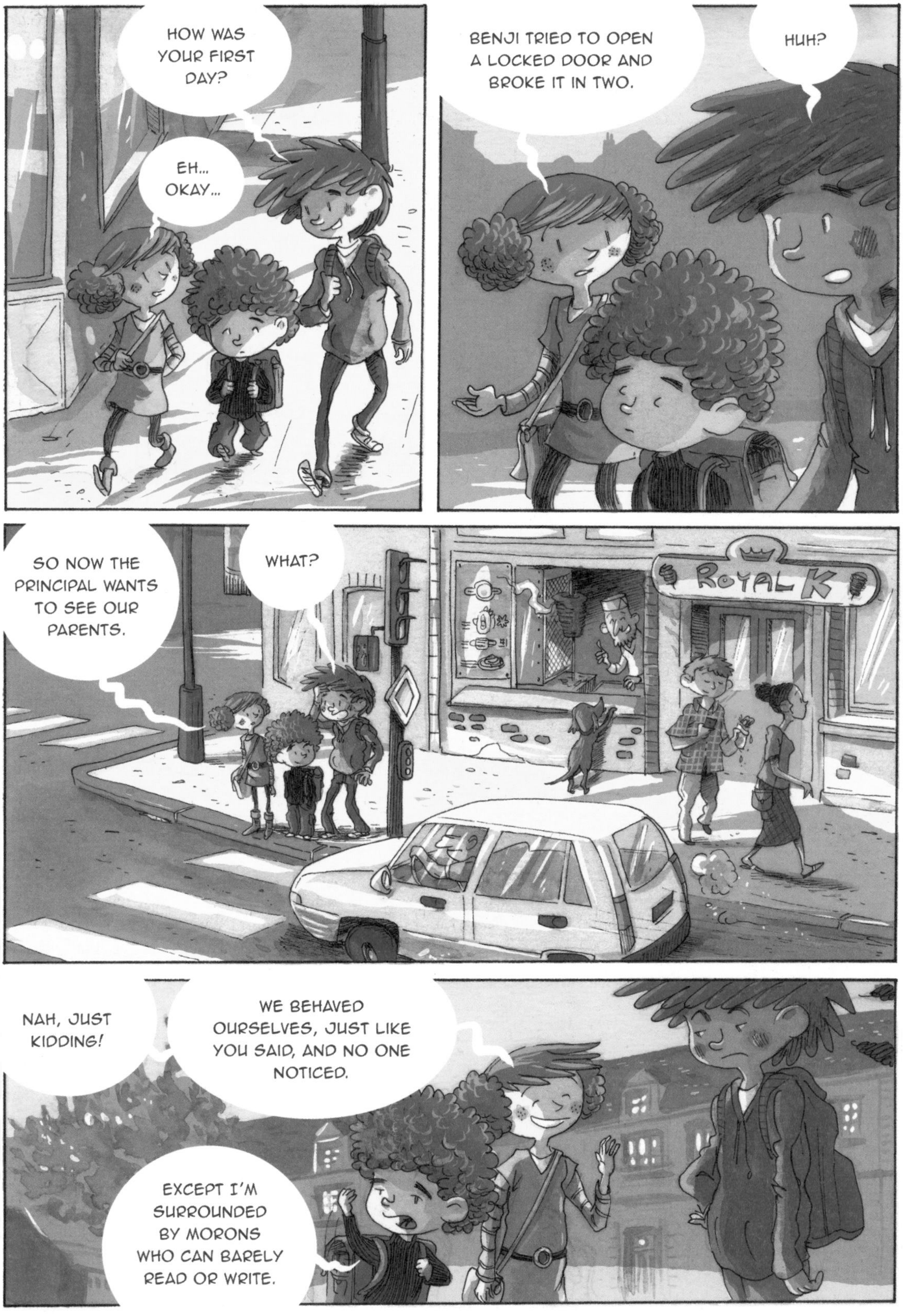
HOW WAS YOUR FIRST DAY?
EH... OKAY...
BENJI TRIED TO OPEN A LOCKED DOOR AND BROKE IT IN TWO.
HUH?
SO NOW THE PRINCIPAL WANTS TO SEE OUR PARENTS.
WHAT?
ROYAL K
NAH, JUST KIDDING!
WE BEHAVED OURSELVES, JUST LIKE YOU SAID, AND NO ONE NOTICED.
EXCEPT I'M SURROUNDED BY MORONS WHO CAN BARELY READ OR WRITE.

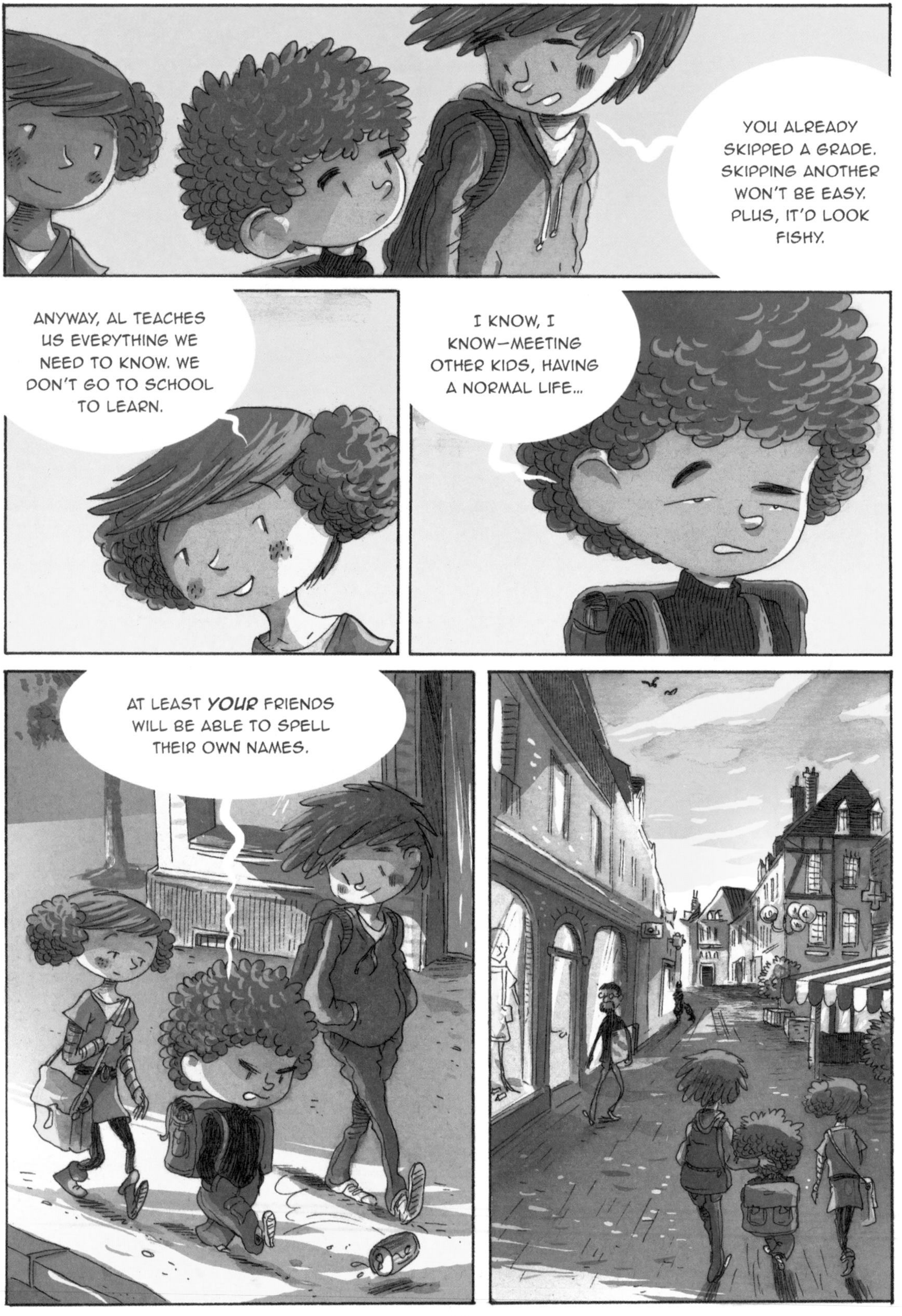

YOU ALREADY SKIPPED A GRADE. SKIPPING ANOTHER WON'T BE EASY. PLUS, IT'D LOOK FISHY.
ANYWAY, AL TEACHES US EVERYTHING WE NEED TO KNOW. WE DON'T GO TO SCHOOL TO LEARN.
I KNOW, I KNOW—MEETING OTHER KIDS, HAVING A NORMAL LIFE...
AT LEAST *YOUR* FRIENDS WILL BE ABLE TO SPELL THEIR OWN NAMES.

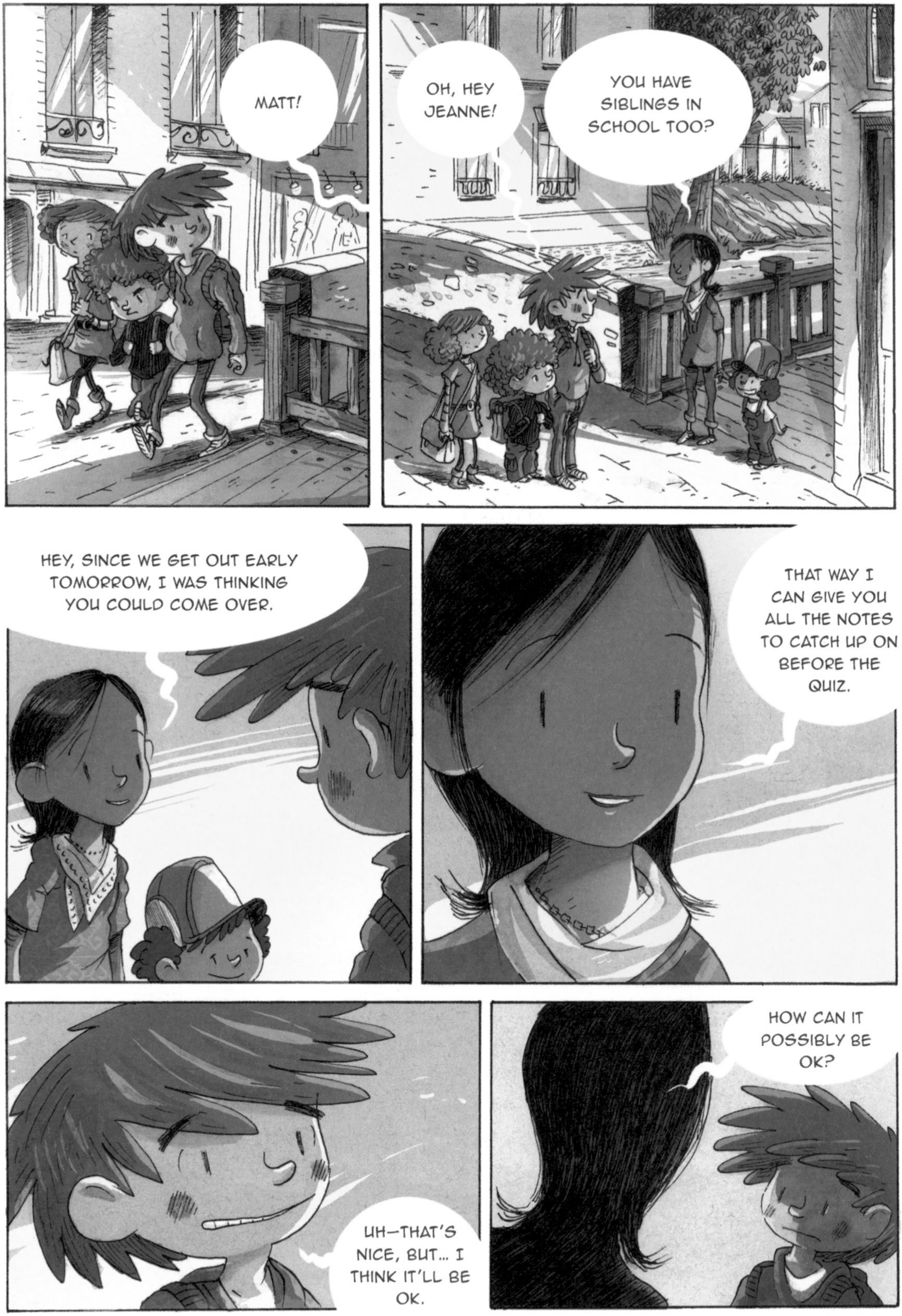
MATT!
OH, HEY JEANNE!
YOU HAVE SIBLINGS IN SCHOOL TOO?
HEY, SINCE WE GET OUT EARLY TOMORROW, I WAS THINKING YOU COULD COME OVER.
THAT WAY I CAN GIVE YOU ALL THE NOTES TO CATCH UP ON BEFORE THE QUIZ.
UH—THAT'S NICE, BUT... I THINK IT'LL BE OK.
HOW CAN IT POSSIBLY BE OK?

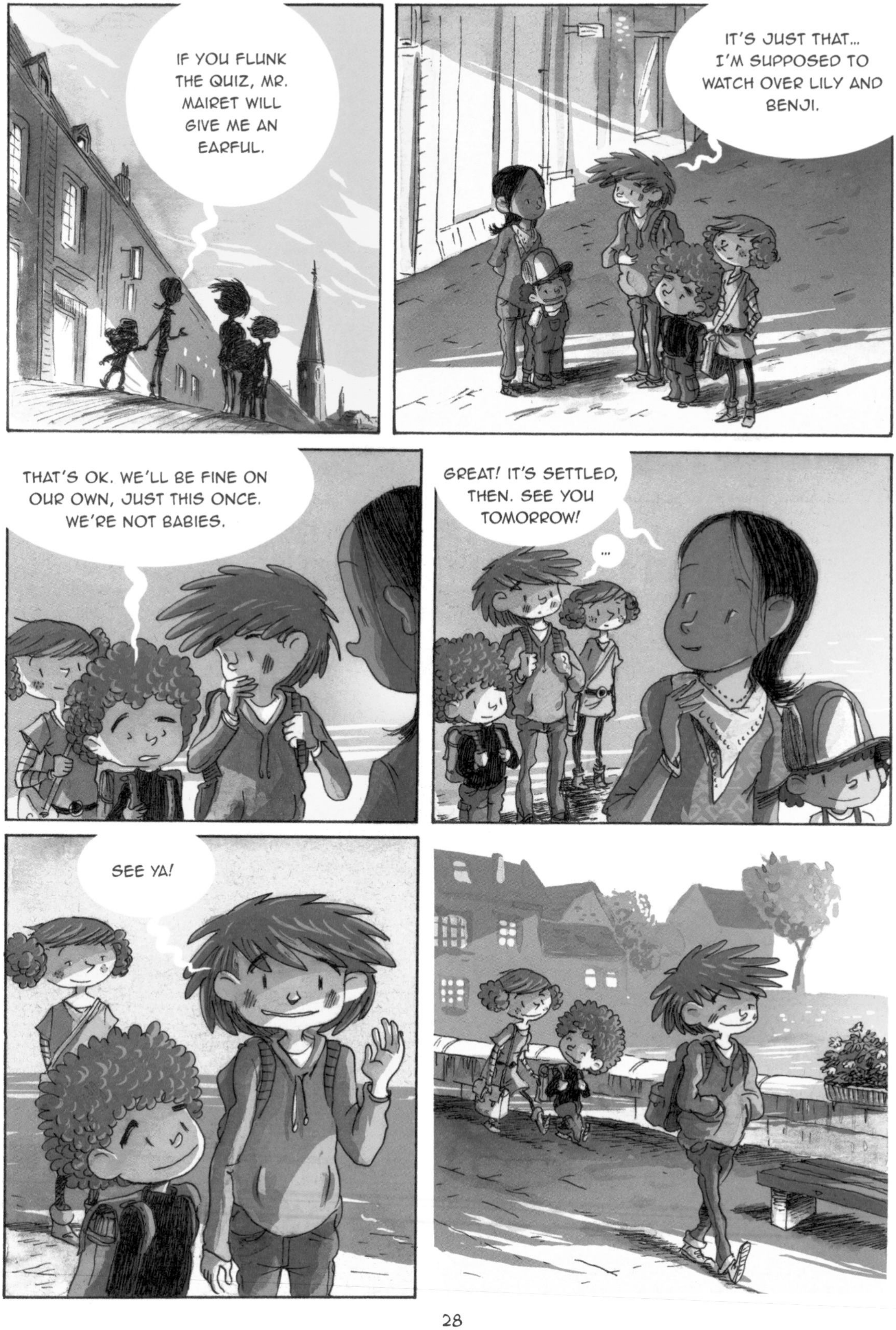
IF YOU FLUNK THE QUIZ, MR. MAIRET WILL GIVE ME AN EARFUL.
IT'S JUST THAT... I'M SUPPOSED TO WATCH OVER LILY AND BENJI.
THAT'S OK. WE'LL BE FINE ON OUR OWN, JUST THIS ONCE. WE'RE NOT BABIES.
GREAT! IT'S SETTLED, THEN. SEE YOU TOMORROW!
...
SEE YA!

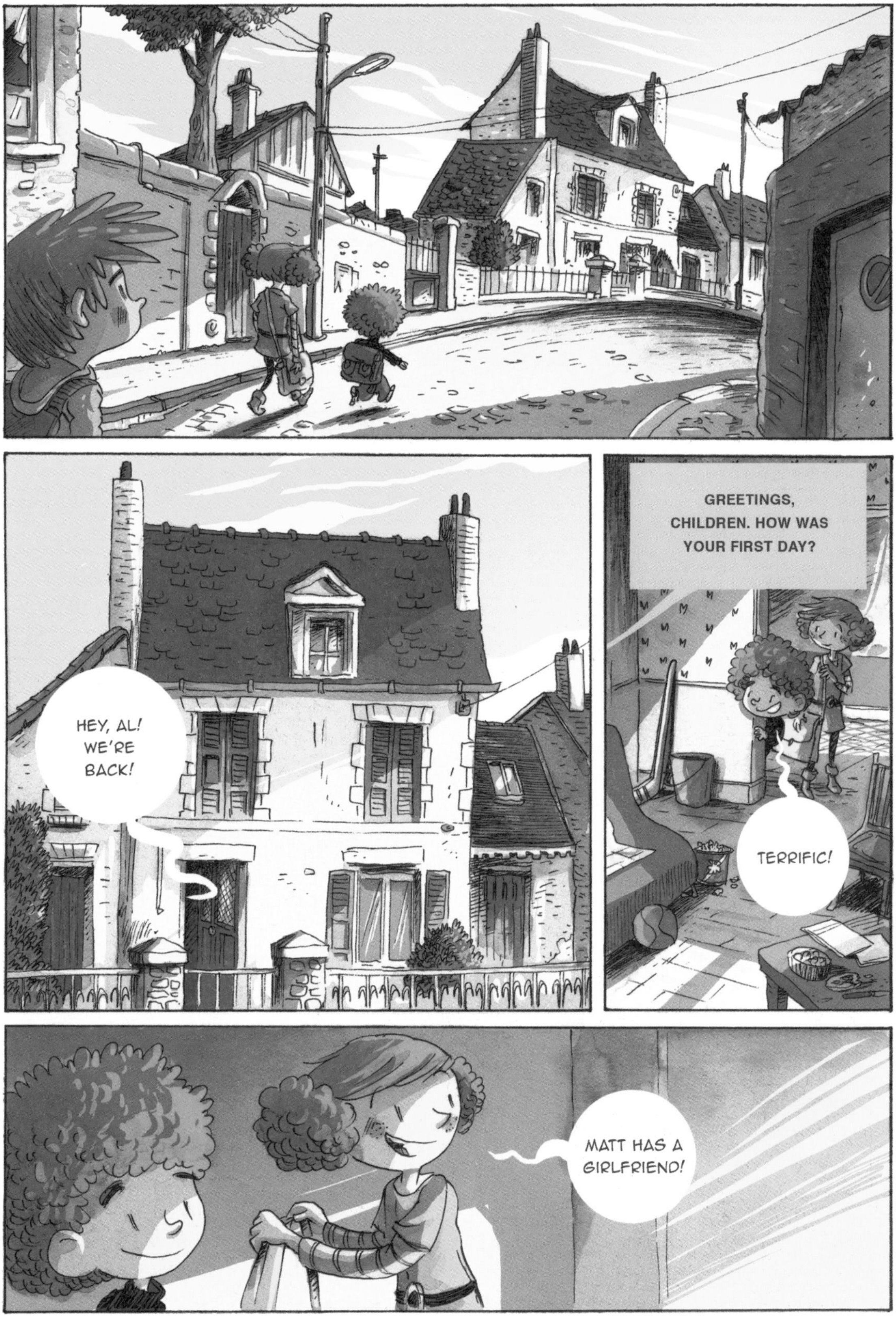
HEY, AL! WE'RE BACK!
GREETINGS, CHILDREN. HOW WAS YOUR FIRST DAY?
TERRIFIC!
MATT HAS A GIRLFRIEND!

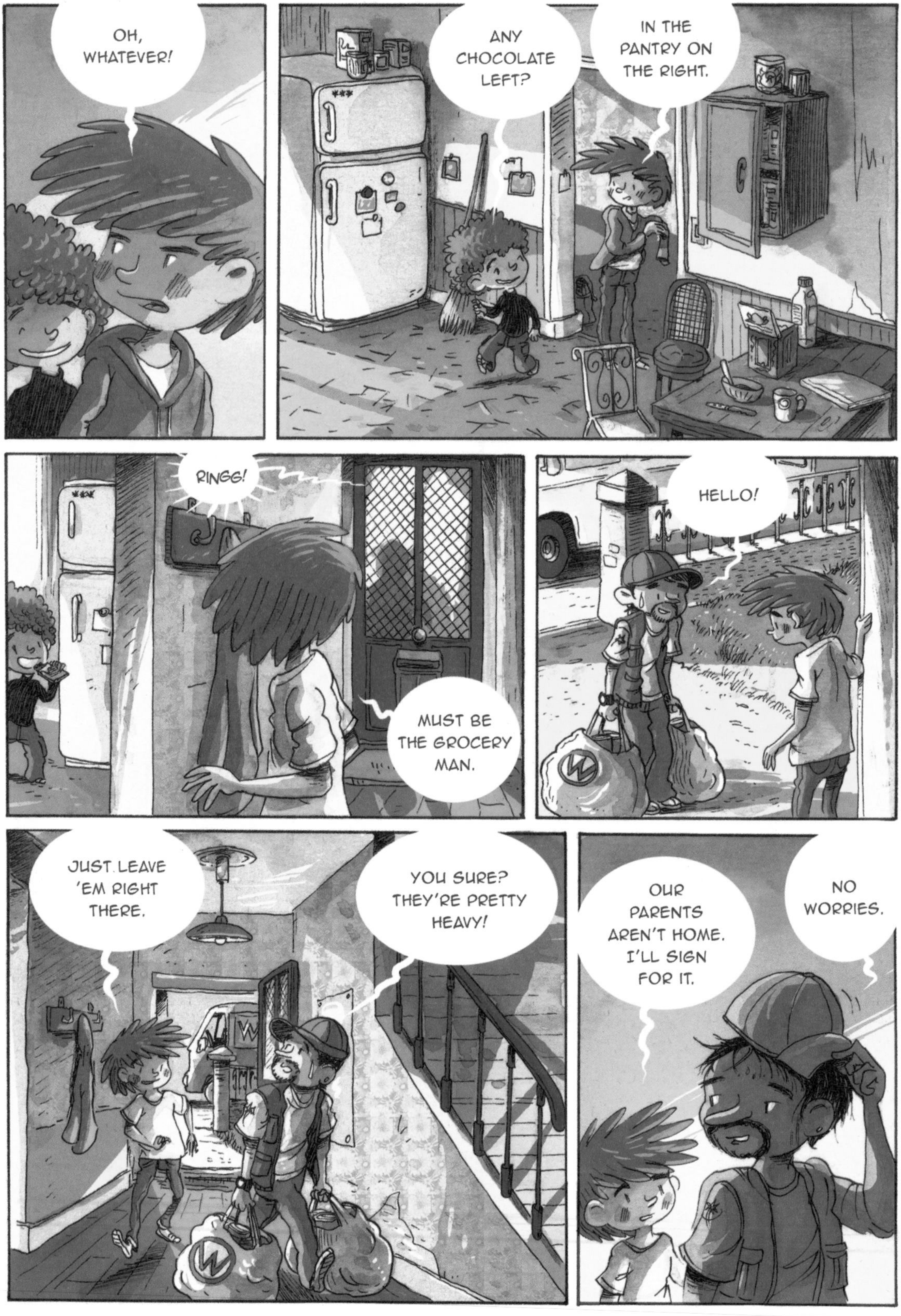
OH, WHATEVER!
ANY CHOCOLATE LEFT?
IN THE PANTRY ON THE RIGHT.
RINGG!
MUST BE THE GROCERY MAN.
HELLO!
JUST LEAVE 'EM RIGHT THERE.
YOU SURE? THEY'RE PRETTY HEAVY!
OUR PARENTS AREN'T HOME. I'LL SIGN FOR IT.
NO WORRIES.

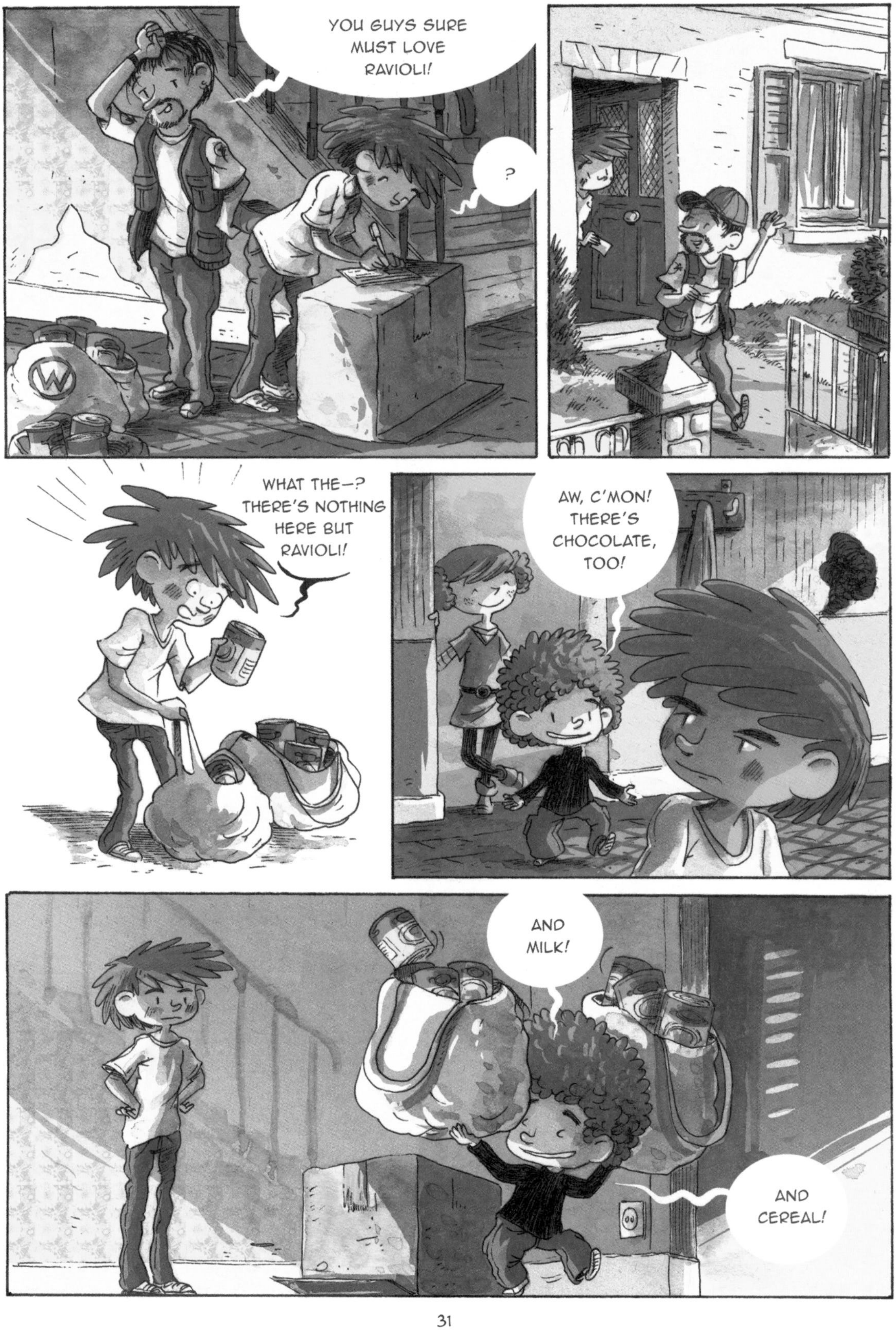
YOU GUYS SURE MUST LOVE RAVIOLI!
?
WHAT THE—? THERE'S NOTHING HERE BUT RAVIOLI!
AW, C'MON! THERE'S CHOCOLATE, TOO!
AND MILK!
AND CEREAL!

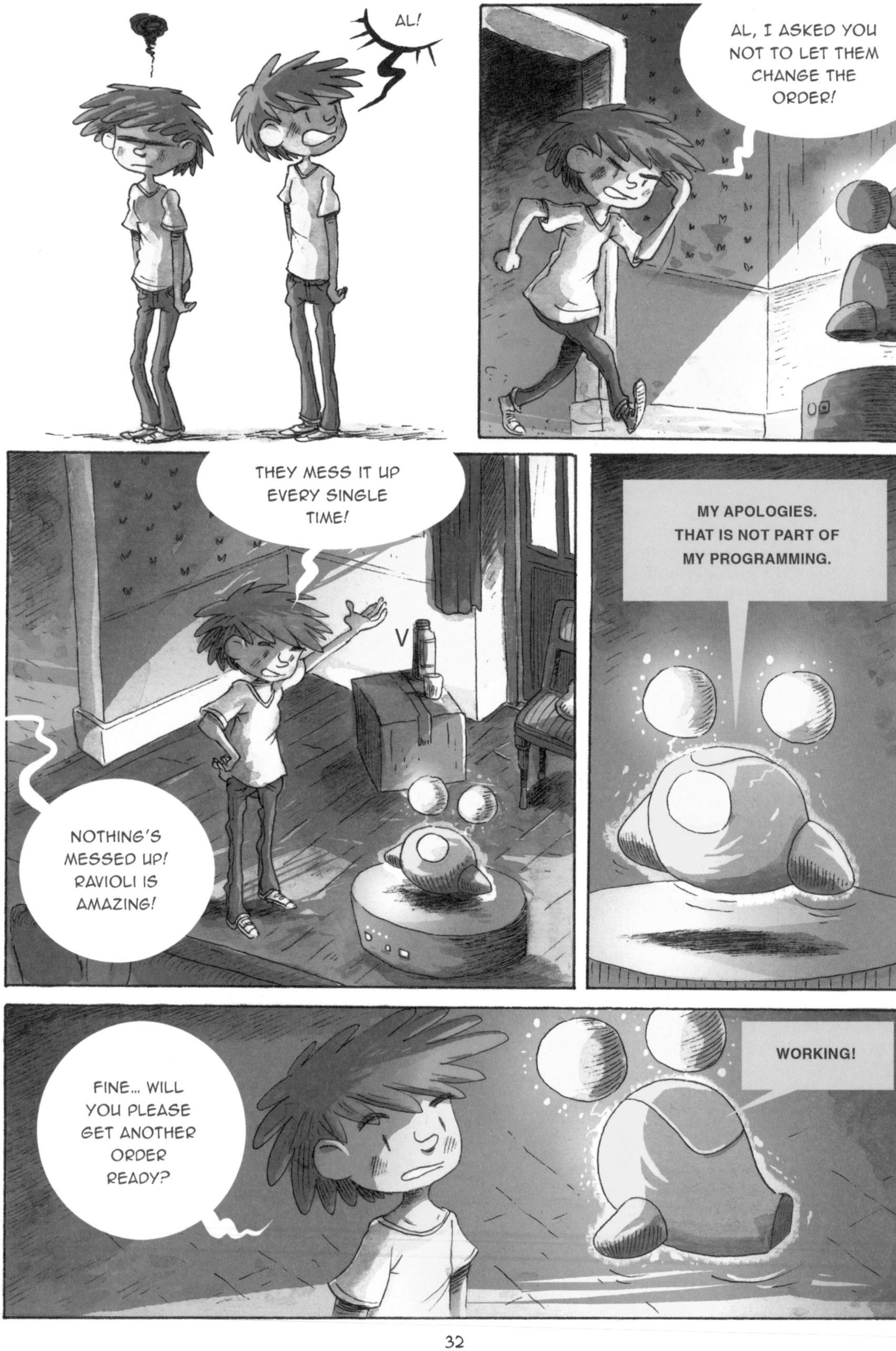
AL!
AL, I ASKED YOU NOT TO LET THEM CHANGE THE ORDER!
THEY MESS IT UP EVERY SINGLE TIME!
V
NOTHING'S MESSED UP! RAVIOLI IS AMAZING!
MY APOLOGIES. THAT IS NOT PART OF MY PROGRAMMING.
FINE... WILL YOU PLEASE GET ANOTHER ORDER READY?
WORKING!

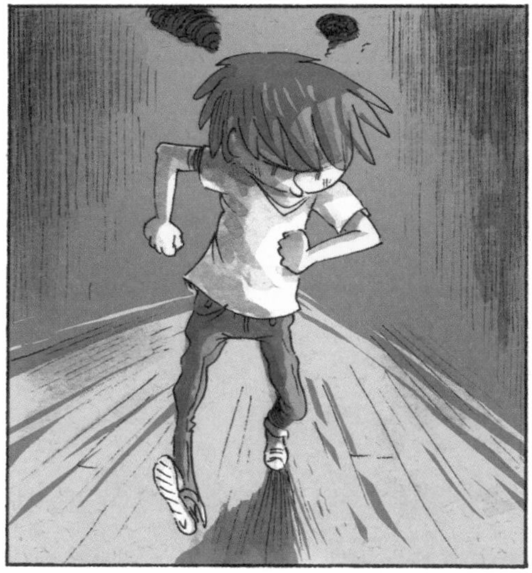

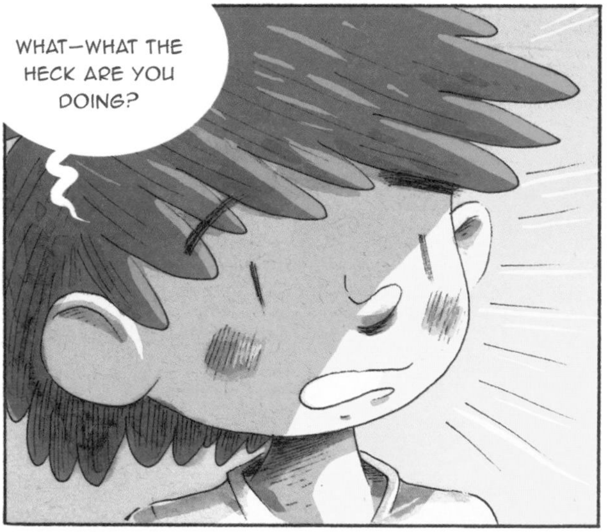
WHAT—WHAT THE HECK ARE YOU DOING?

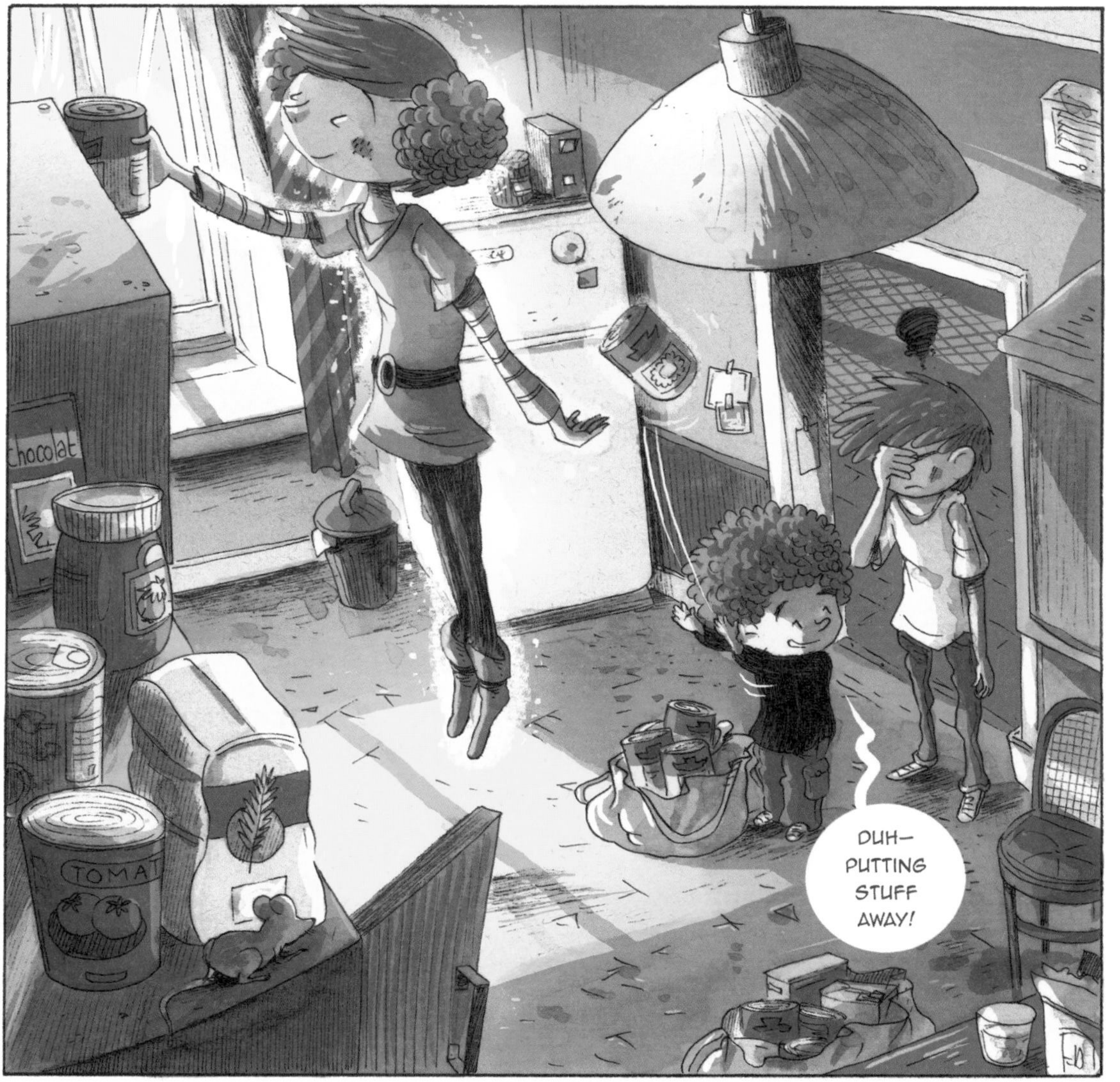
Chocolat
TOMAT
DUH—PUTTING STUFF AWAY!

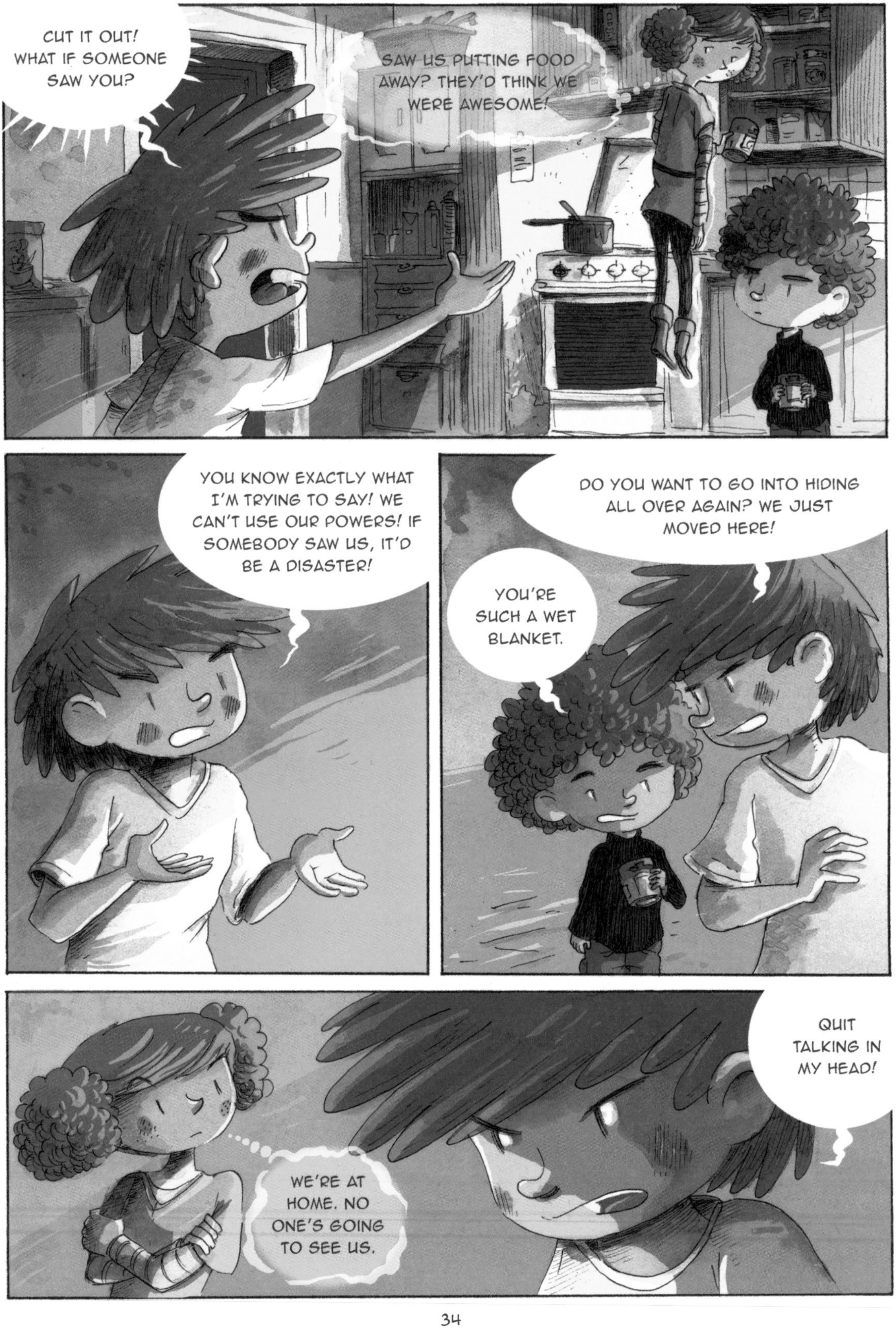
CUT IT OUT! WHAT IF SOMEONE SAW YOU?
SAW US PUTTING FOOD AWAY? THEY'D THINK WE WERE AWESOME!
YOU KNOW EXACTLY WHAT I'M TRYING TO SAY! WE CAN'T USE OUR POWERS! IF SOMEBODY SAW US, IT'D BE A DISASTER!
DO YOU WANT TO GO INTO HIDING ALL OVER AGAIN? WE JUST MOVED HERE!
YOU'RE SUCH A WET BLANKET.
QUIT TALKING IN MY HEAD!
WE'RE AT HOME. NO ONE'S GOING TO SEE US.

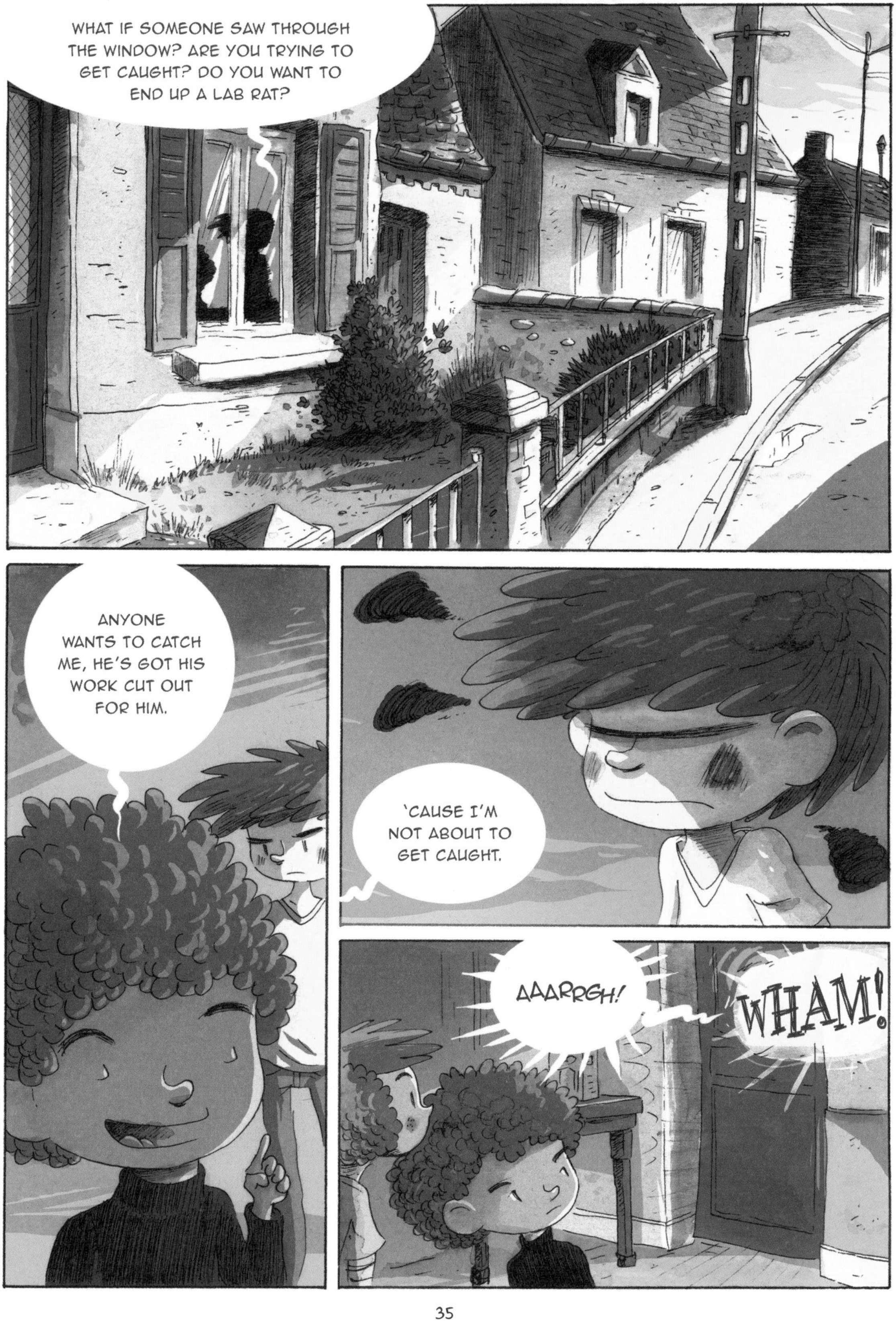
WHAT IF SOMEONE SAW THROUGH THE WINDOW? ARE YOU TRYING TO GET CAUGHT? DO YOU WANT TO END UP A LAB RAT?
ANYONE WANTS TO CATCH ME, HE'S GOT HIS WORK CUT OUT FOR HIM.
'CAUSE I'M NOT ABOUT TO GET CAUGHT.
AAARRGH!
WHAM!

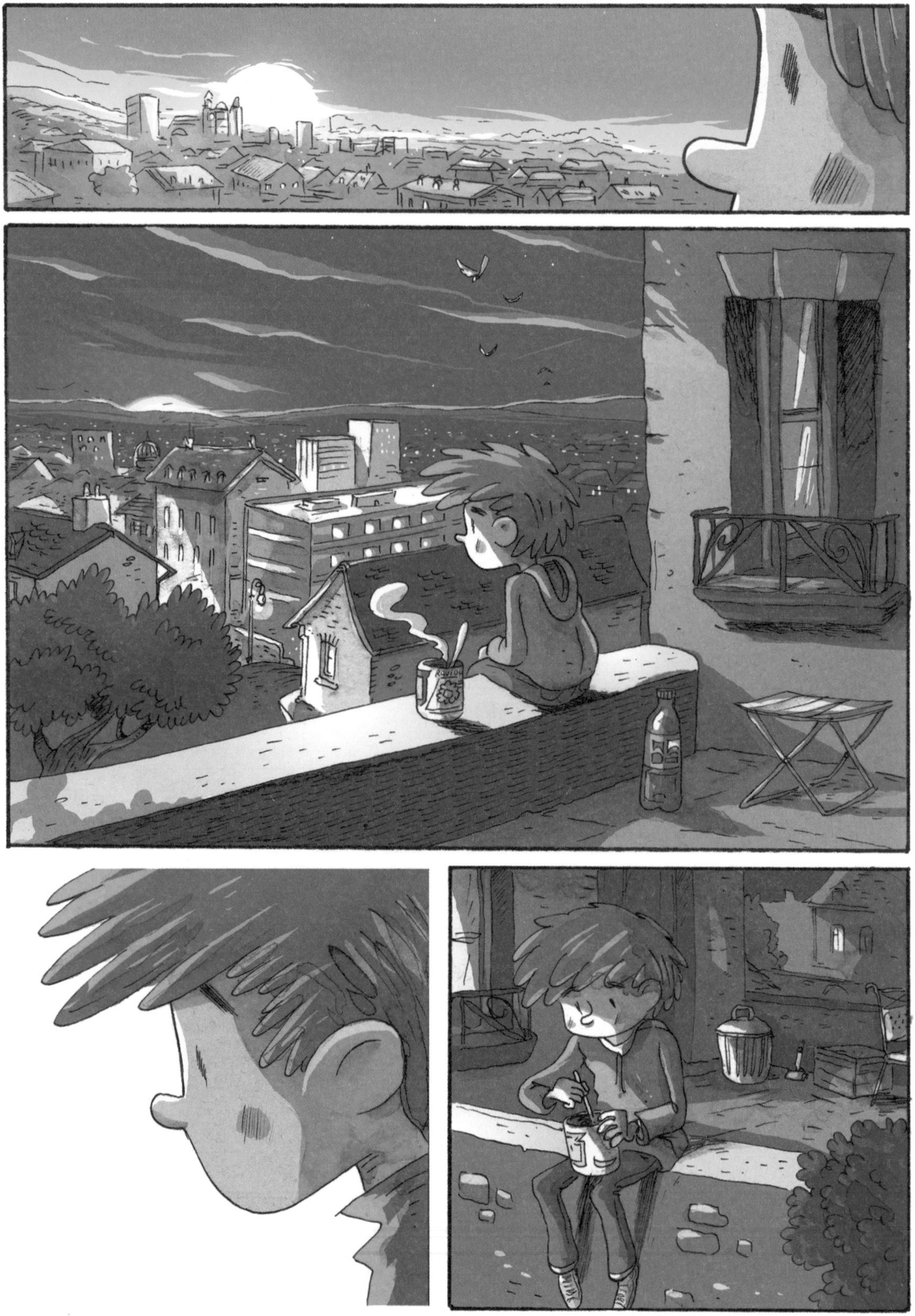

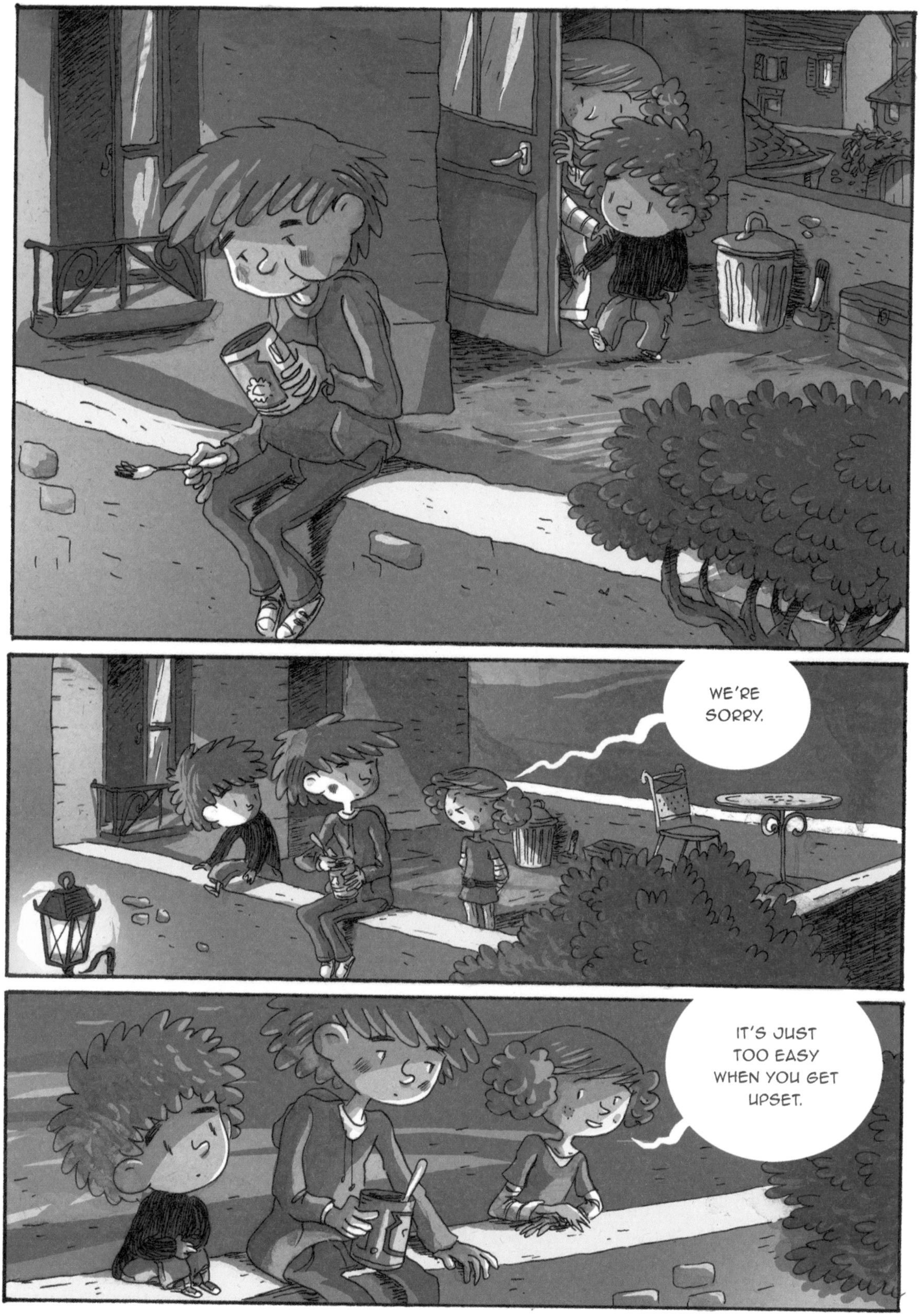
WE'RE SORRY.
IT'S JUST TOO EASY WHEN YOU GET UPSET.

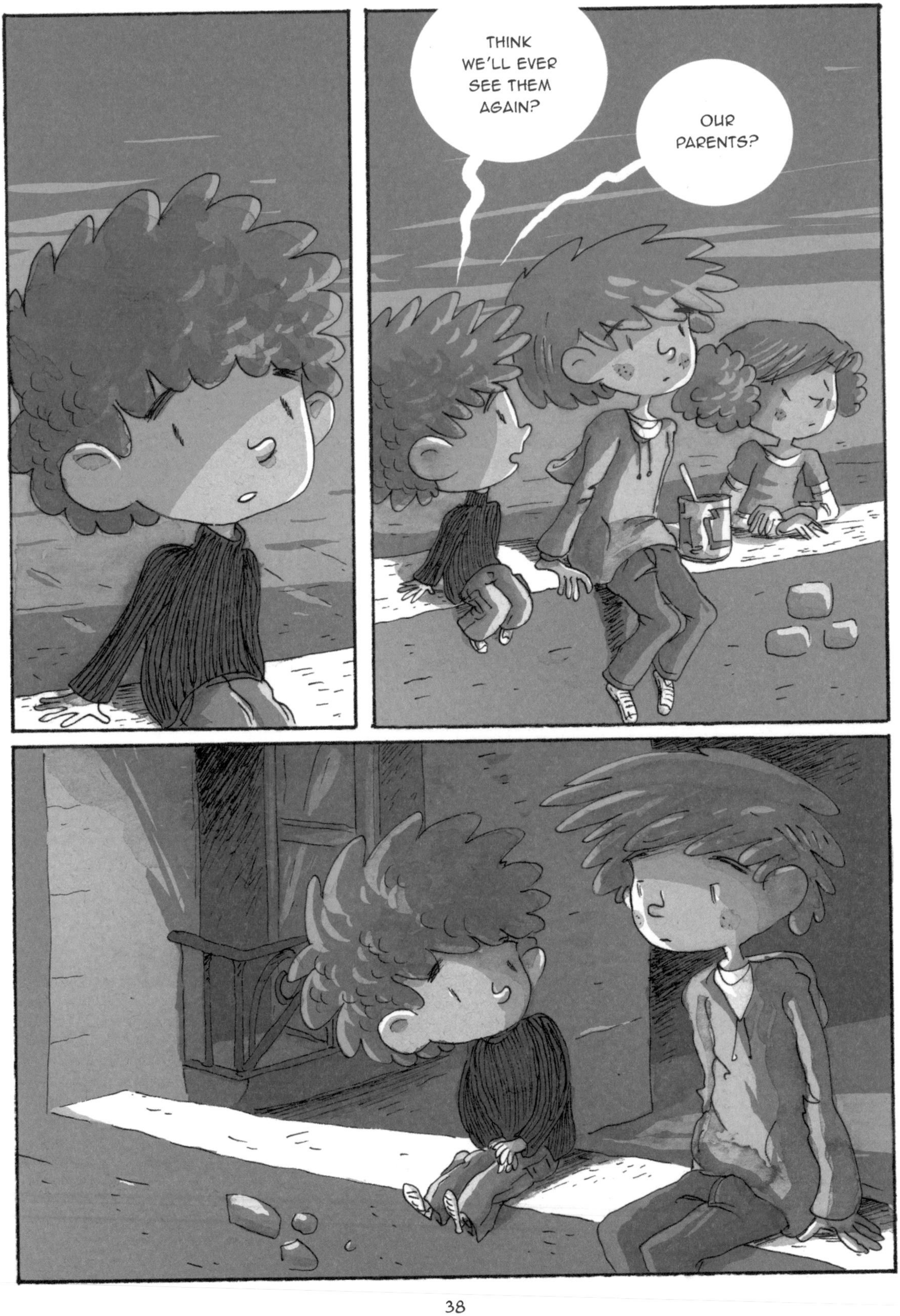
THINK WE'LL EVER SEE THEM AGAIN?
OUR PARENTS?

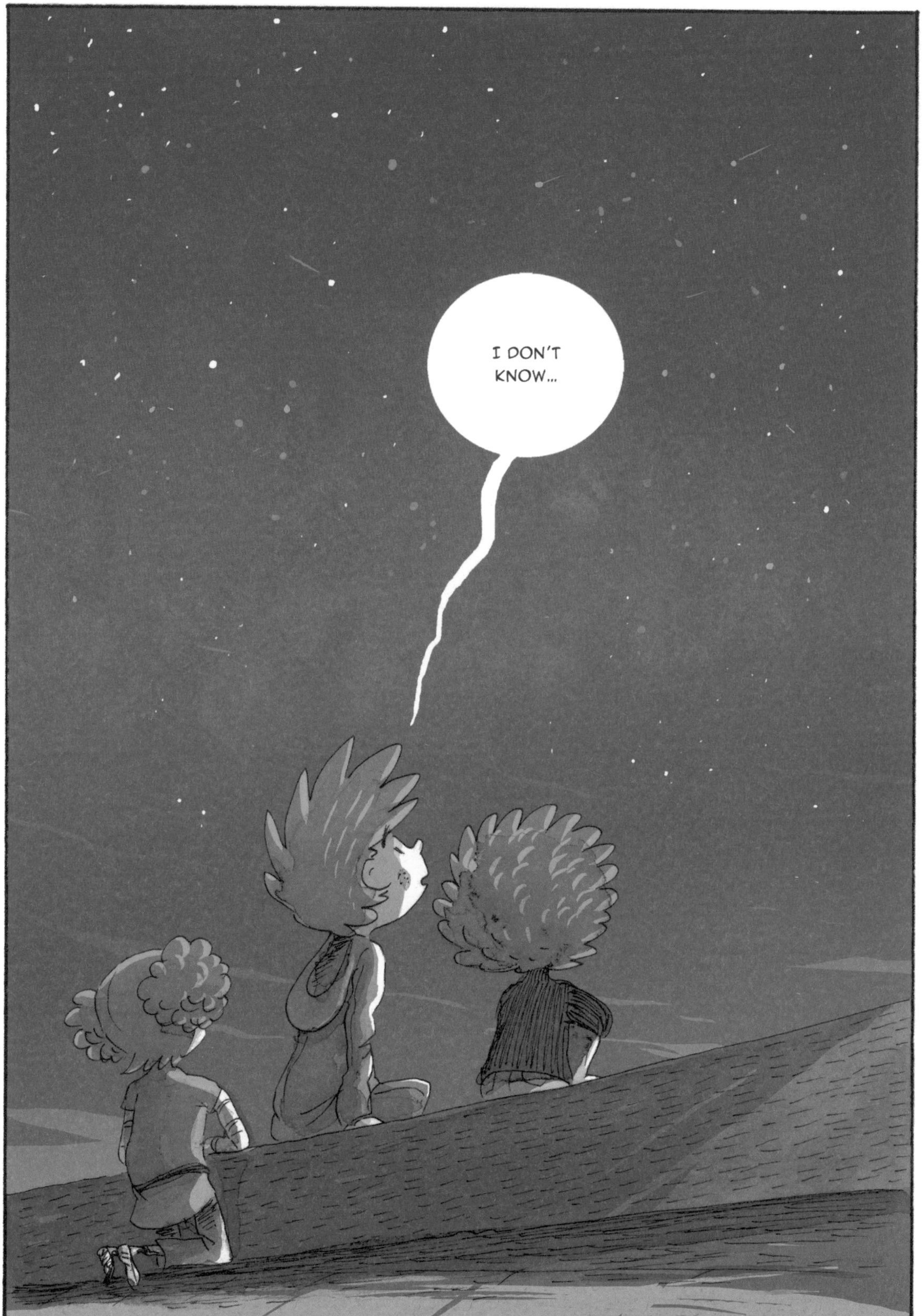
I DON'T KNOW...

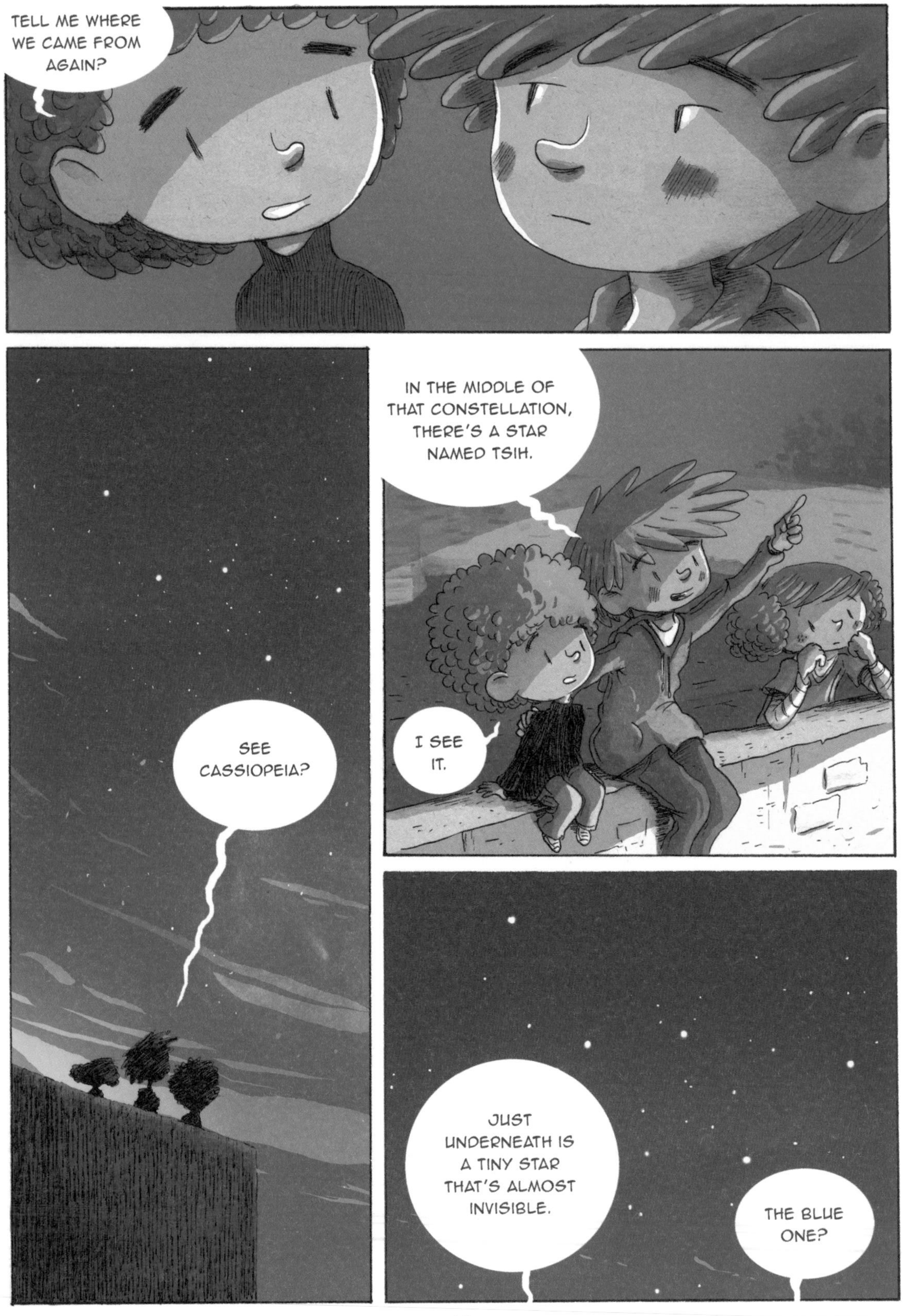
TELL ME WHERE WE CAME FROM AGAIN?
SEE CASSIOPEIA?
IN THE MIDDLE OF THAT CONSTELLATION, THERE'S A STAR NAMED TSIH.
I SEE IT.
JUST UNDERNEATH IS A TINY STAR THAT'S ALMOST INVISIBLE.
THE BLUE ONE?

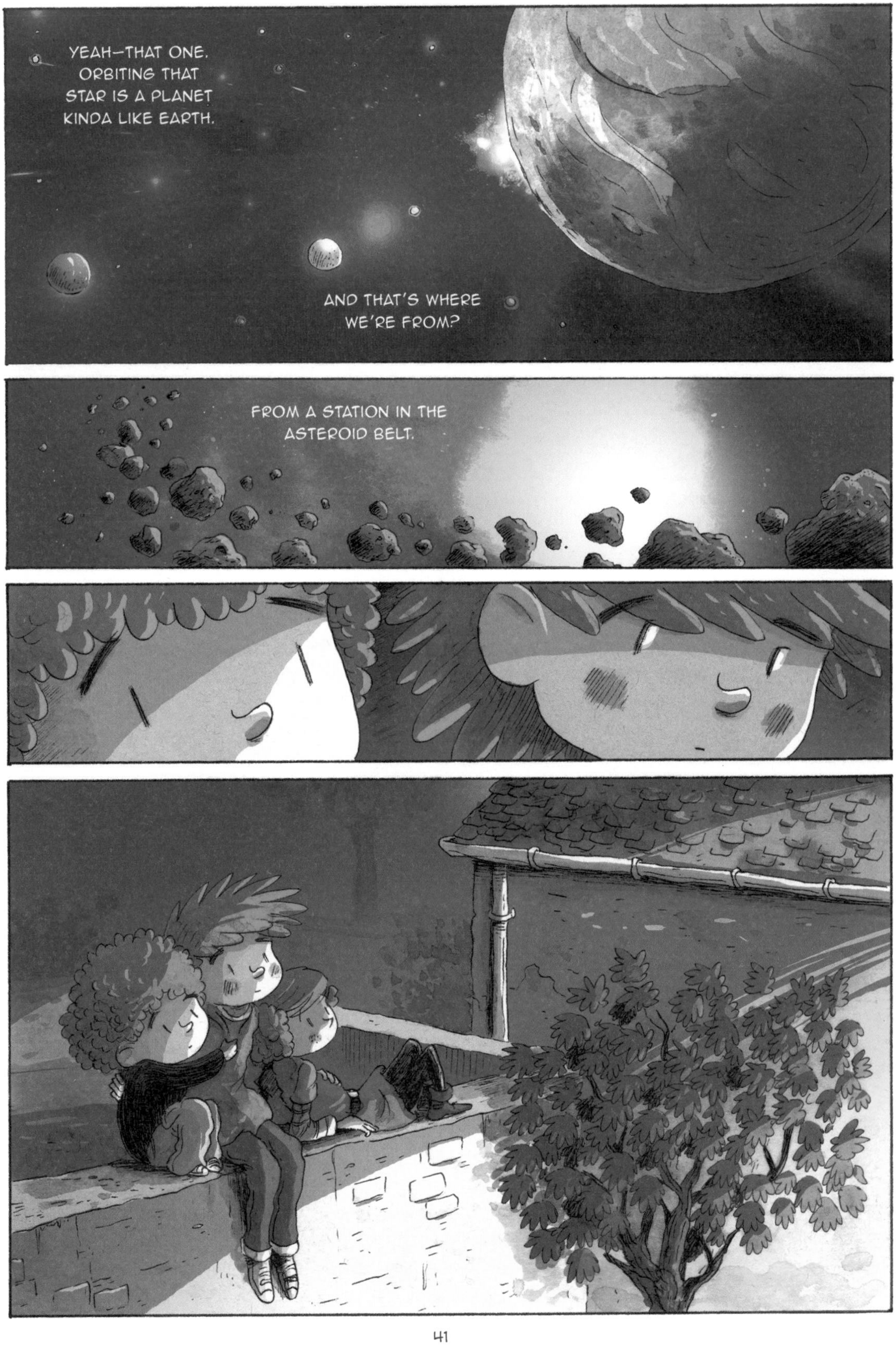
YEAH—THAT ONE. ORBITING THAT STAR IS A PLANET KINDA LIKE EARTH.
AND THAT'S WHERE WE'RE FROM?
FROM A STATION IN THE ASTEROID BELT.

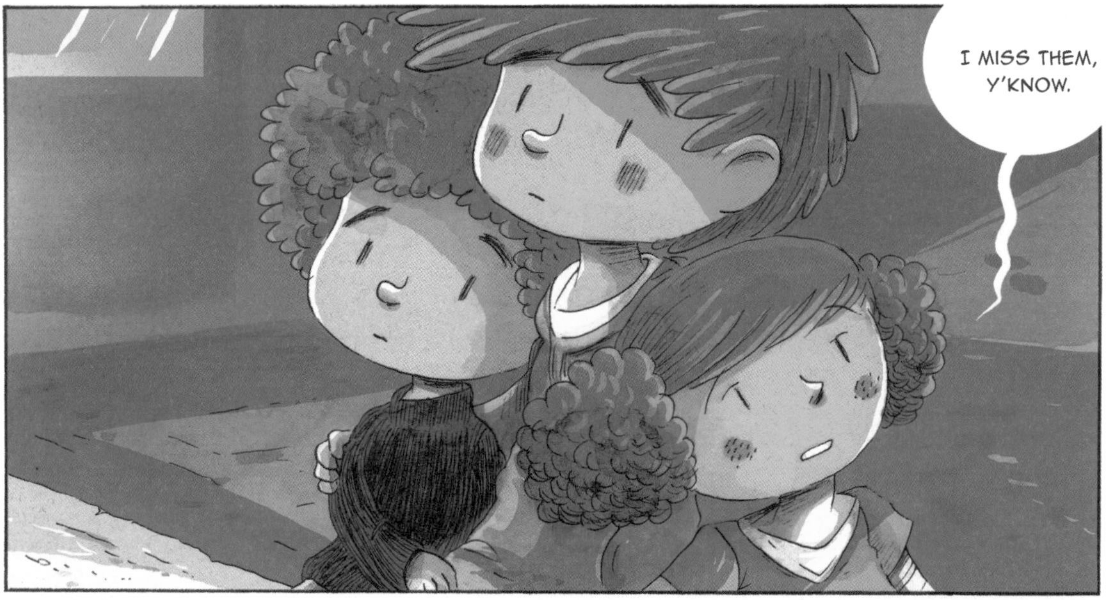
I MISS THEM, Y'KNOW.

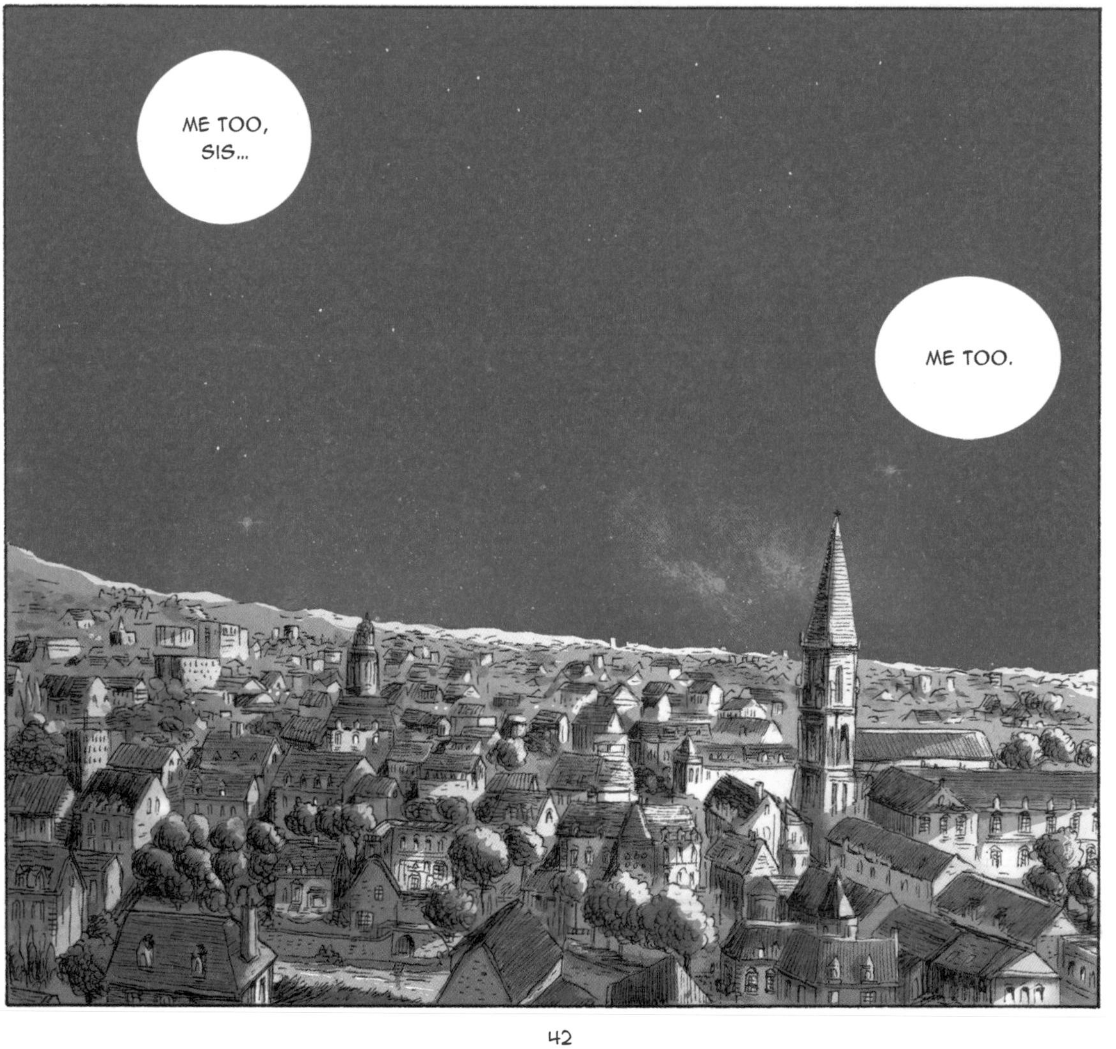
ME TOO, SIS...
ME TOO.

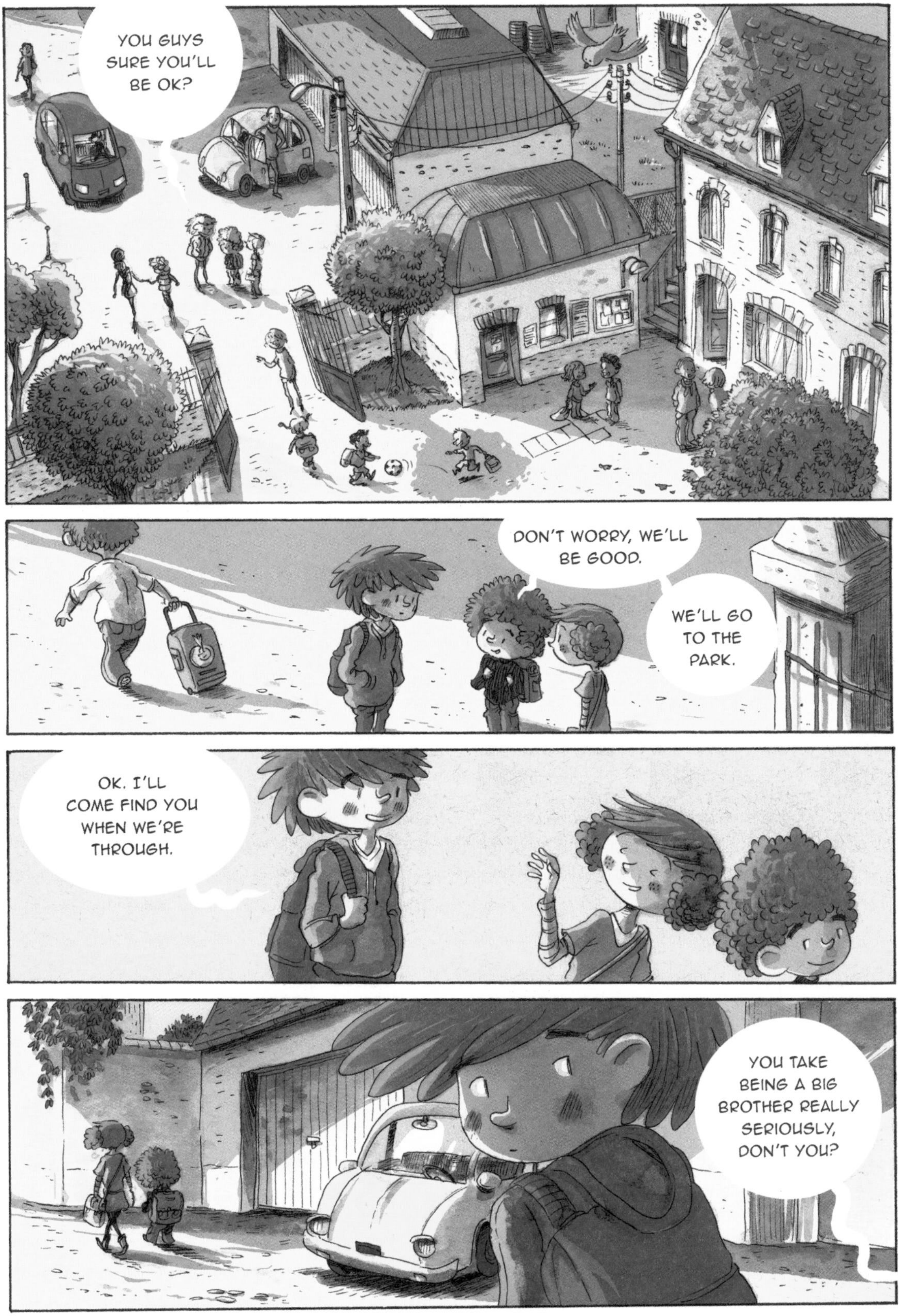
YOU GUYS SURE YOU'LL BE OK?
DON'T WORRY, WE'LL BE GOOD.
WE'LL GO TO THE PARK.
OK. I'LL COME FIND YOU WHEN WE'RE THROUGH.
YOU TAKE BEING A BIG BROTHER REALLY SERIOUSLY, DON'T YOU?

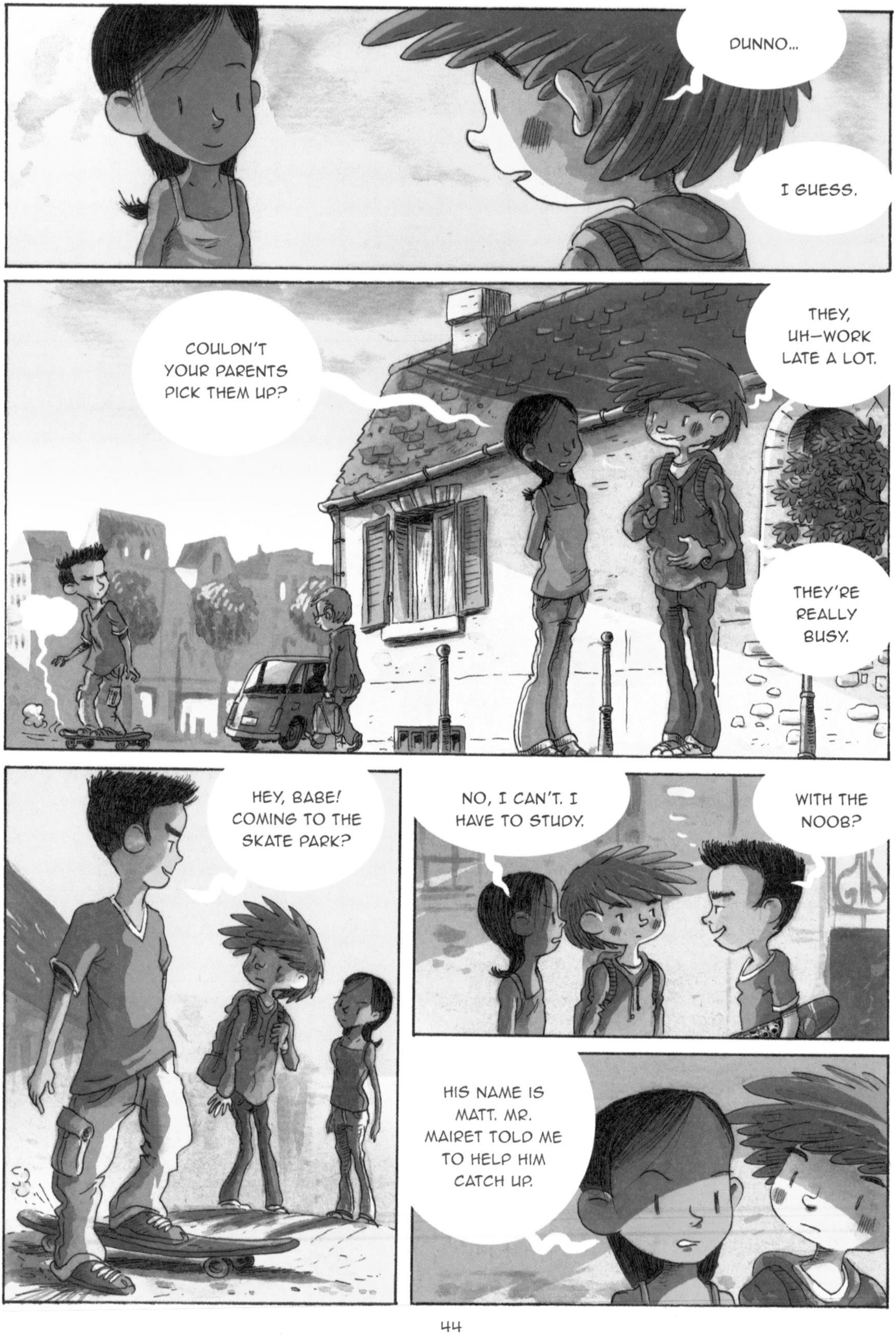
DUNNO...
I GUESS.
COULDN'T YOUR PARENTS PICK THEM UP?
THEY, UH—WORK LATE A LOT.
THEY'RE REALLY BUSY.
HEY, BABE! COMING TO THE SKATE PARK?
NO, I CAN'T. I HAVE TO STUDY.
WITH THE NOOB?
HIS NAME IS MATT. MR. MAIRET TOLD ME TO HELP HIM CATCH UP.

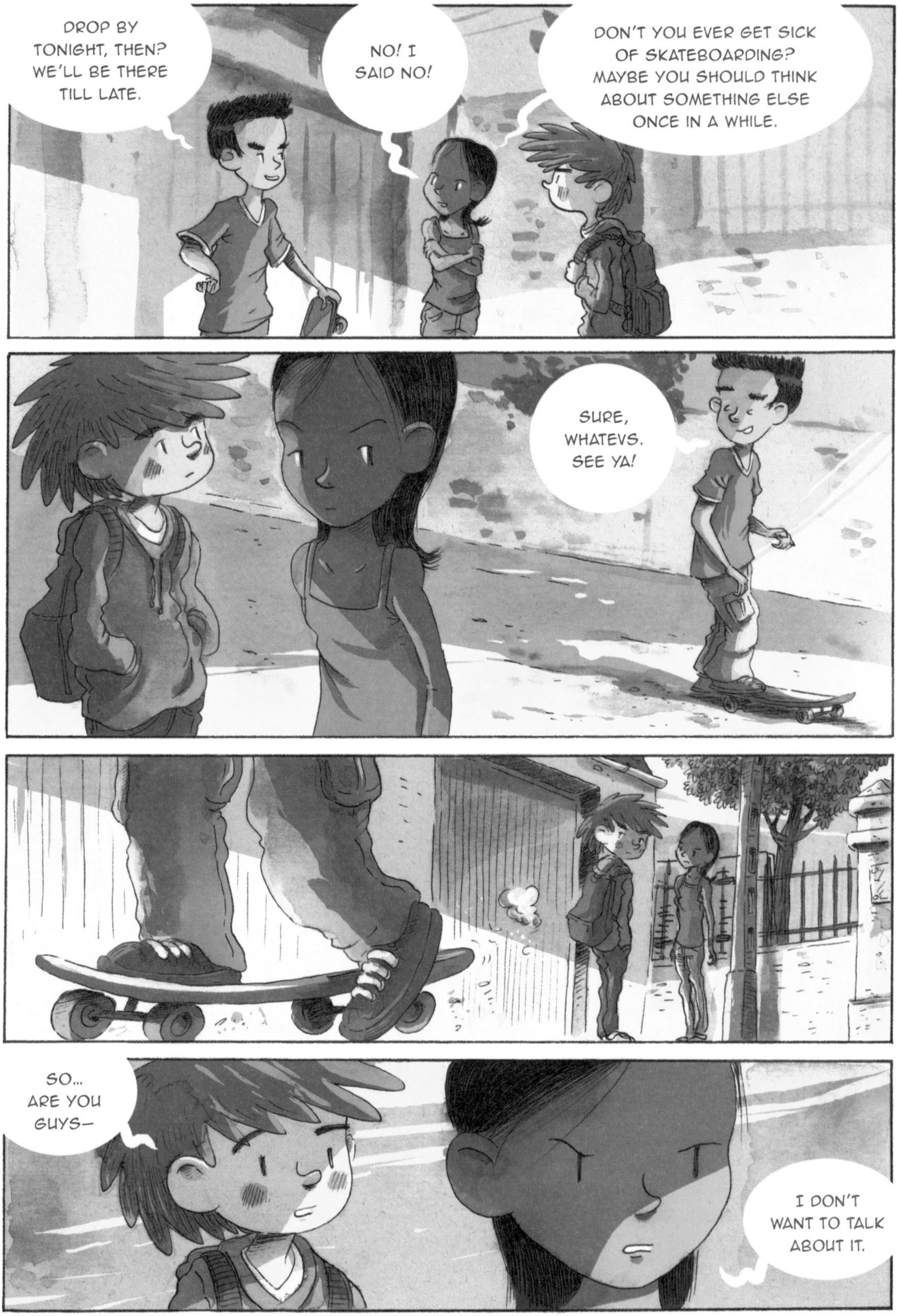
DROP BY TONIGHT, THEN? WE'LL BE THERE TILL LATE.
NO! I SAID NO!
DON'T YOU EVER GET SICK OF SKATEBOARDING? MAYBE YOU SHOULD THINK ABOUT SOMETHING ELSE ONCE IN A WHILE.
SURE, WHATEVS. SEE YA!
SO... ARE YOU GUYS—
I DON'T WANT TO TALK ABOUT IT.

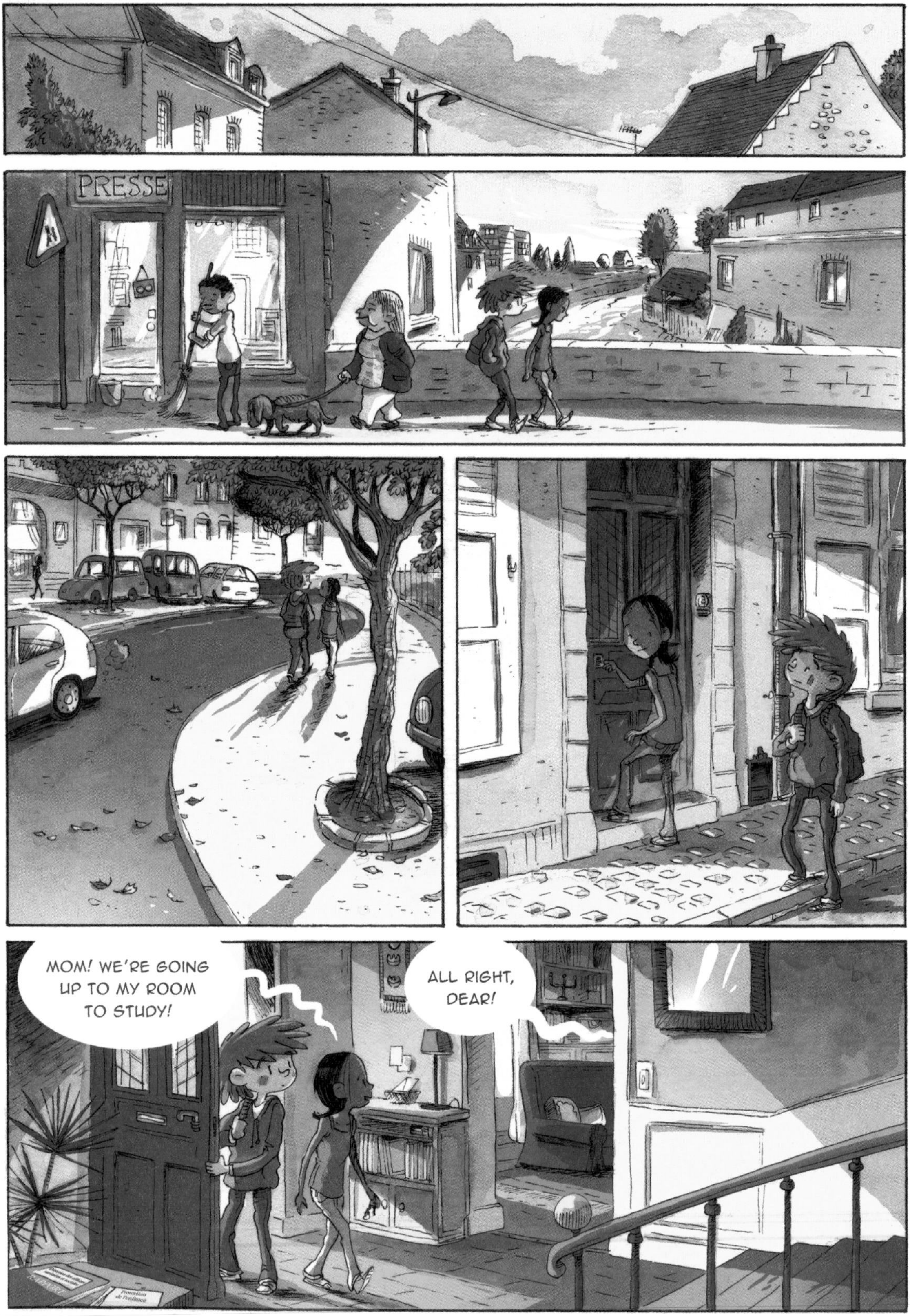
PRESSE
MOM! WE'RE GOING UP TO MY ROOM TO STUDY!
ALL RIGHT, DEAR!

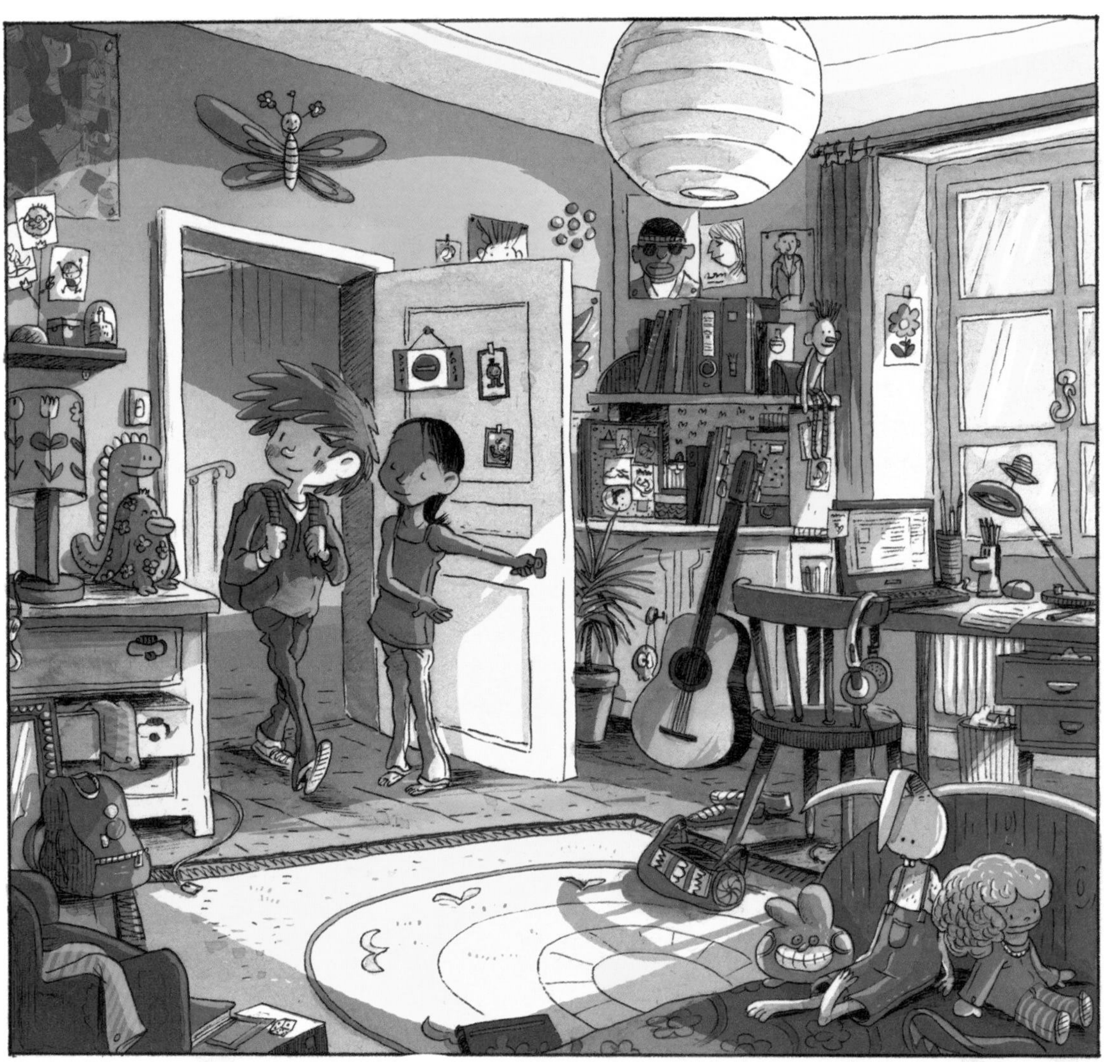

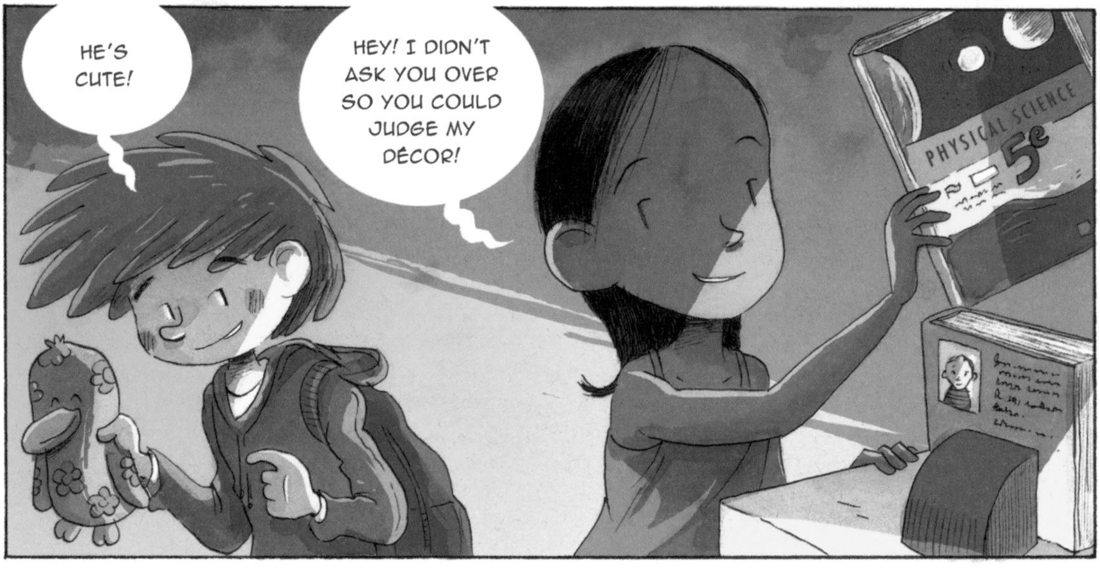
HE'S CUTE!
HEY! I DIDN'T ASK YOU OVER SO YOU COULD JUDGE MY DÉCOR!
PHYSICAL SCIENCE
5e

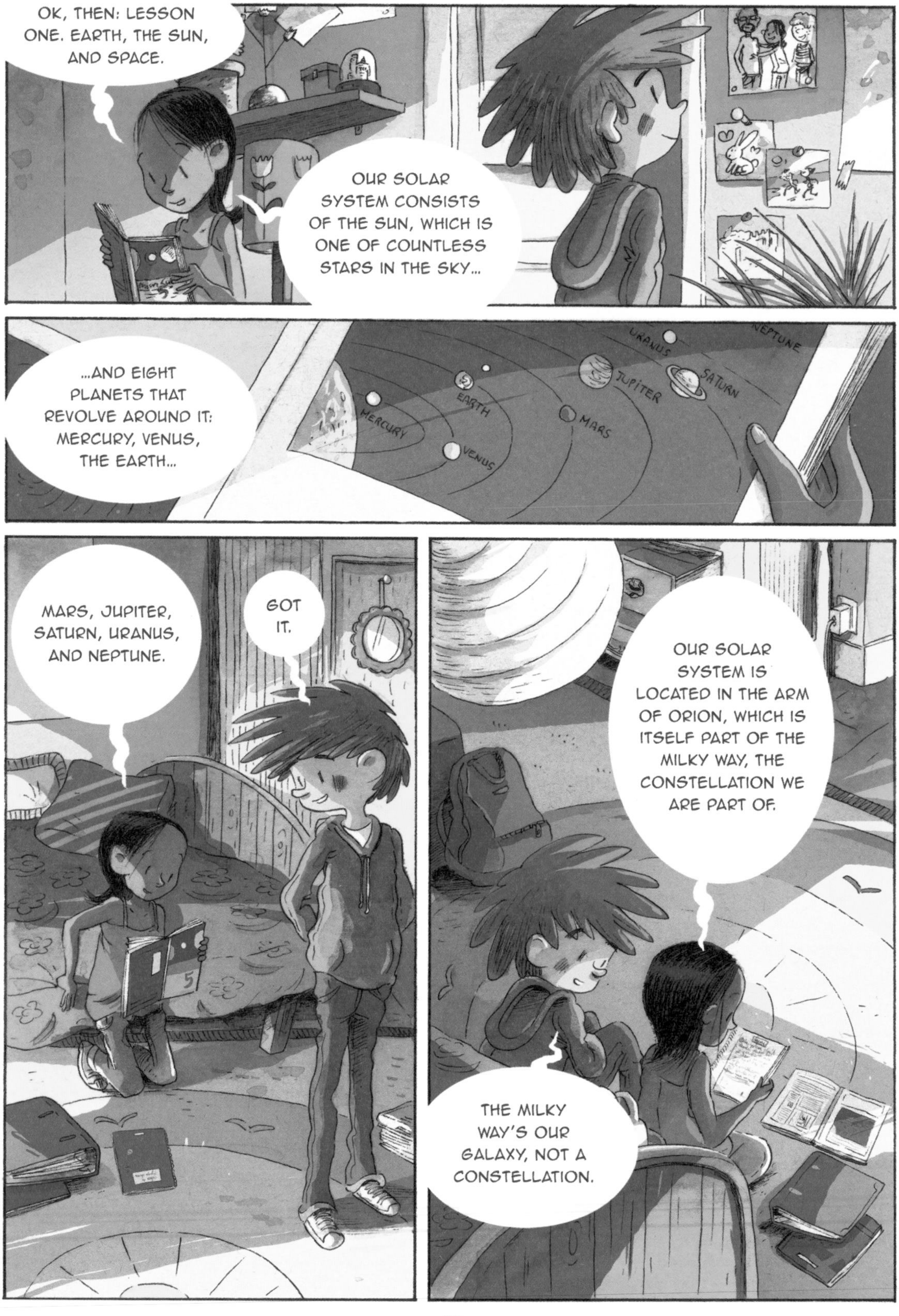

OK, THEN: LESSON ONE. EARTH, THE SUN, AND SPACE.
OUR SOLAR SYSTEM CONSISTS OF THE SUN, WHICH IS ONE OF COUNTLESS STARS IN THE SKY...
...AND EIGHT PLANETS THAT REVOLVE AROUND IT: MERCURY, VENUS, THE EARTH...
MERCURY
VENUS
EARTH
MARS
JUPITER
SATURN
URANUS
NEPTUNE
MARS, JUPITER, SATURN, URANUS, AND NEPTUNE.
GOT IT.
OUR SOLAR SYSTEM IS LOCATED IN THE ARM OF ORION, WHICH IS ITSELF PART OF THE MILKY WAY, THE CONSTELLATION WE ARE PART OF.
THE MILKY WAY'S OUR GALAXY, NOT A CONSTELLATION.

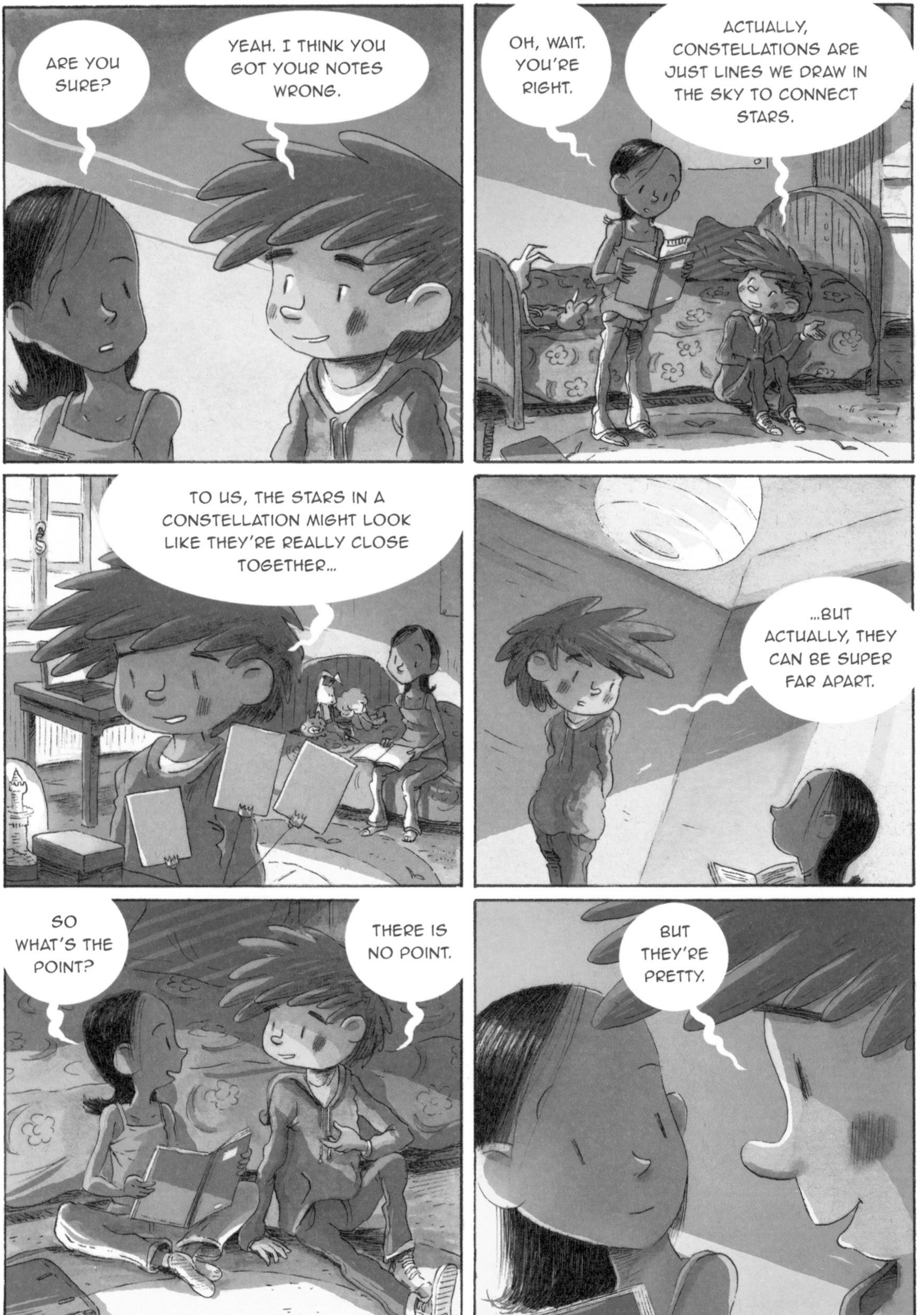

ARE YOU SURE?
YEAH. I THINK YOU GOT YOUR NOTES WRONG.
OH, WAIT. YOU'RE RIGHT.
ACTUALLY, CONSTELLATIONS ARE JUST LINES WE DRAW IN THE SKY TO CONNECT STARS.
TO US, THE STARS IN A CONSTELLATION MIGHT LOOK LIKE THEY'RE REALLY CLOSE TOGETHER...
...BUT ACTUALLY, THEY CAN BE SUPER FAR APART.
SO WHAT'S THE POINT?
THERE IS NO POINT.
BUT THEY'RE PRETTY.

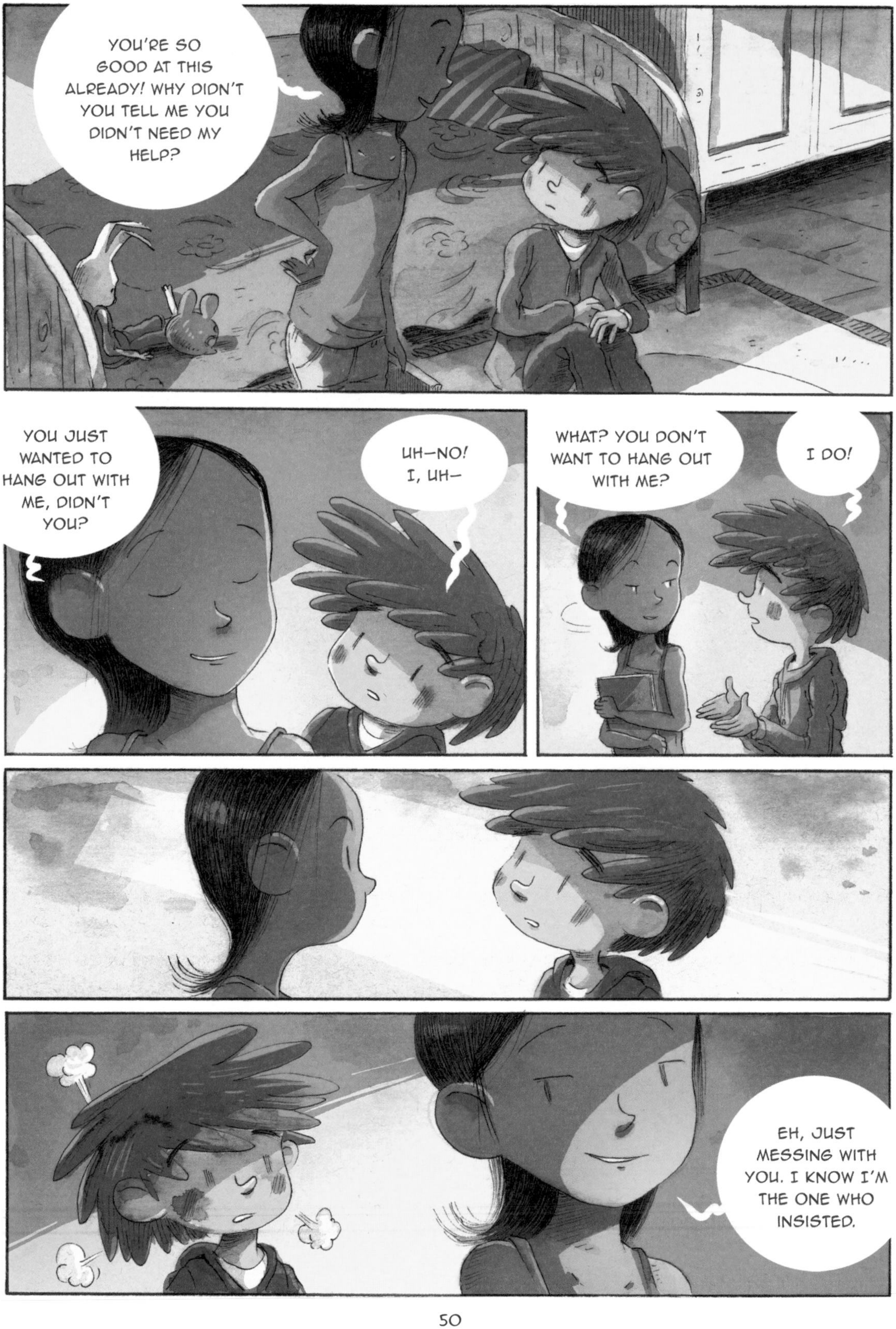
YOU'RE SO GOOD AT THIS ALREADY! WHY DIDN'T YOU TELL ME YOU DIDN'T NEED MY HELP?
YOU JUST WANTED TO HANG OUT WITH ME, DIDN'T YOU?
UH—NO! I, UH—
WHAT? YOU DON'T WANT TO HANG OUT WITH ME?
I DO!
EH, JUST MESSING WITH YOU. I KNOW I'M THE ONE WHO INSISTED.

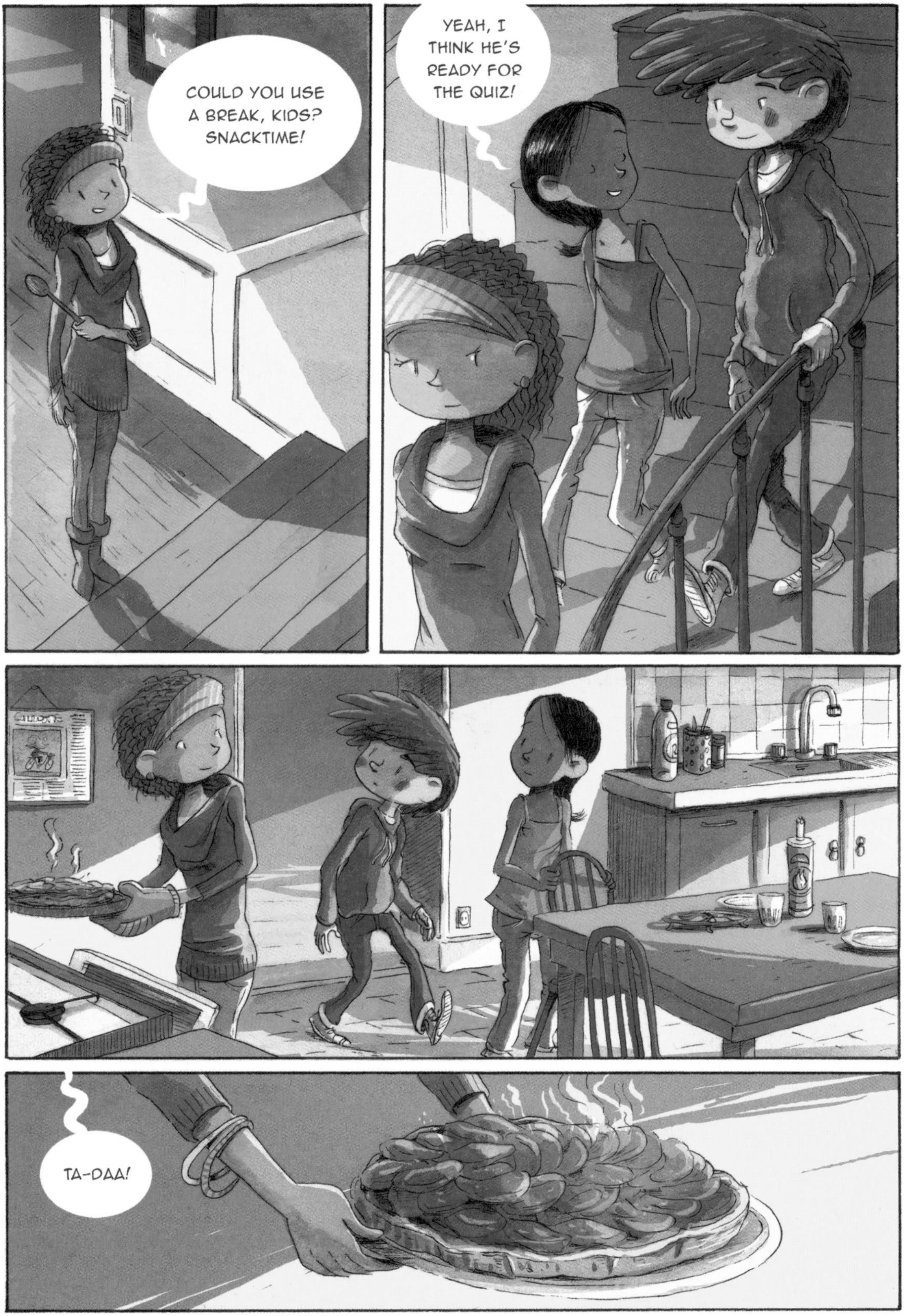
COULD YOU USE A BREAK, KIDS? SNACKTIME!
YEAH, I THINK HE'S READY FOR THE QUIZ!
TA-DAA!

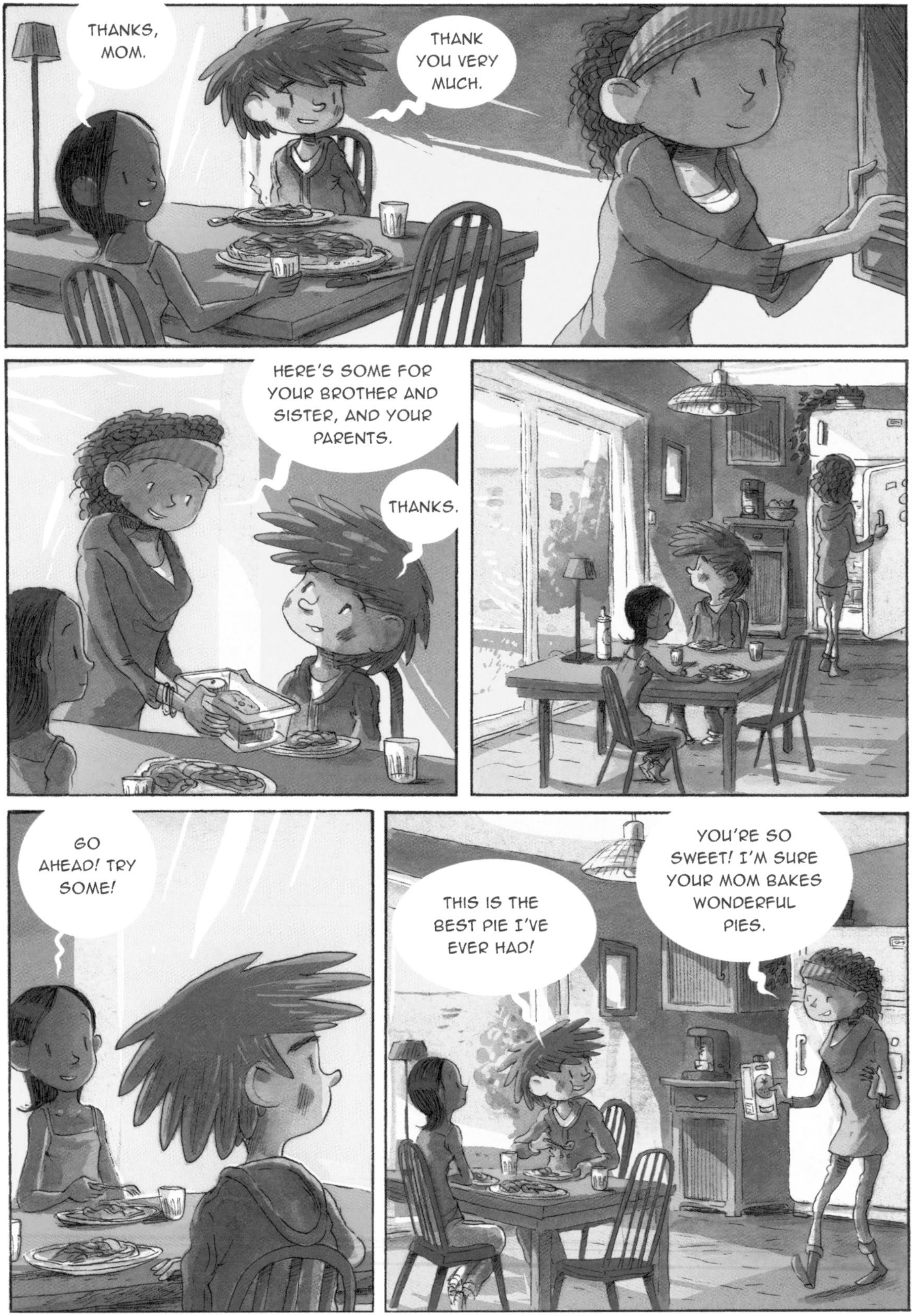
THANKS, MOM.
THANK YOU VERY MUCH.
HERE'S SOME FOR YOUR BROTHER AND SISTER, AND YOUR PARENTS.
THANKS.
GO AHEAD! TRY SOME!
THIS IS THE BEST PIE I'VE EVER HAD!
YOU'RE SO SWEET! I'M SURE YOUR MOM BAKES WONDERFUL PIES.

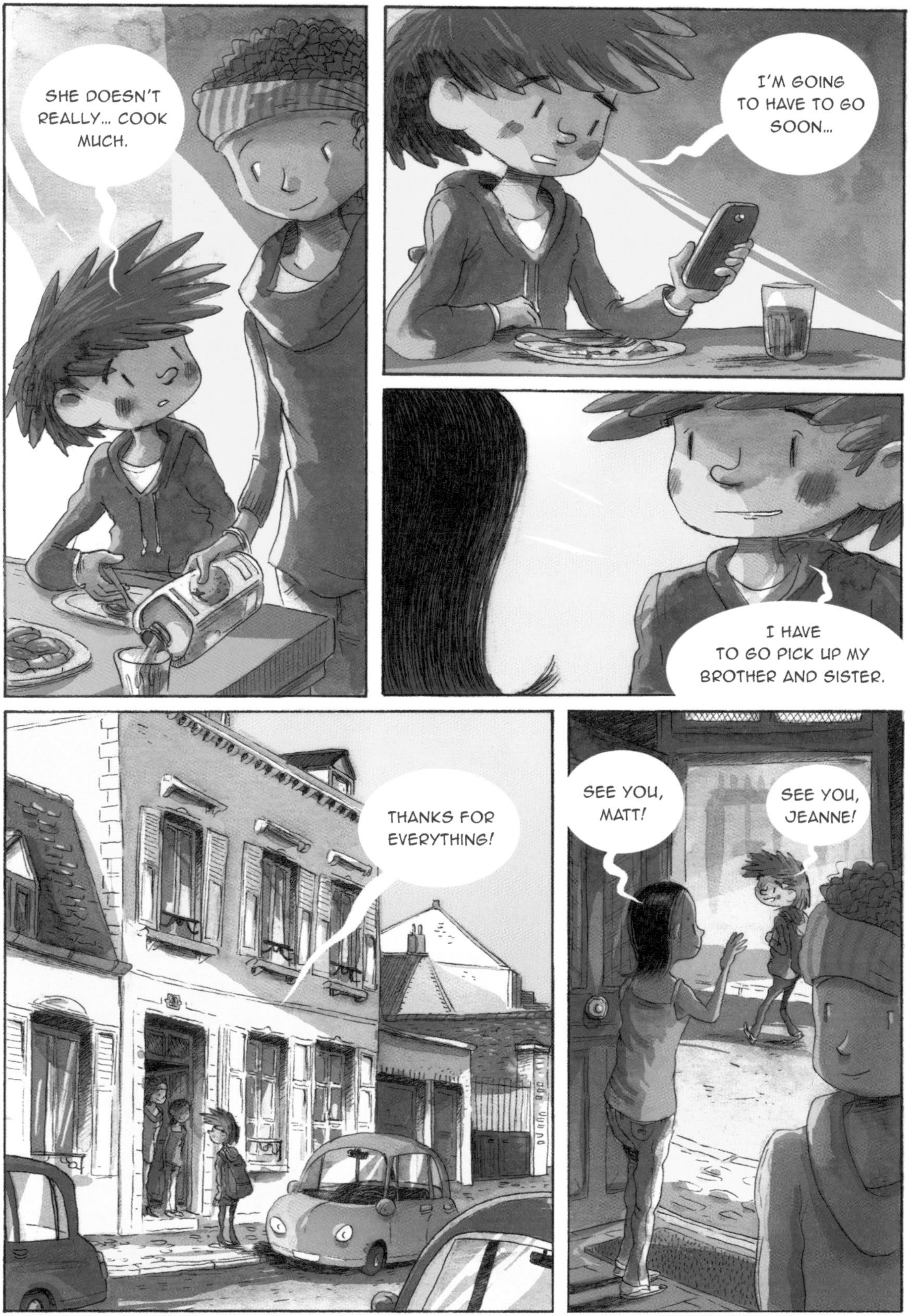
SHE DOESN'T REALLY... COOK MUCH.
I'M GOING TO HAVE TO GO SOON...
I HAVE TO GO PICK UP MY BROTHER AND SISTER.
THANKS FOR EVERYTHING!
SEE YOU, MATT!
SEE YOU, JEANNE!

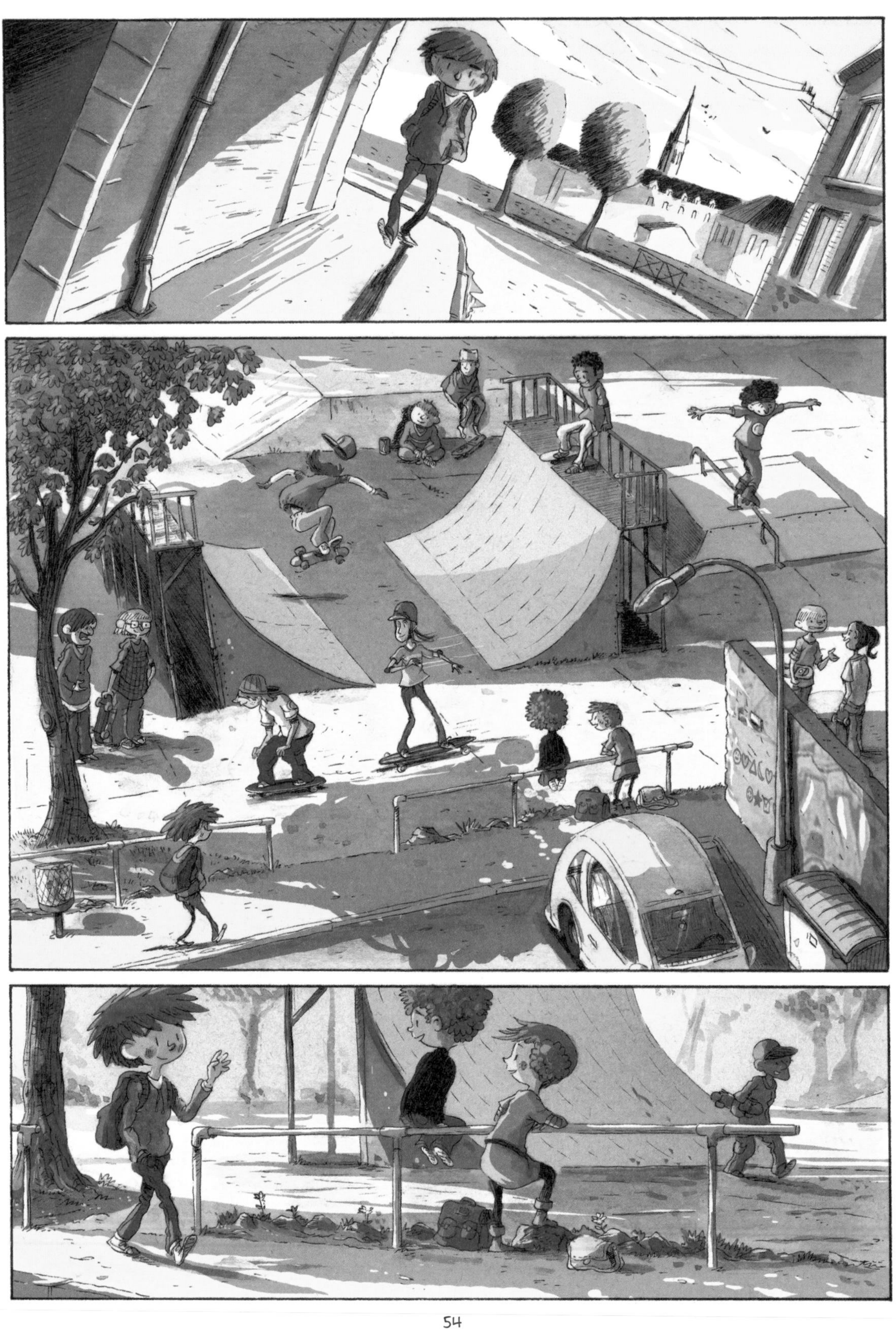

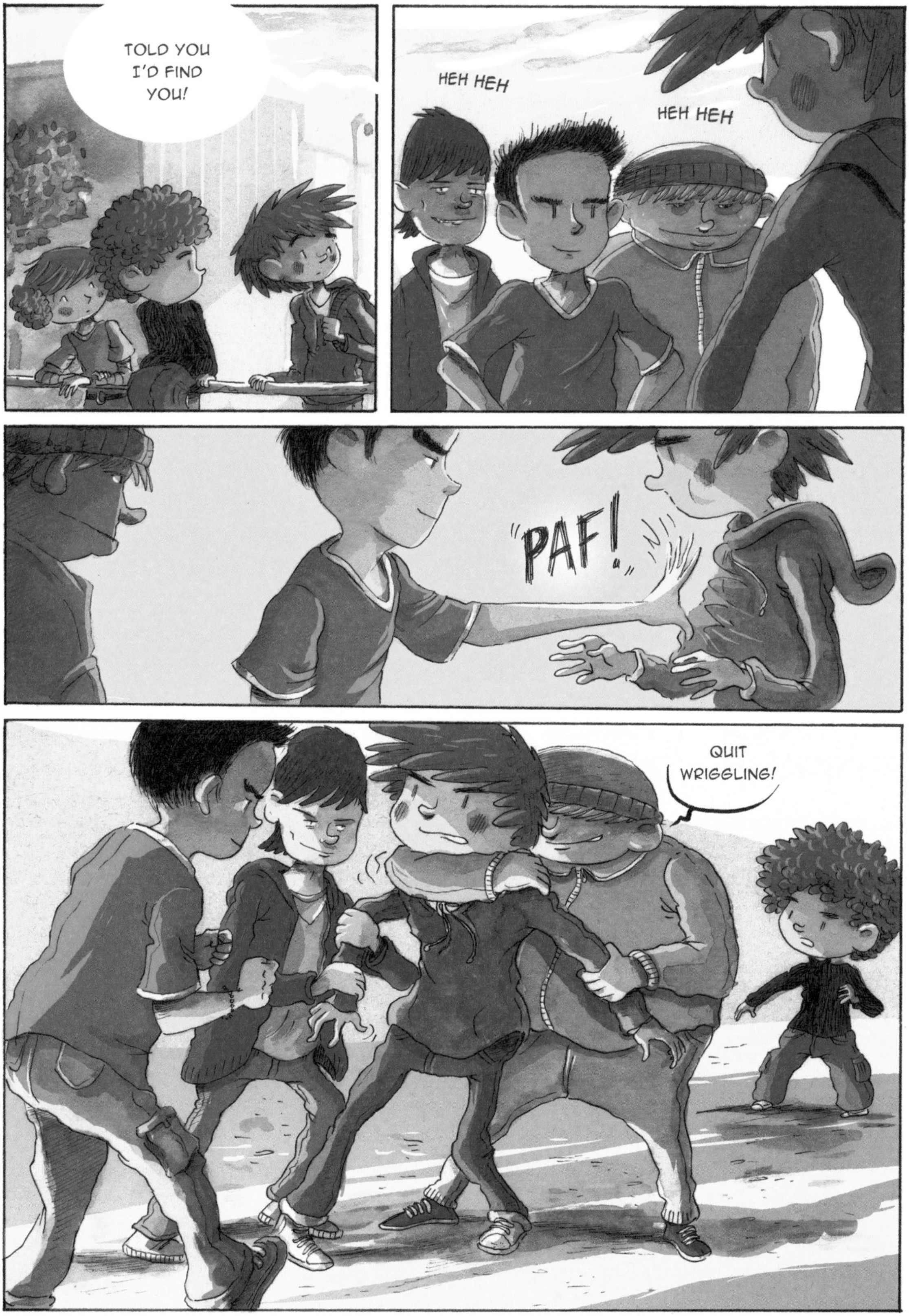
TOLD YOU I'D FIND YOU!
HEH HEH
HEH HEH
PAF!
QUIT WRIGGLING!

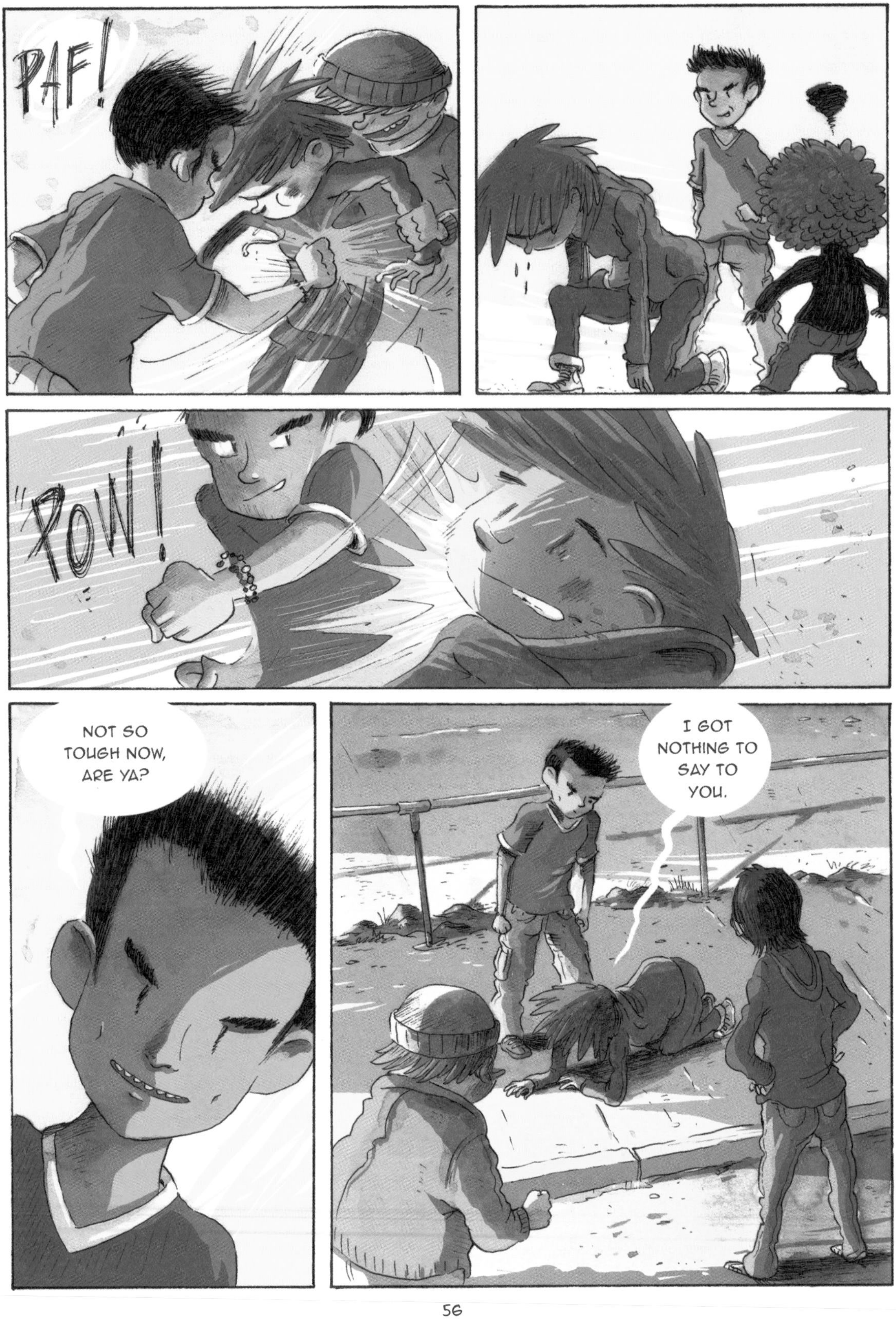
PAF!
POW!
NOT SO TOUGH NOW, ARE YA?
I GOT NOTHING TO SAY TO YOU.

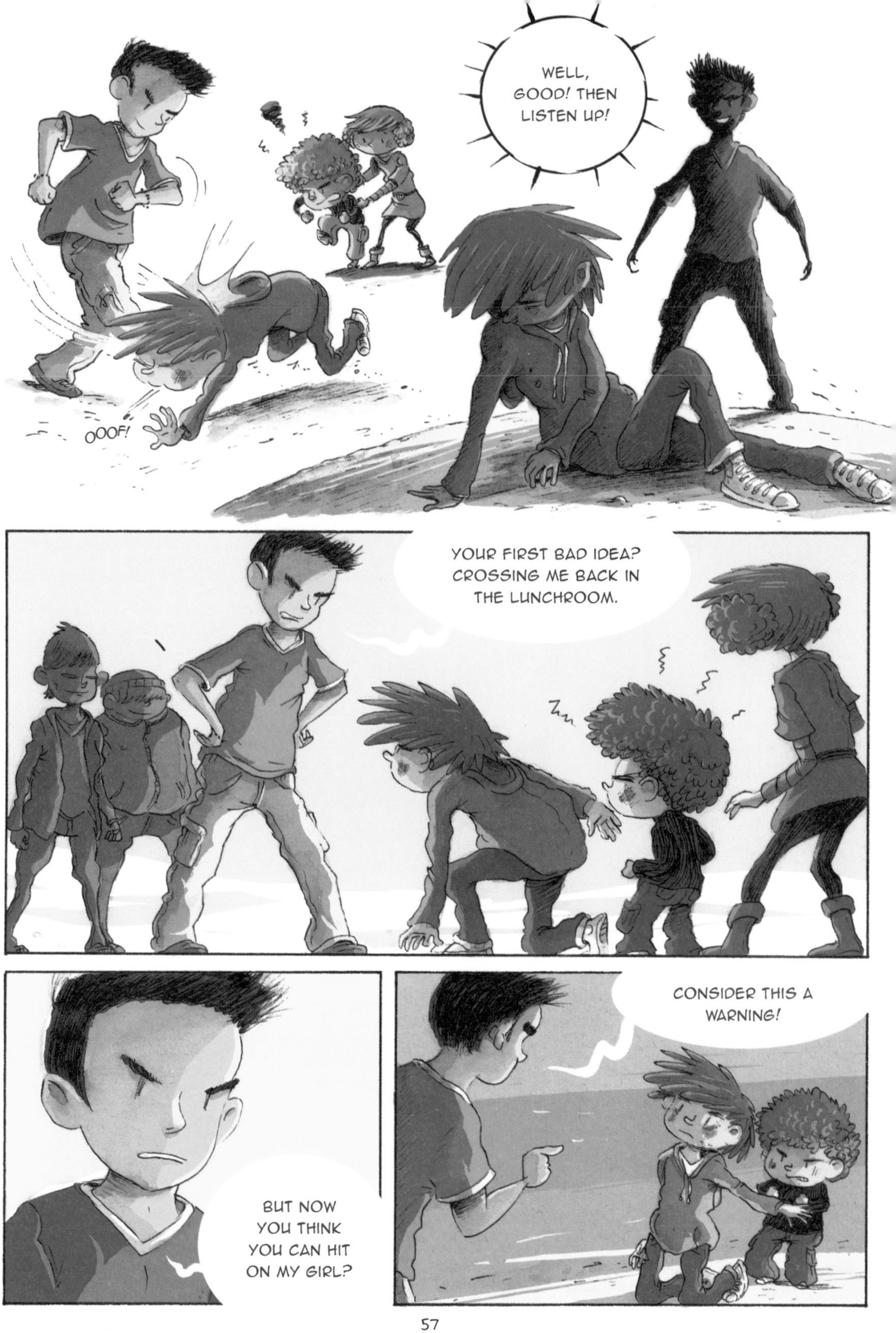
OOOF!
WELL, GOOD! THEN LISTEN UP!
YOUR FIRST BAD IDEA? CROSSING ME BACK IN THE LUNCHROOM.
BUT NOW YOU THINK YOU CAN HIT ON MY GIRL?
CONSIDER THIS A WARNING!

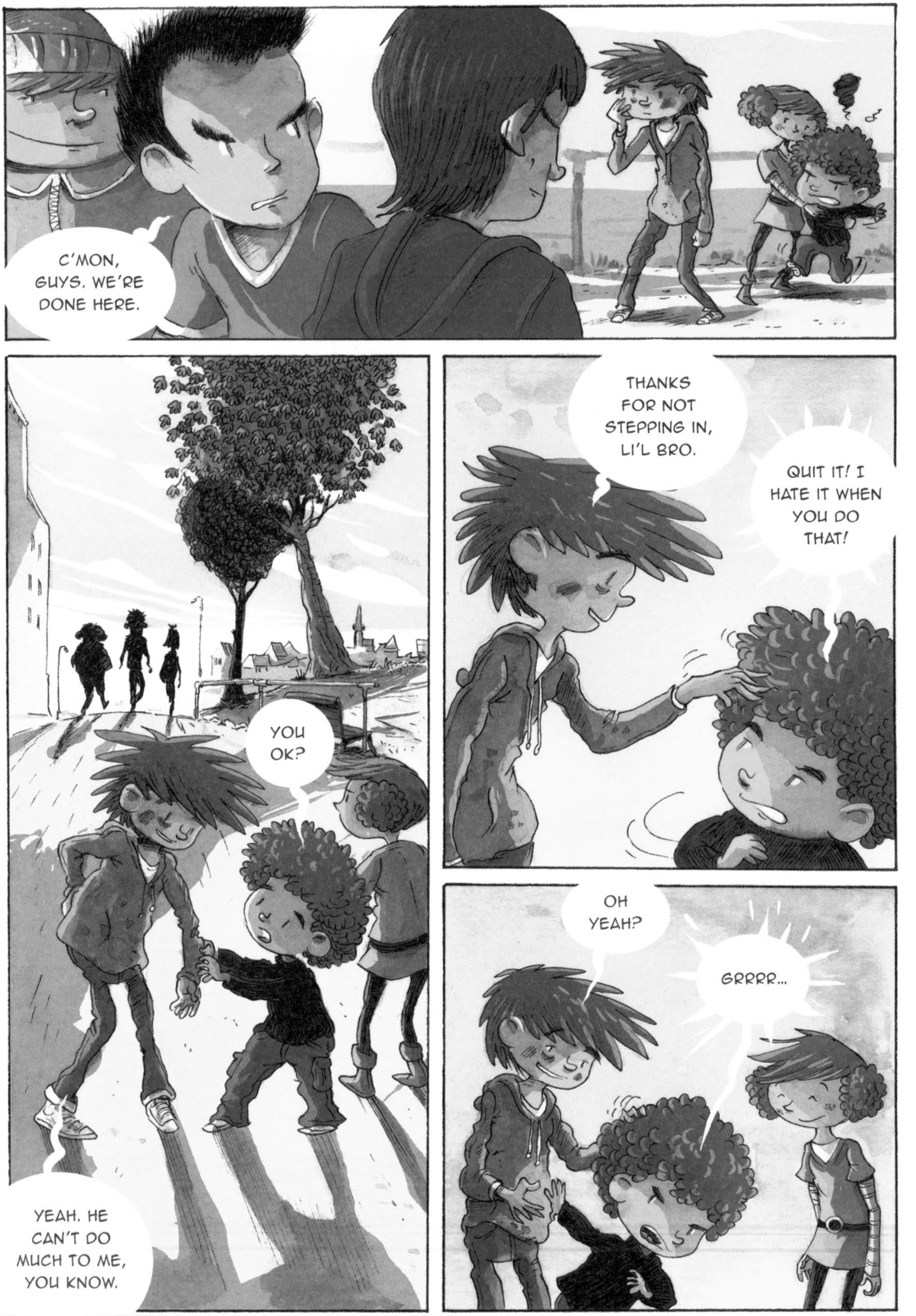
C'MON, GUYS. WE'RE DONE HERE.
YOU OK?
YEAH. HE CAN'T DO MUCH TO ME, YOU KNOW.
THANKS FOR NOT STEPPING IN, LI'L BRO.
QUIT IT! I HATE IT WHEN YOU DO THAT!
OH YEAH?
GRRRR...

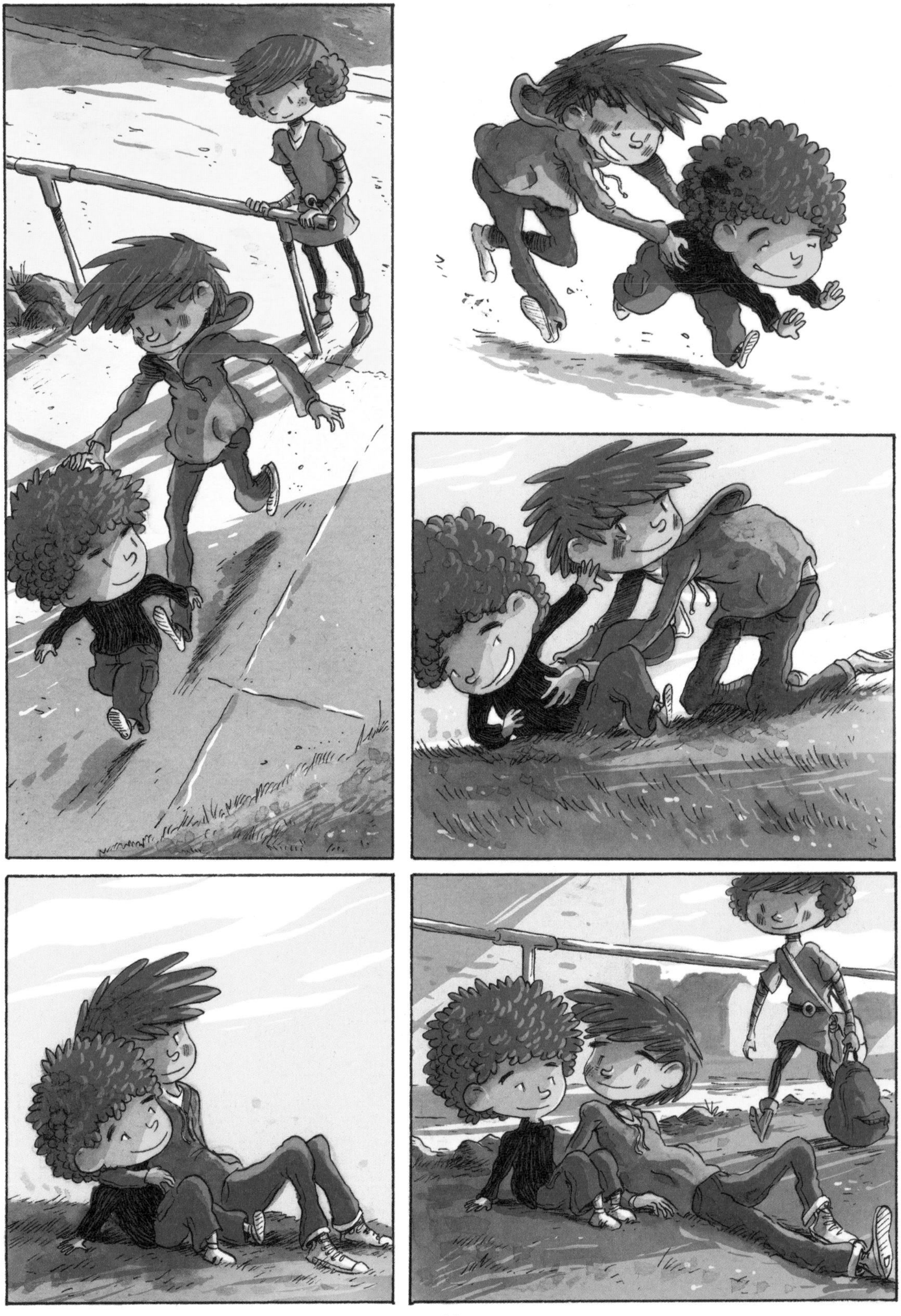

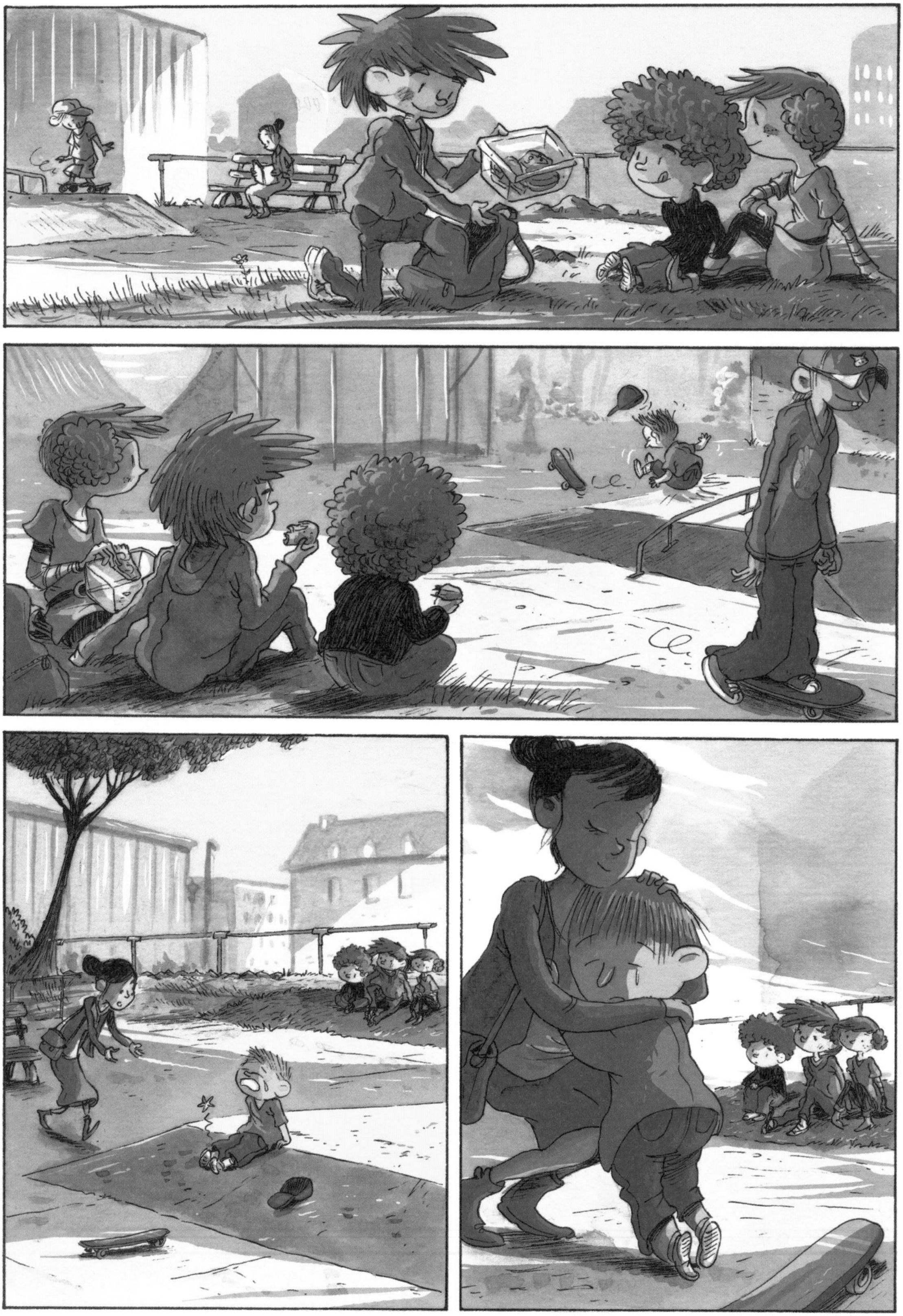

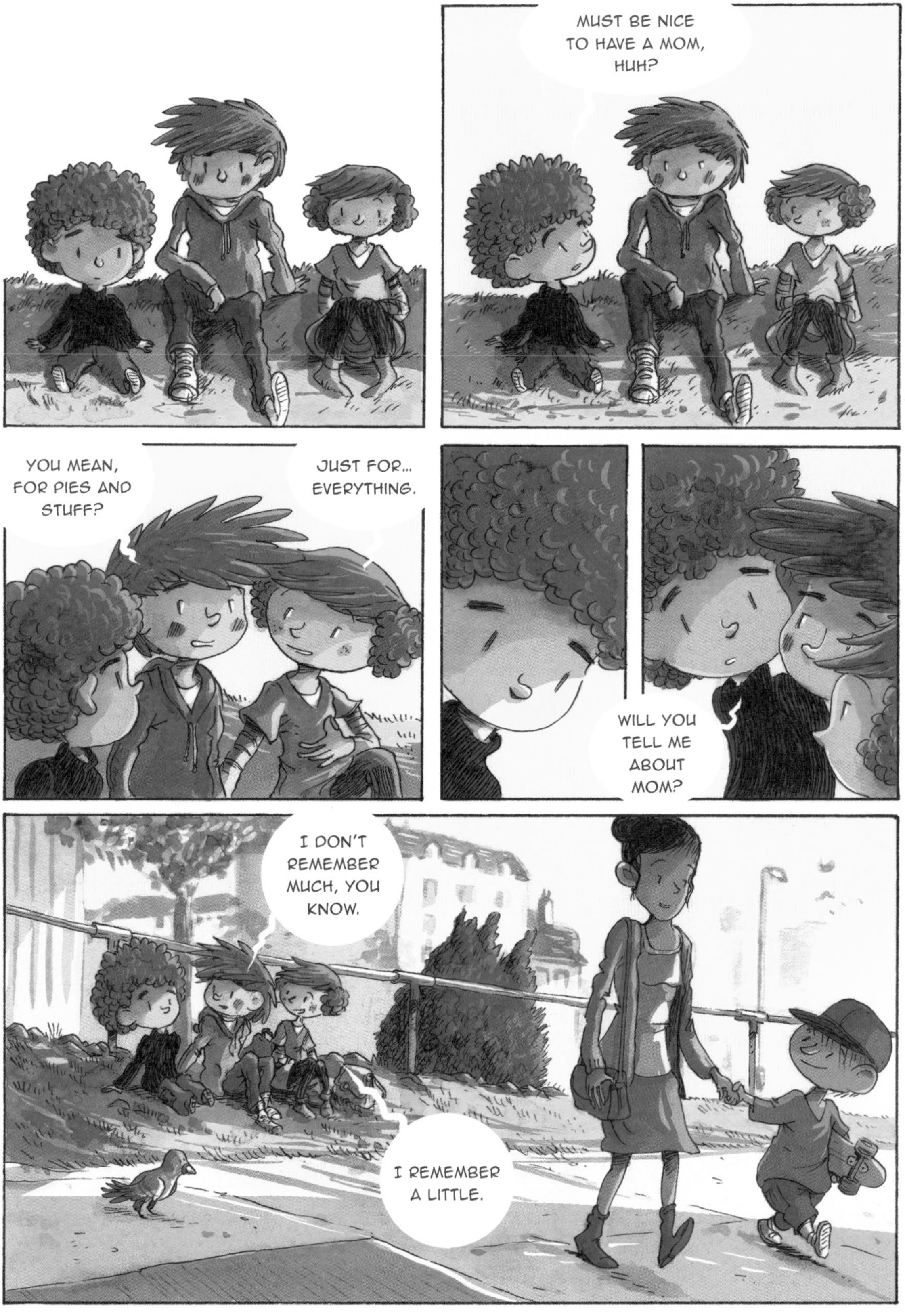
MUST BE NICE TO HAVE A MOM, HUH?
YOU MEAN, FOR PIES AND STUFF?
JUST FOR... EVERYTHING.
WILL YOU TELL ME ABOUT MOM?
I DON'T REMEMBER MUCH, YOU KNOW.
I REMEMBER A LITTLE.

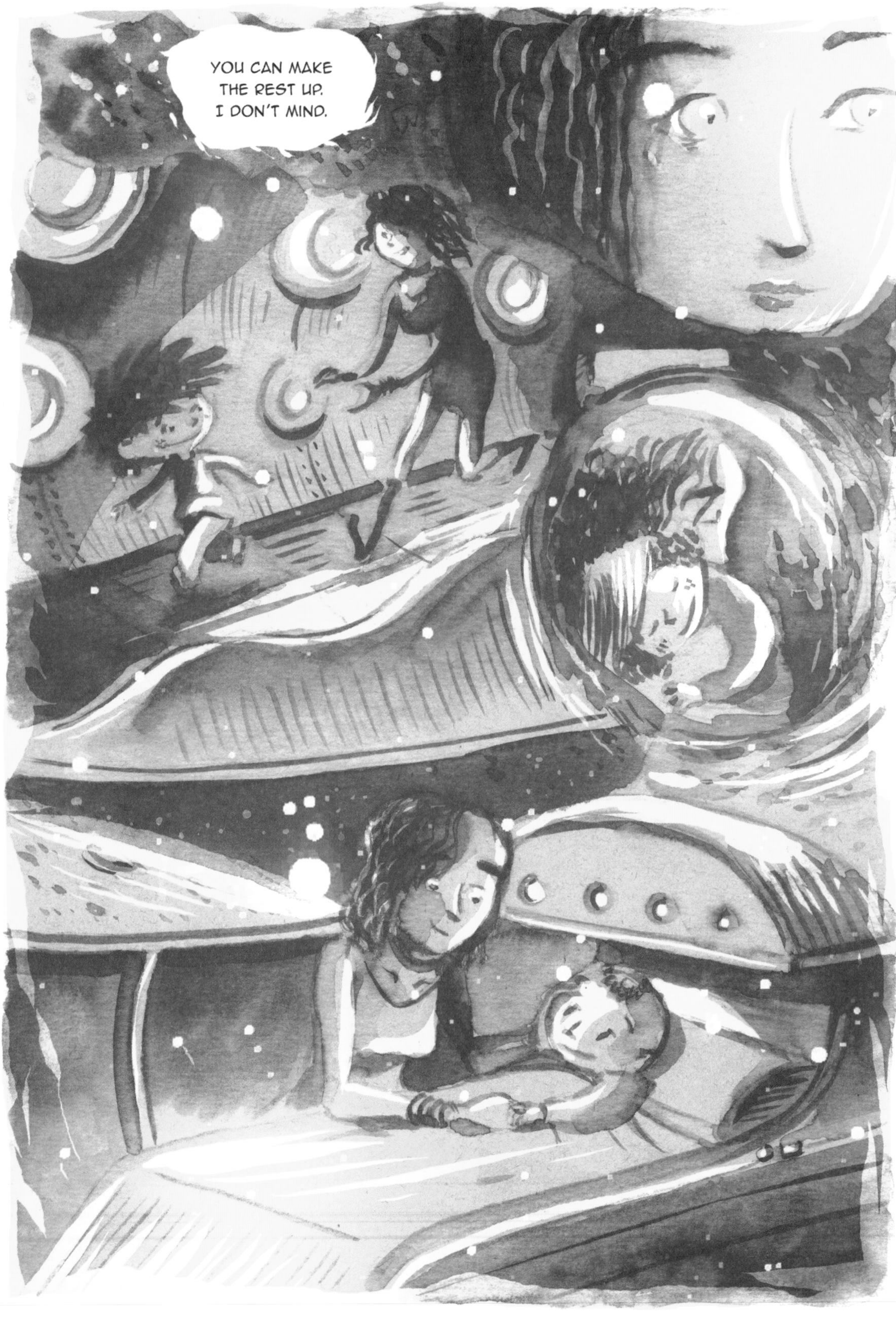
YOU CAN MAKE THE REST UP. I DON'T MIND.

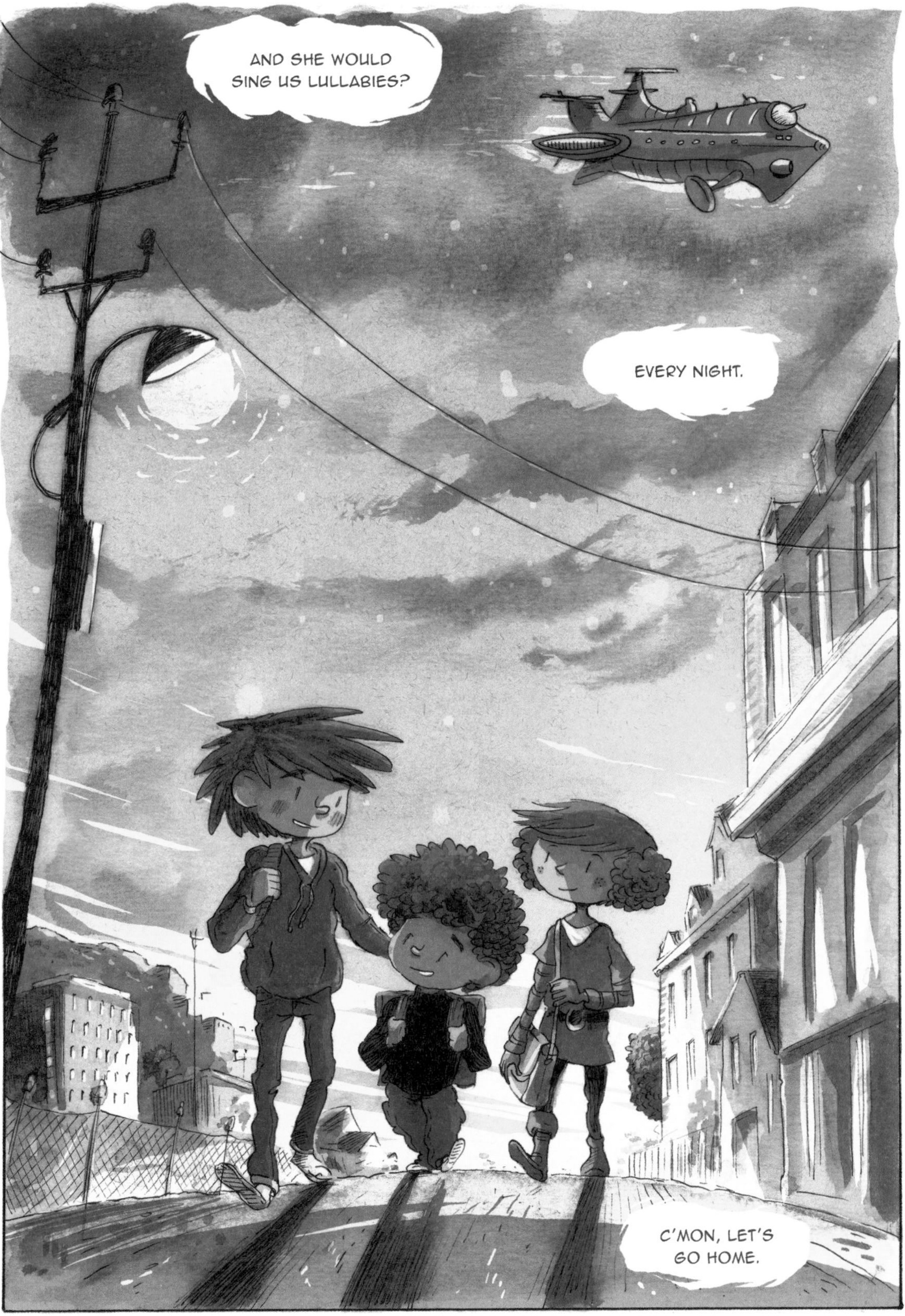
AND SHE WOULD SING US LULLABIES?
EVERY NIGHT.
C'MON, LET'S GO HOME.

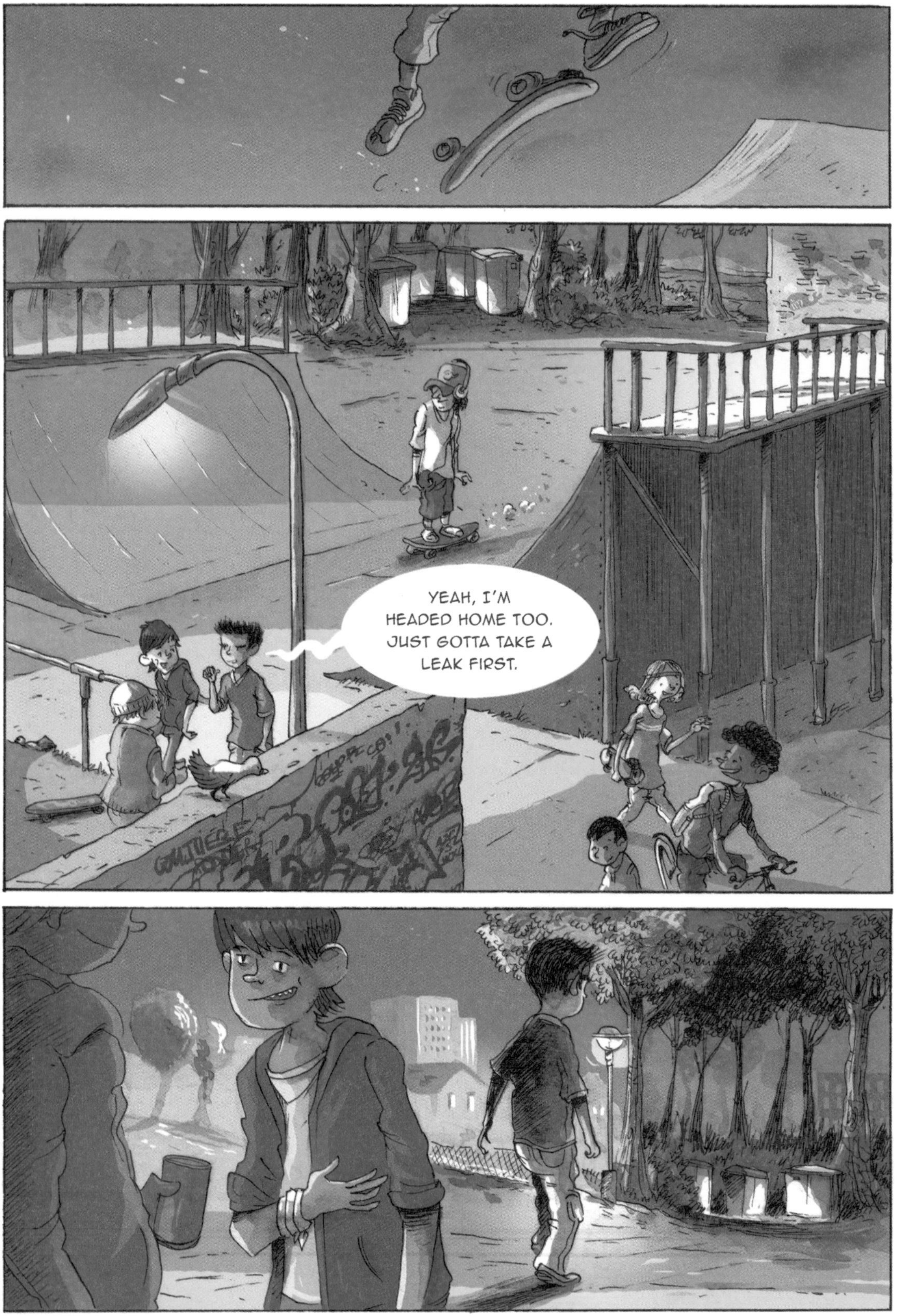
YEAH, I'M HEADED HOME TOO. JUST GOTTA TAKE A LEAK FIRST.

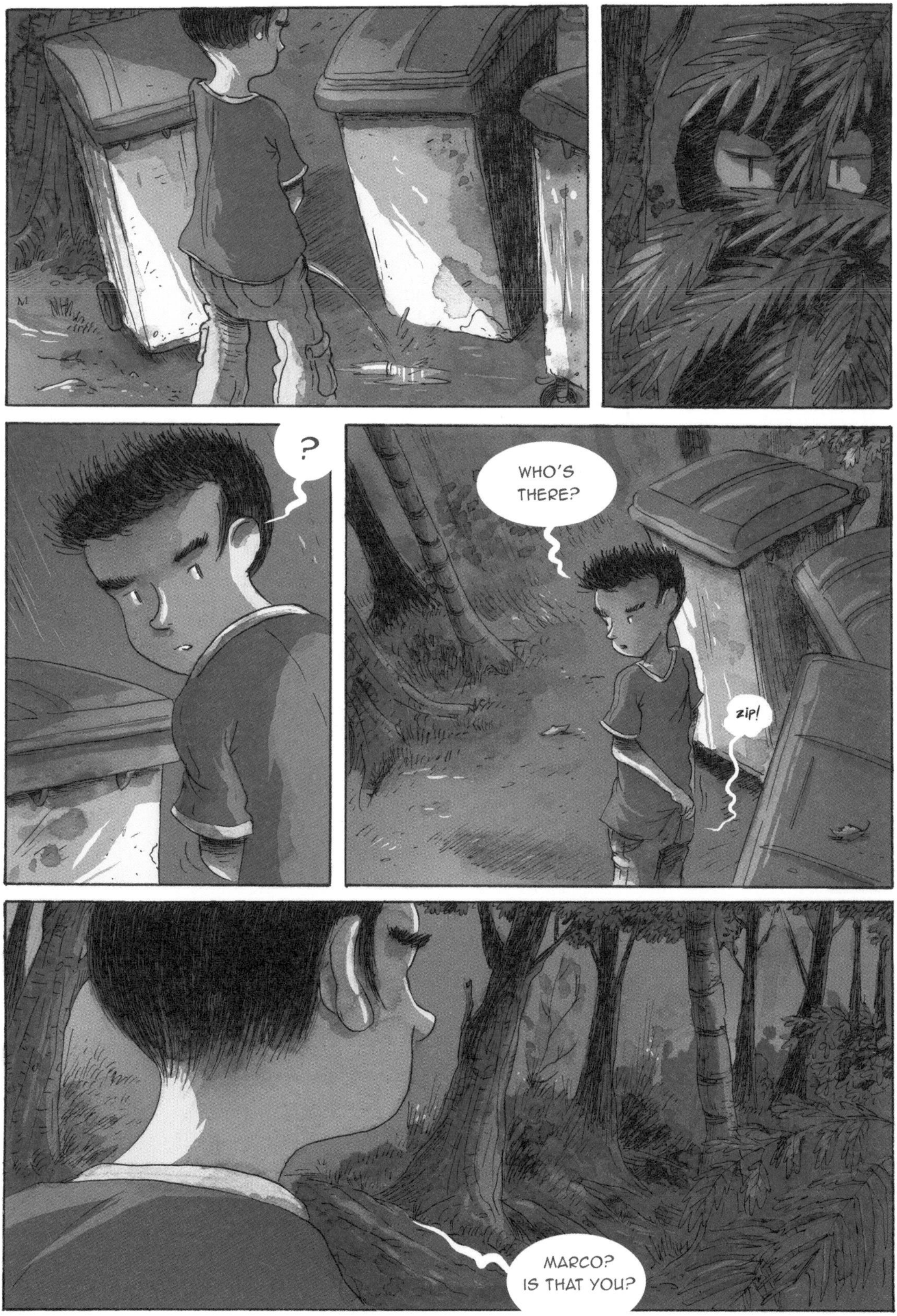
?
WHO'S THERE?
zip!
MARCO? IS THAT YOU?

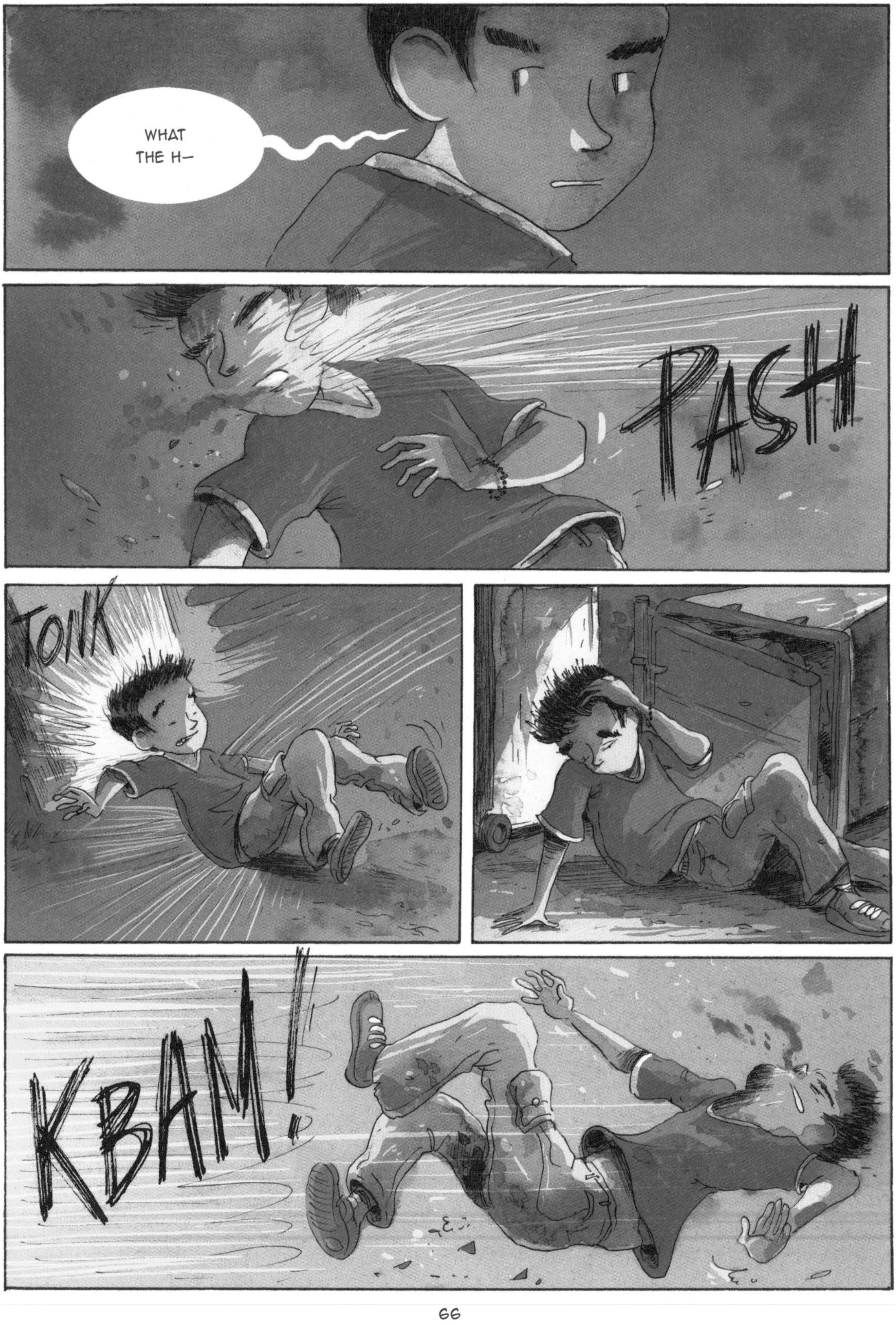
WHAT THE H—
PASH
TONK
KBAM!!

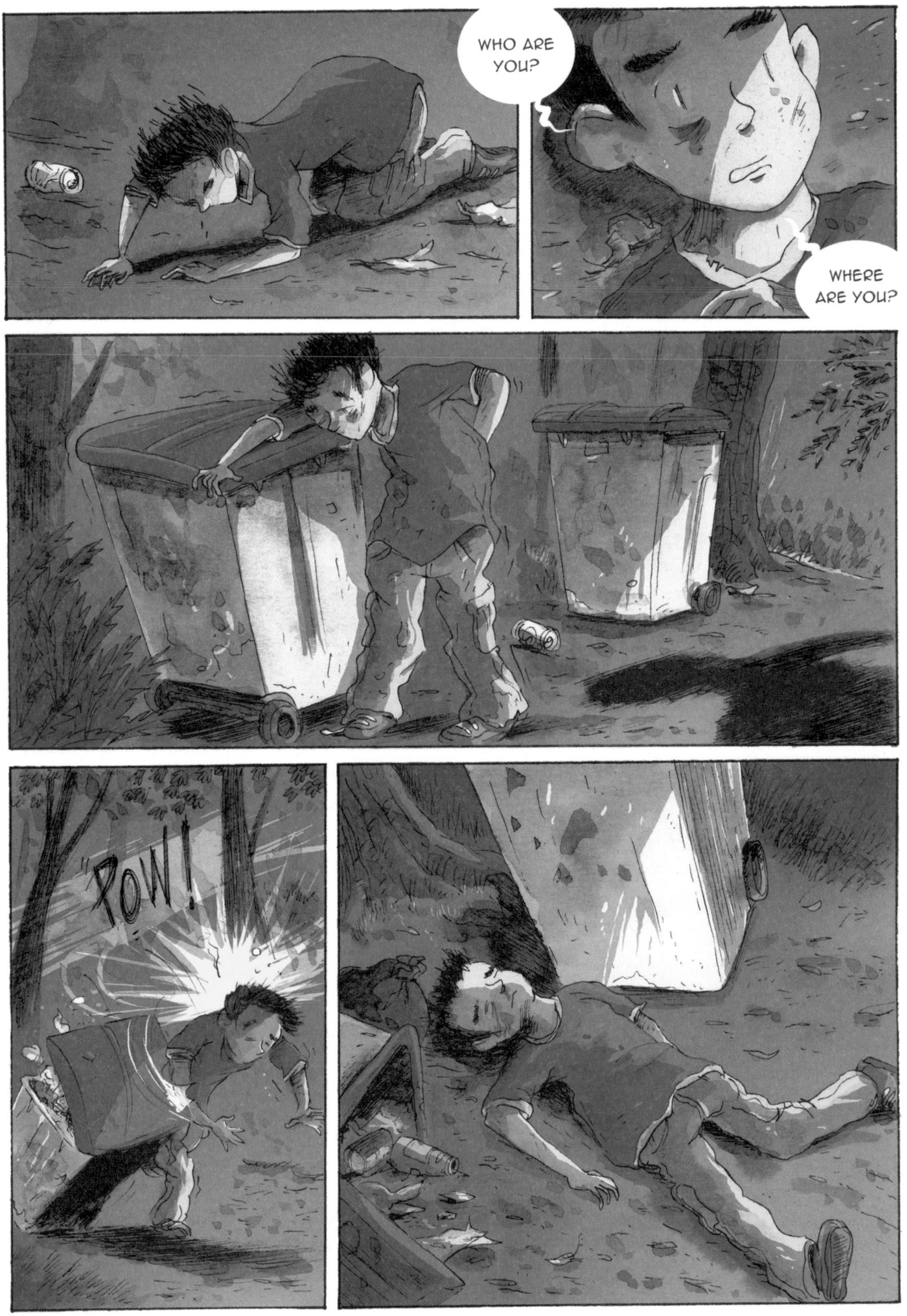
WHO ARE YOU?
WHERE ARE YOU?
POW!

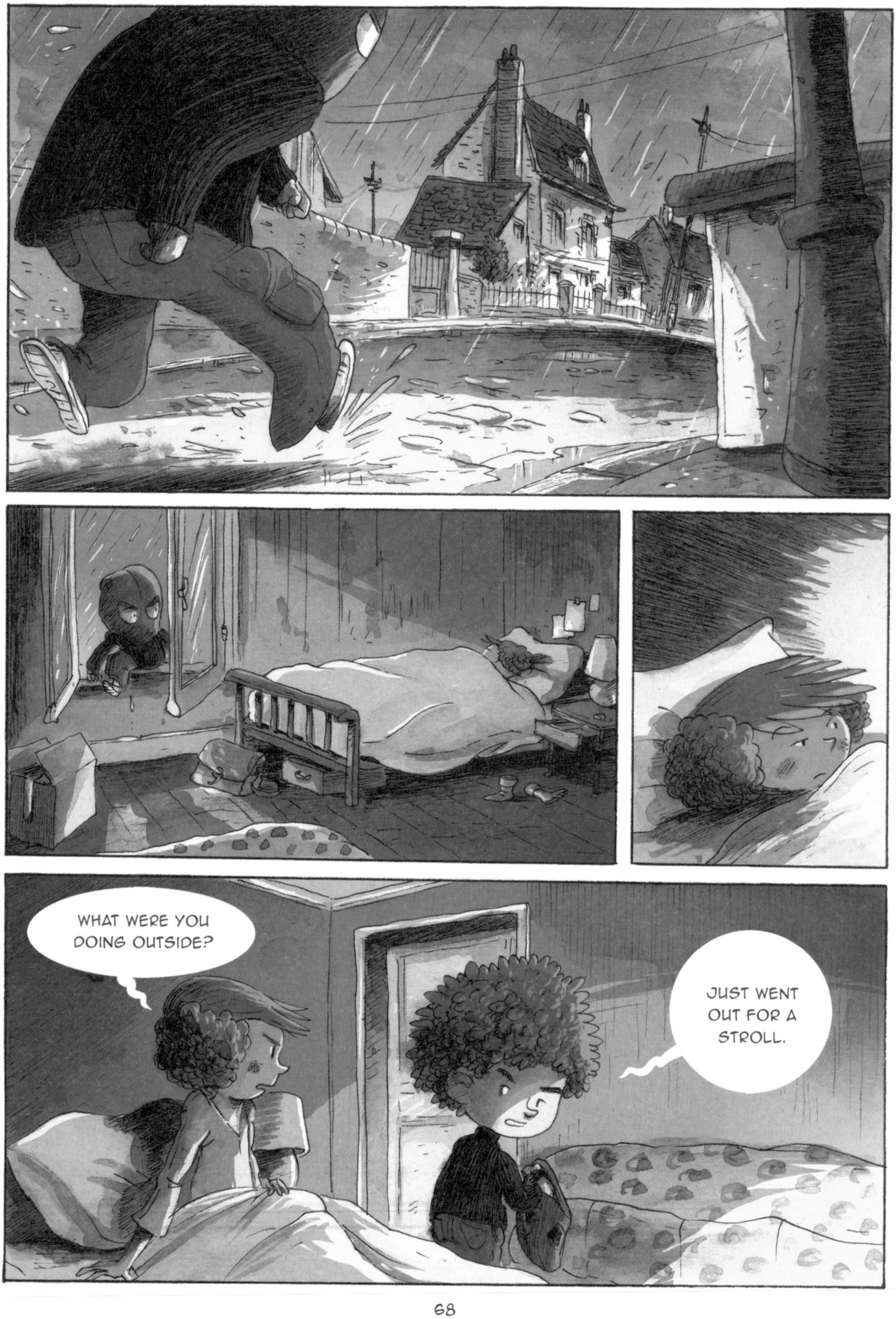
WHAT WERE YOU DOING OUTSIDE?
JUST WENT OUT FOR A STROLL.

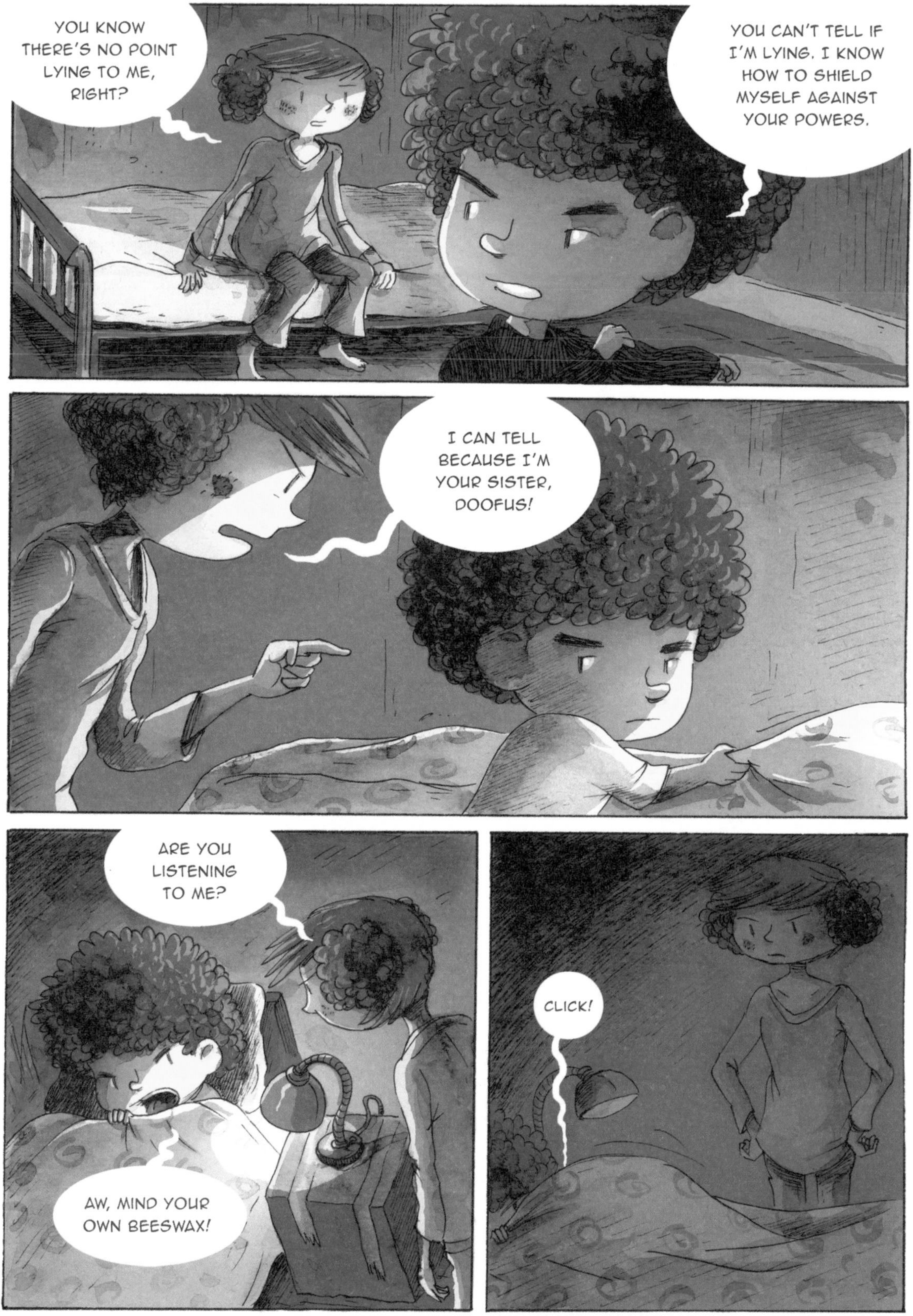
YOU KNOW THERE'S NO POINT LYING TO ME, RIGHT?
YOU CAN'T TELL IF I'M LYING. I KNOW HOW TO SHIELD MYSELF AGAINST YOUR POWERS.
I CAN TELL BECAUSE I'M YOUR SISTER, DOOFUS!
ARE YOU LISTENING TO ME?
AW, MIND YOUR OWN BEESWAX!
CLICK!

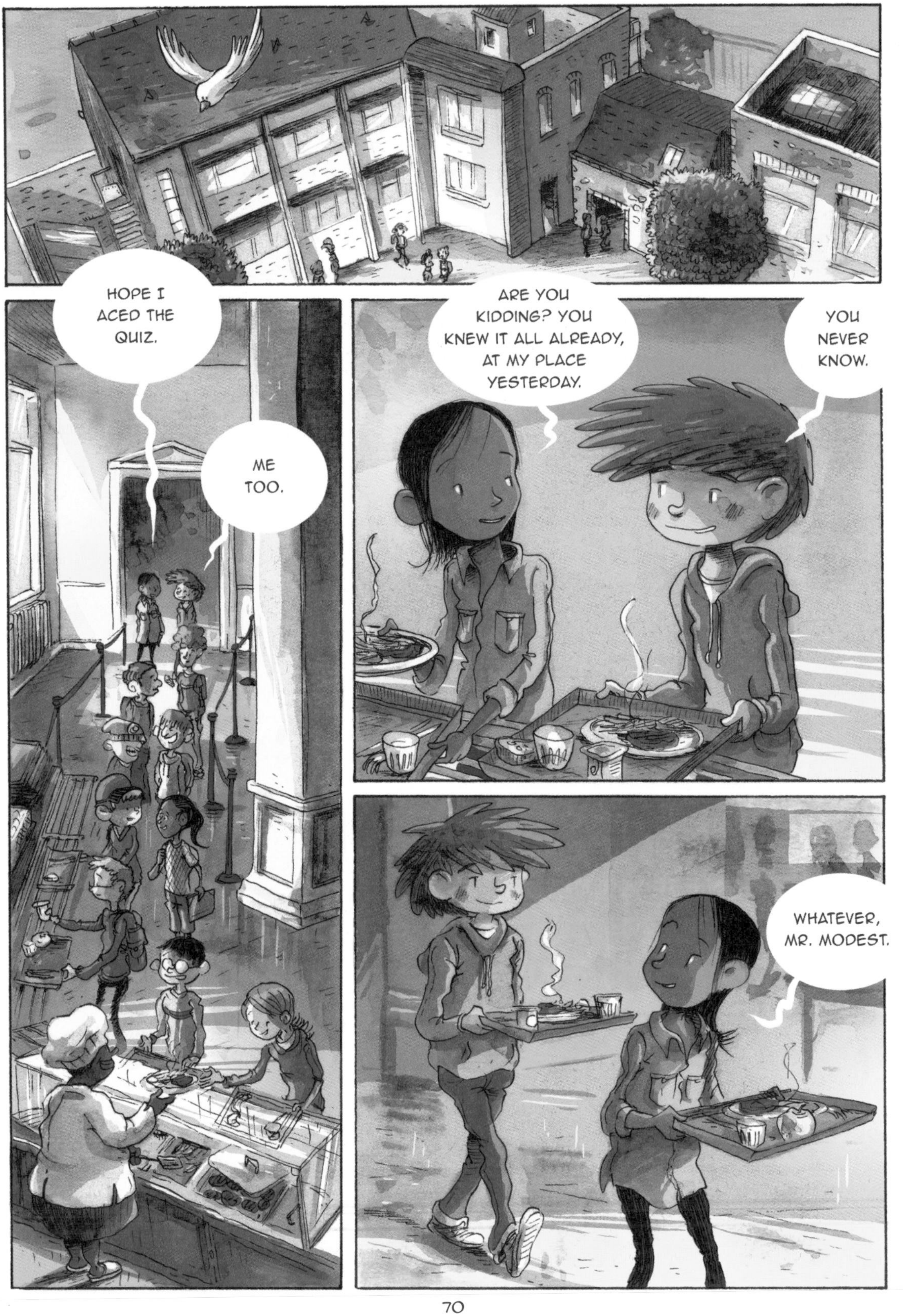
HOPE I ACED THE QUIZ.
ME TOO.
ARE YOU KIDDING? YOU KNEW IT ALL ALREADY, AT MY PLACE YESTERDAY.
YOU NEVER KNOW.
WHATEVER, MR. MODEST.

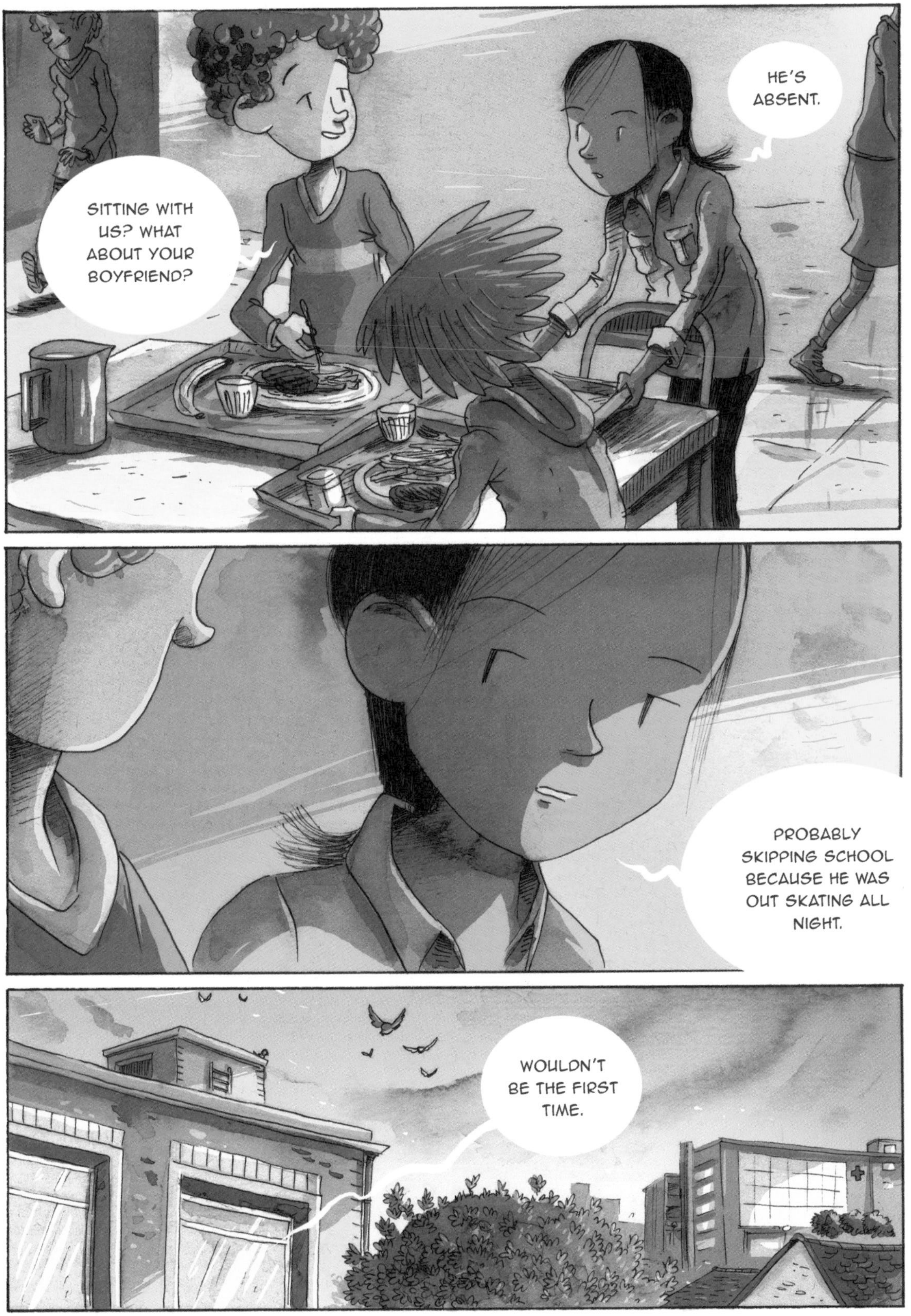
SITTING WITH US? WHAT ABOUT YOUR BOYFRIEND?
HE'S ABSENT.
PROBABLY SKIPPING SCHOOL BECAUSE HE WAS OUT SKATING ALL NIGHT.
WOULDN'T BE THE FIRST TIME.

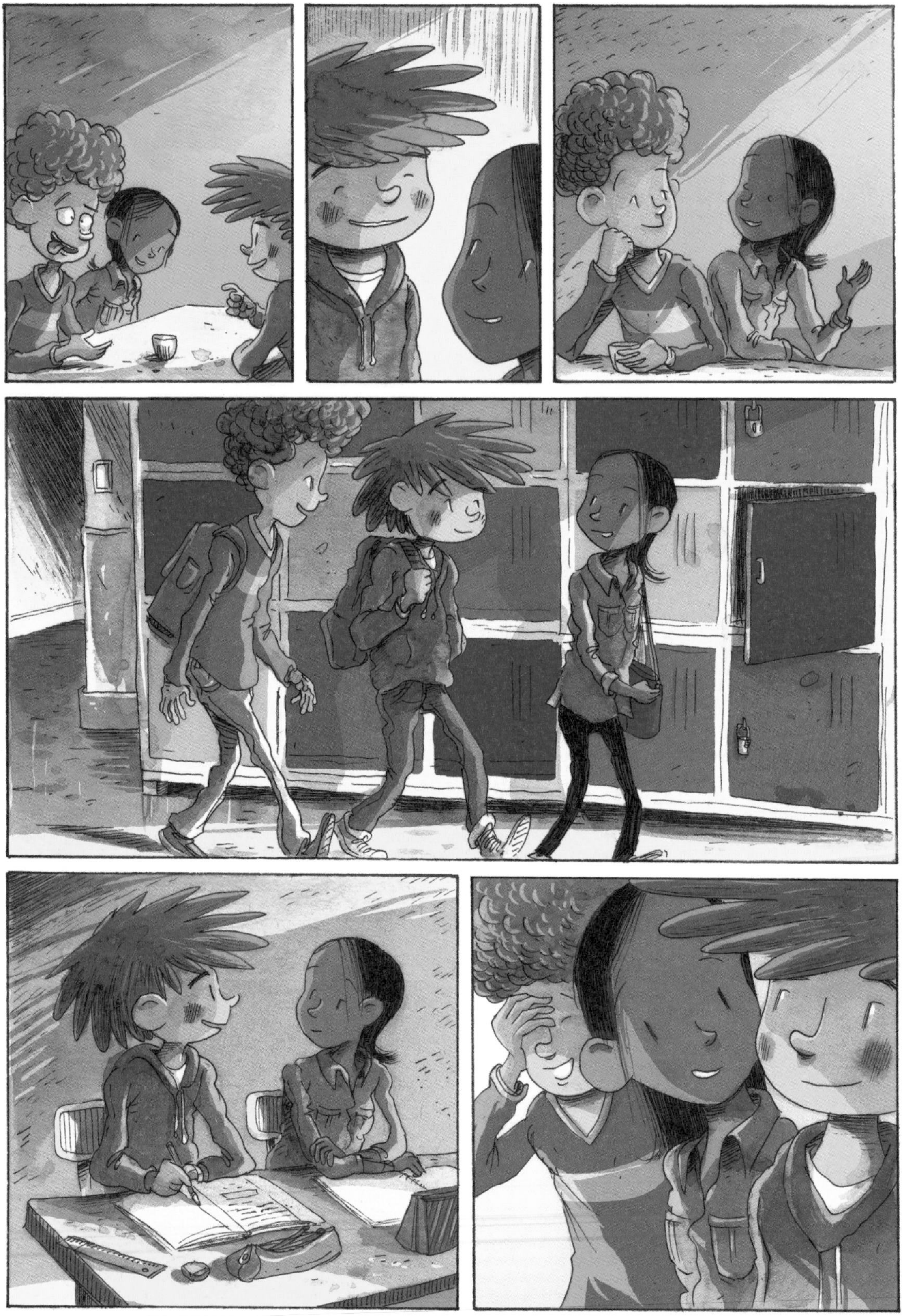

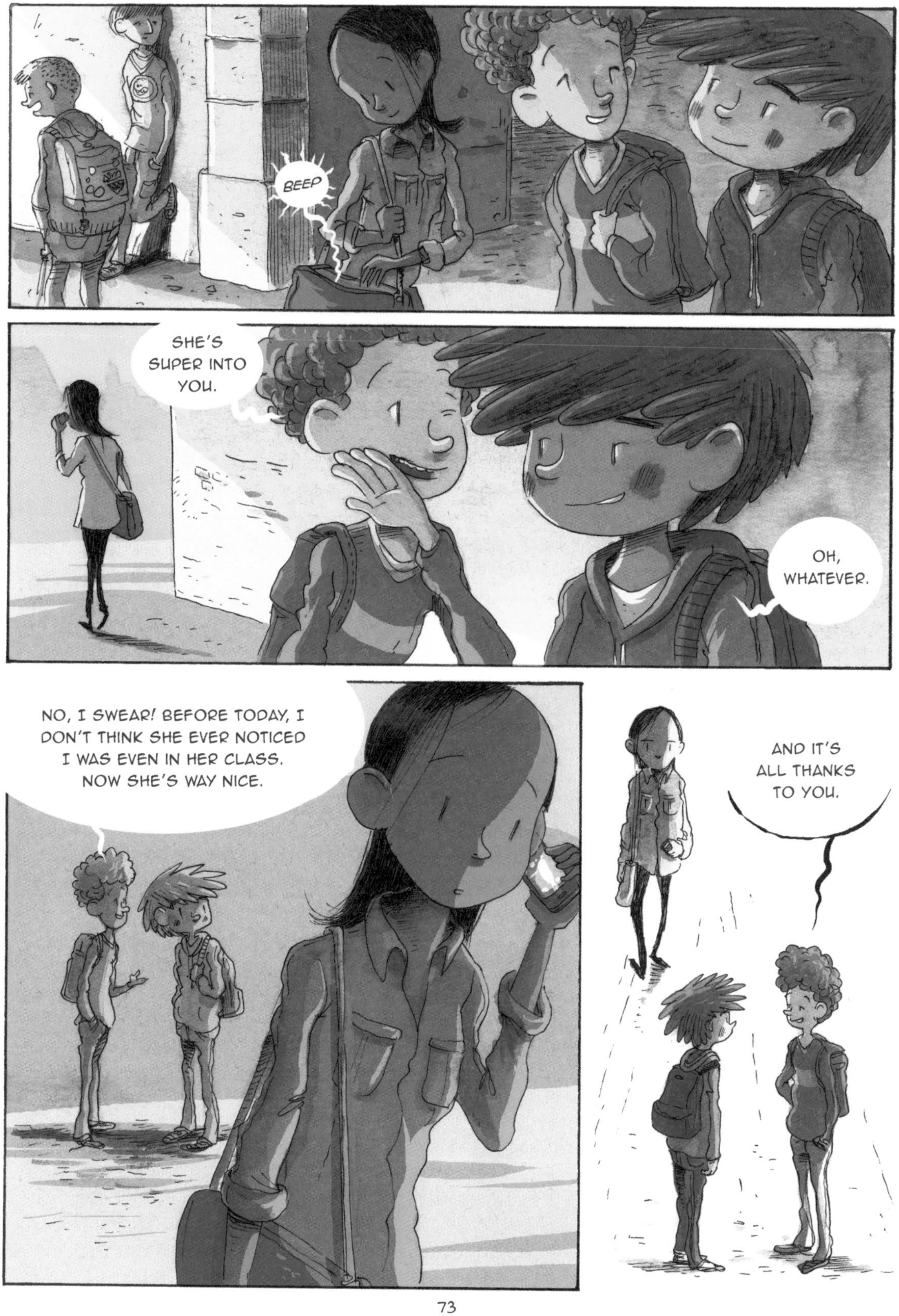
BEEP
SHE'S SUPER INTO YOU.
OH, WHATEVER.
NO, I SWEAR! BEFORE TODAY, I DON'T THINK SHE EVER NOTICED I WAS EVEN IN HER CLASS. NOW SHE'S WAY NICE.
AND IT'S ALL THANKS TO YOU.

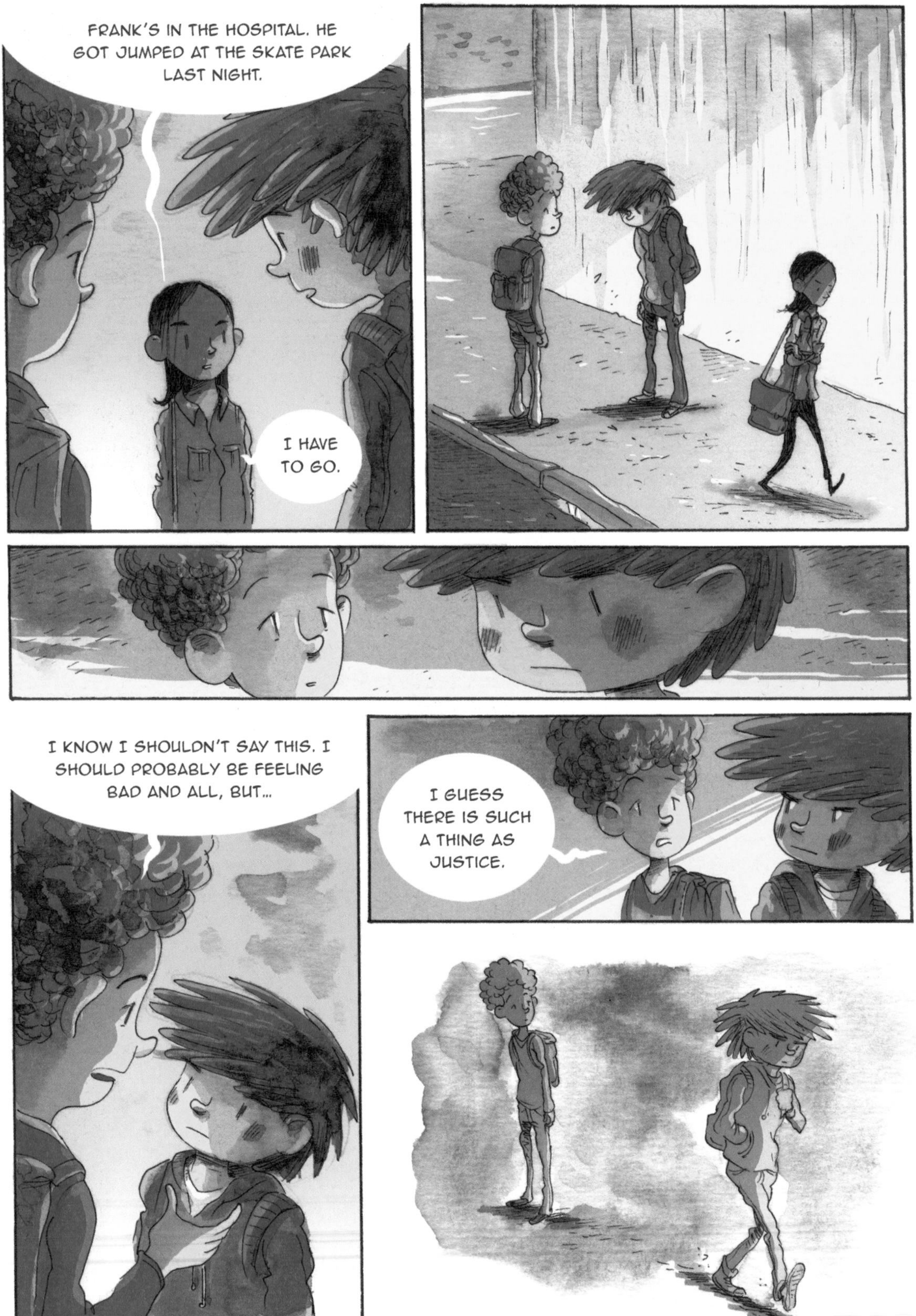
FRANK'S IN THE HOSPITAL. HE GOT JUMPED AT THE SKATE PARK LAST NIGHT.
I HAVE TO GO.
I KNOW I SHOULDN'T SAY THIS. I SHOULD PROBABLY BE FEELING BAD AND ALL, BUT...
I GUESS THERE IS SUCH A THING AS JUSTICE.

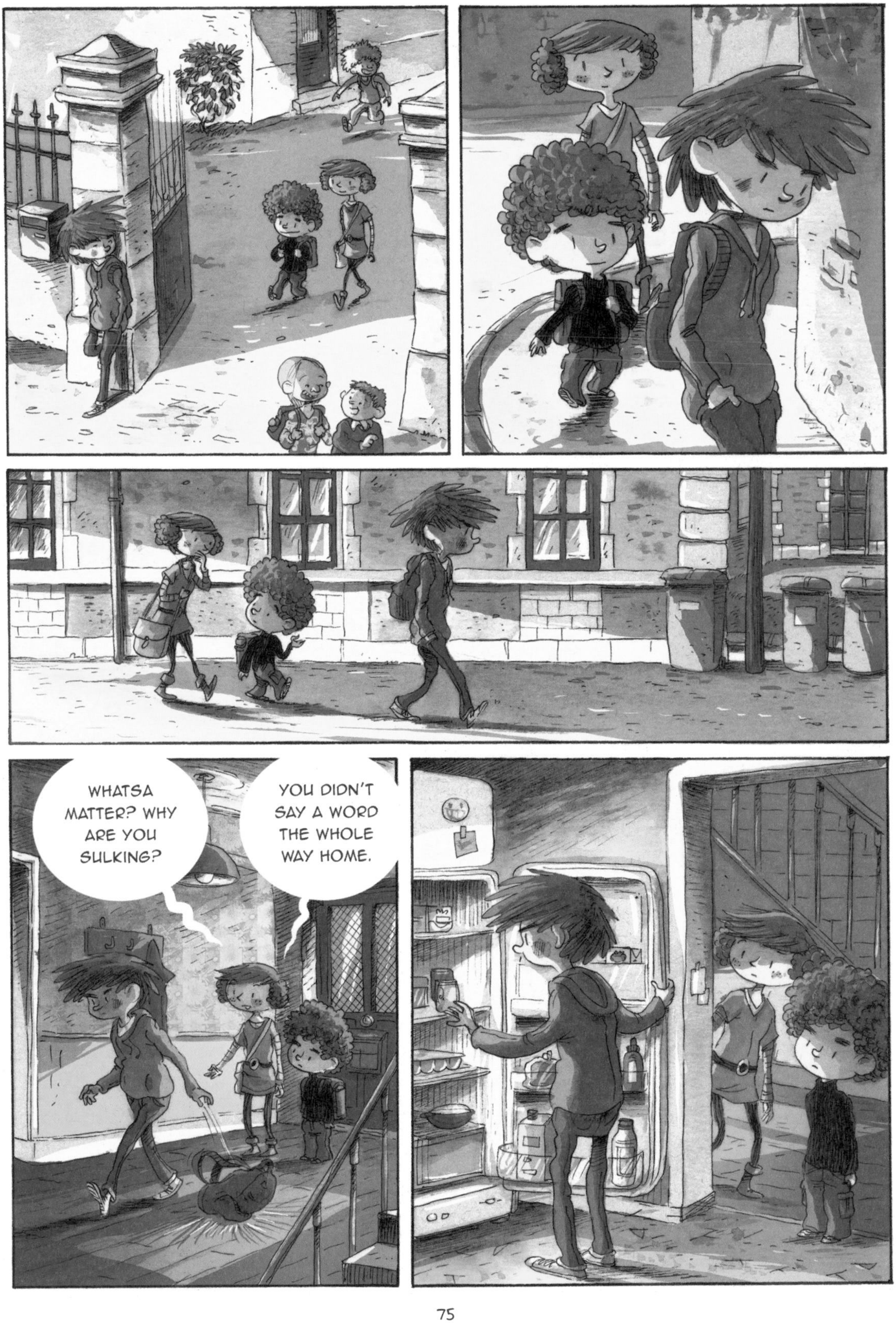
WHATSA MATTER? WHY ARE YOU SULKING?
YOU DIDN'T SAY A WORD THE WHOLE WAY HOME.

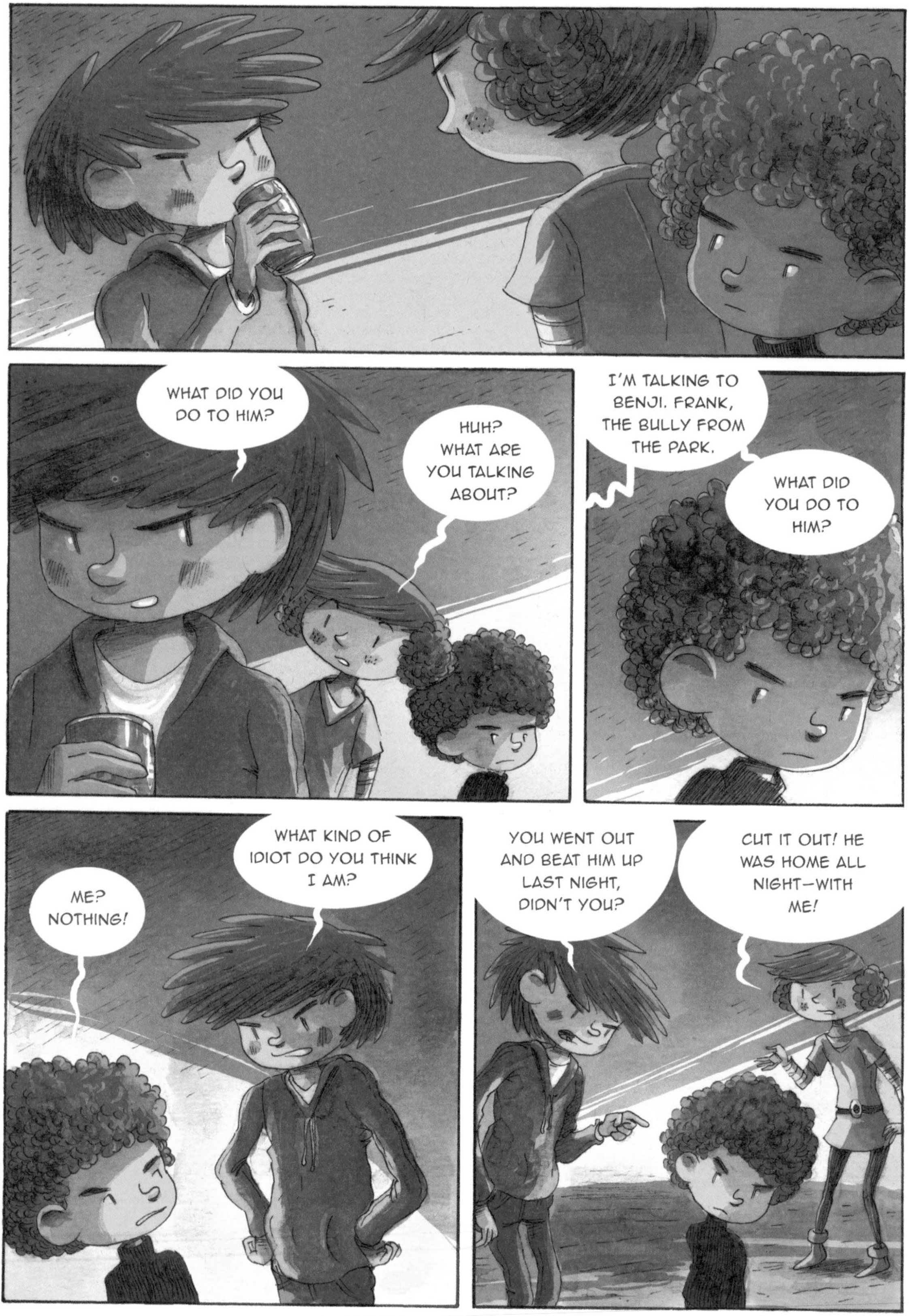
WHAT DID YOU DO TO HIM?
HUH? WHAT ARE YOU TALKING ABOUT?
I'M TALKING TO BENJI. FRANK, THE BULLY FROM THE PARK.
WHAT DID YOU DO TO HIM?
ME? NOTHING!
WHAT KIND OF IDIOT DO YOU THINK I AM?
YOU WENT OUT AND BEAT HIM UP LAST NIGHT, DIDN'T YOU?
CUT IT OUT! HE WAS HOME ALL NIGHT—WITH ME!

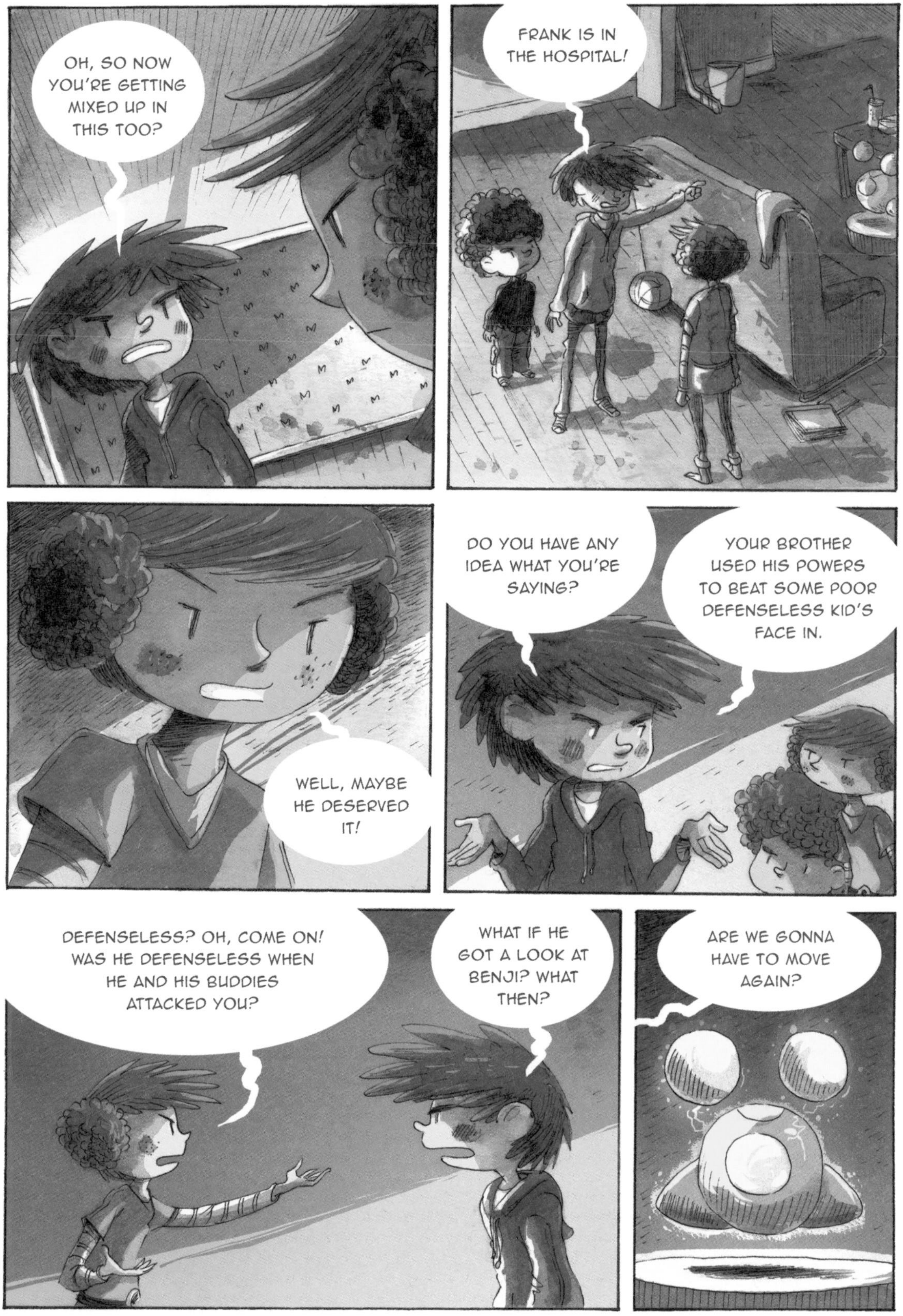
OH, SO NOW YOU'RE GETTING MIXED UP IN THIS TOO?
FRANK IS IN THE HOSPITAL!
WELL, MAYBE HE DESERVED IT!
DO YOU HAVE ANY IDEA WHAT YOU'RE SAYING?
YOUR BROTHER USED HIS POWERS TO BEAT SOME POOR DEFENSELESS KID'S FACE IN.
DEFENSELESS? OH, COME ON! WAS HE DEFENSELESS WHEN HE AND HIS BUDDIES ATTACKED YOU?
WHAT IF HE GOT A LOOK AT BENJI? WHAT THEN?
ARE WE GONNA HAVE TO MOVE AGAIN?

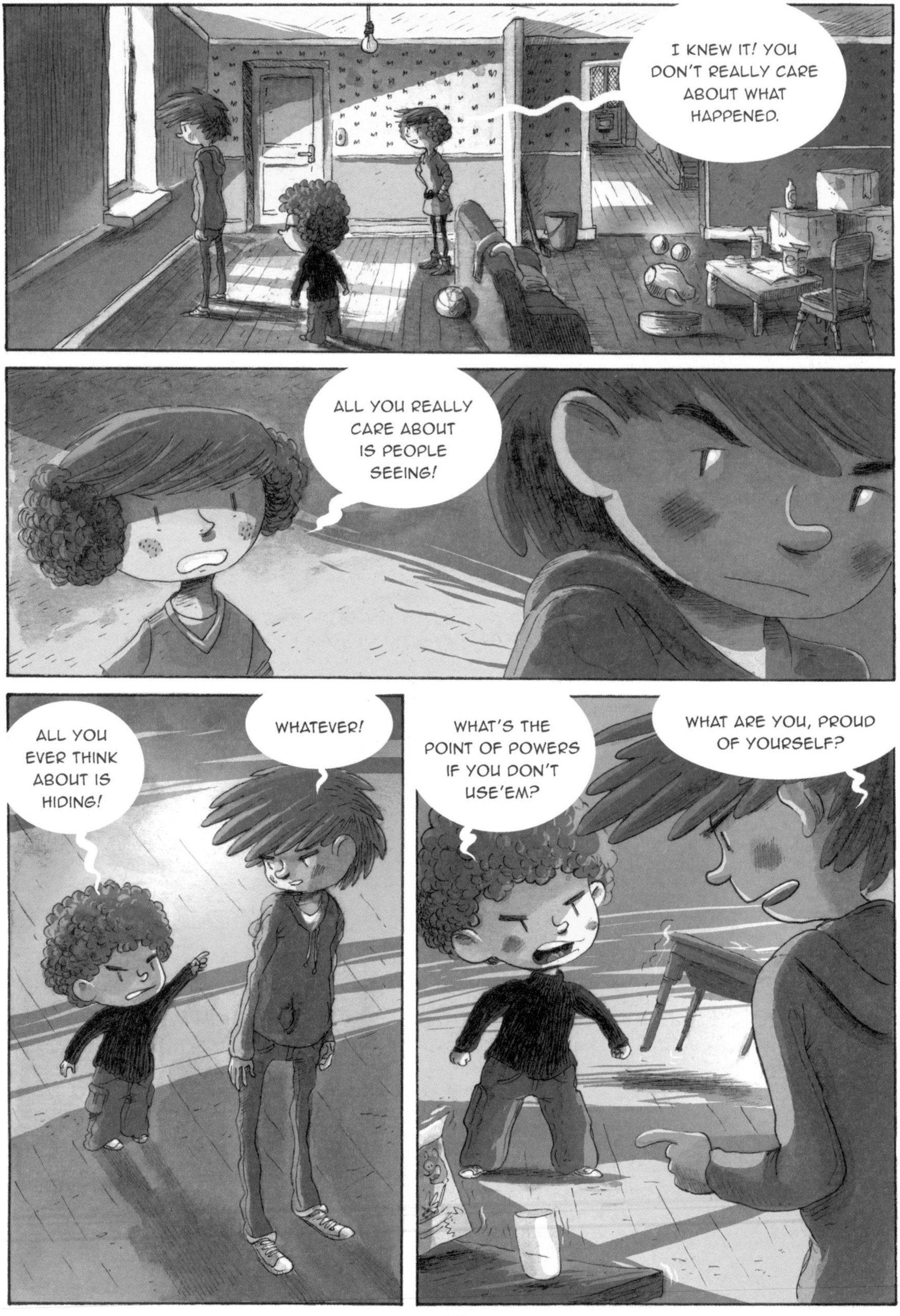
I KNEW IT! YOU DON'T REALLY CARE ABOUT WHAT HAPPENED.
ALL YOU REALLY CARE ABOUT IS PEOPLE SEEING!
ALL YOU EVER THINK ABOUT IS HIDING!
WHATEVER!
WHAT'S THE POINT OF POWERS IF YOU DON'T USE'EM?
WHAT ARE YOU, PROUD OF YOURSELF?

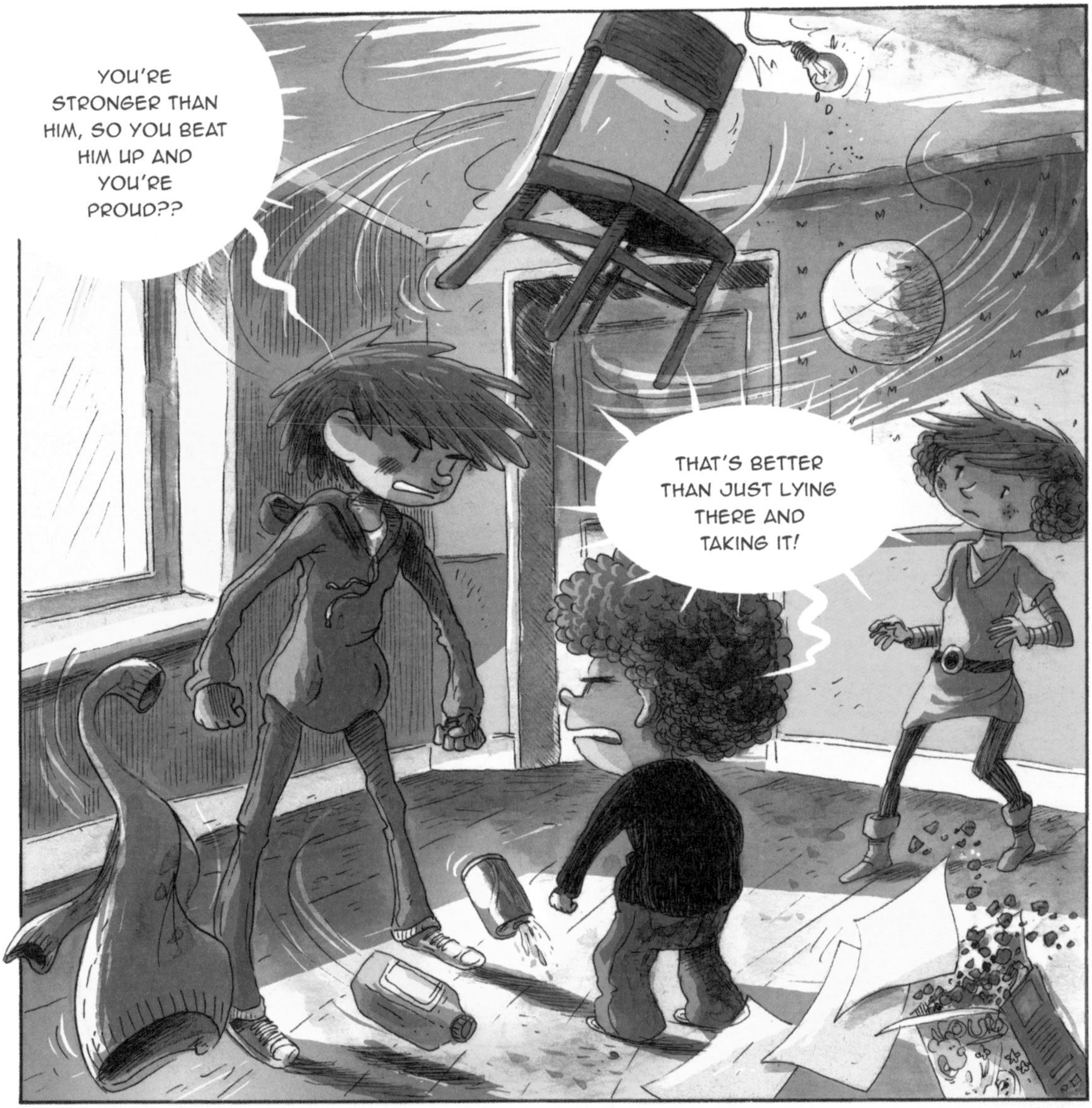
YOU'RE STRONGER THAN HIM, SO YOU BEAT HIM UP AND YOU'RE PROUD??
THAT'S BETTER THAN JUST LYING THERE AND TAKING IT!

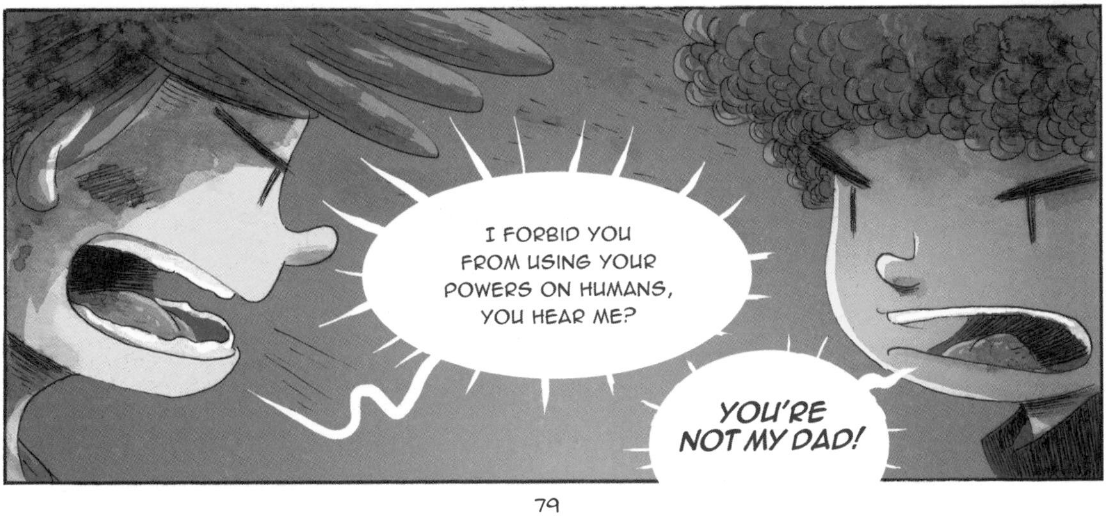
I FORBID YOU FROM USING YOUR POWERS ON HUMANS, YOU HEAR ME?
YOU'RE NOT MY DAD!

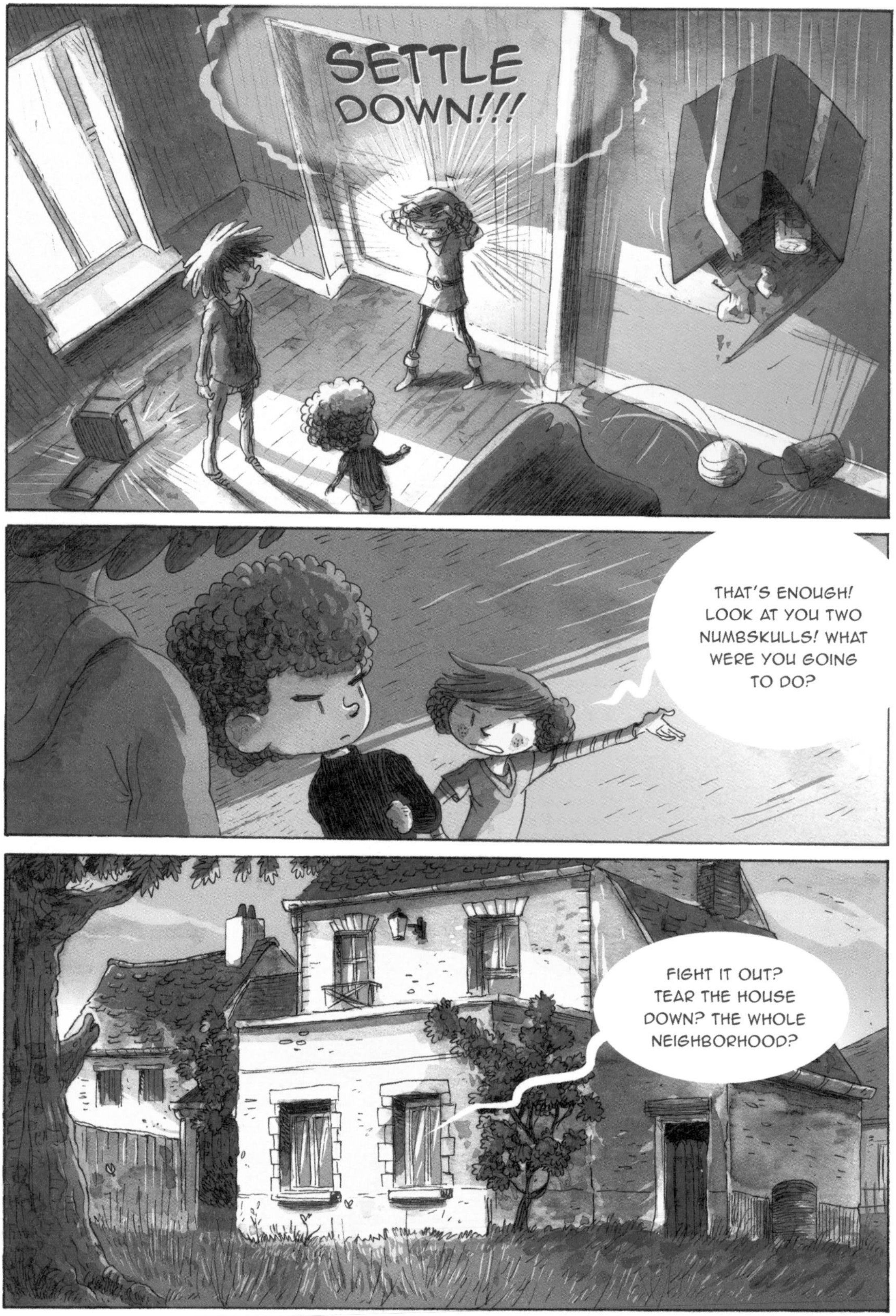
SETTLE DOWN!!!
THAT'S ENOUGH! LOOK AT YOU TWO NUMBSKULLS! WHAT WERE YOU GOING TO DO?
FIGHT IT OUT? TEAR THE HOUSE DOWN? THE WHOLE NEIGHBORHOOD?

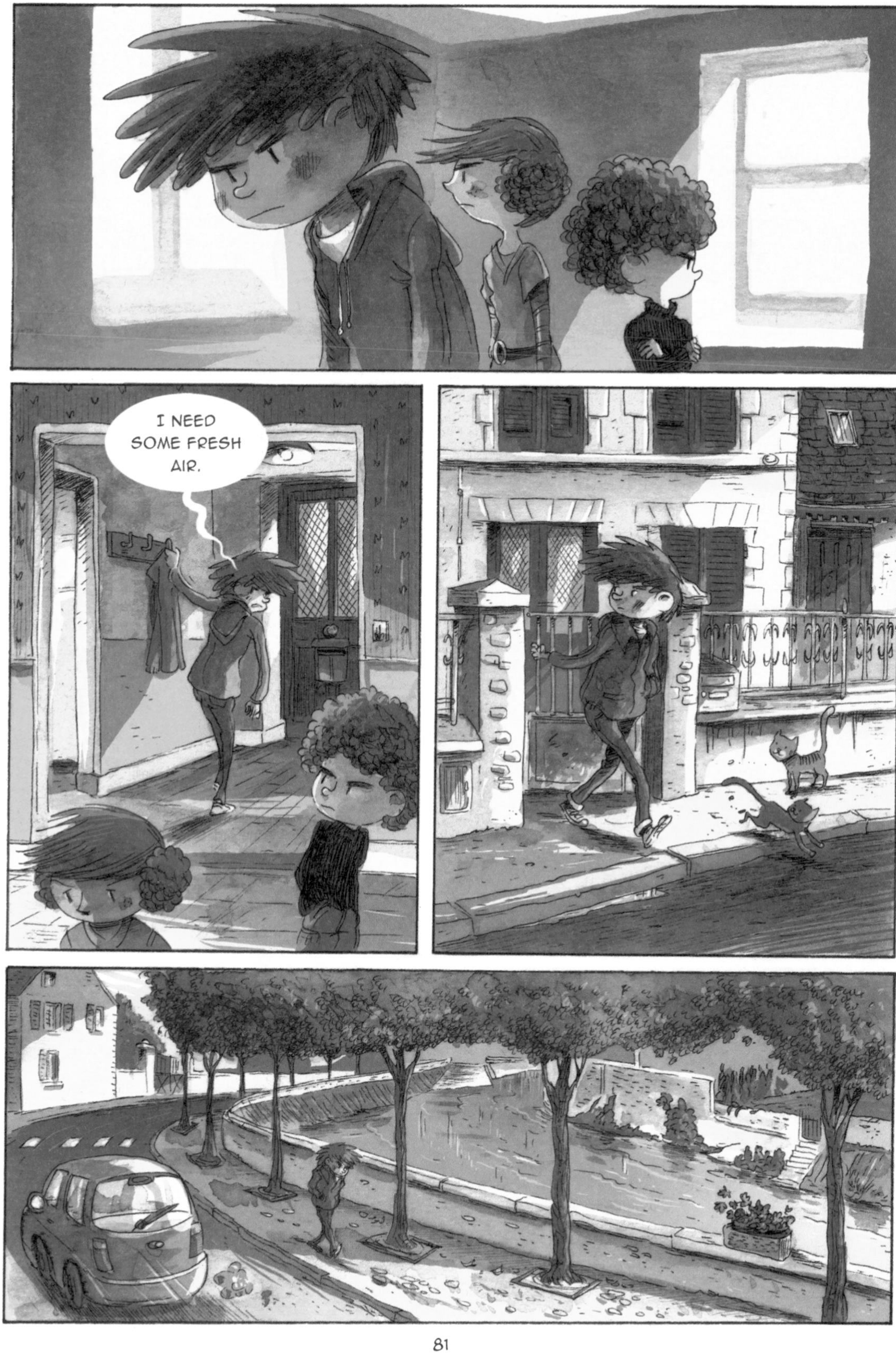
I NEED SOME FRESH AIR.

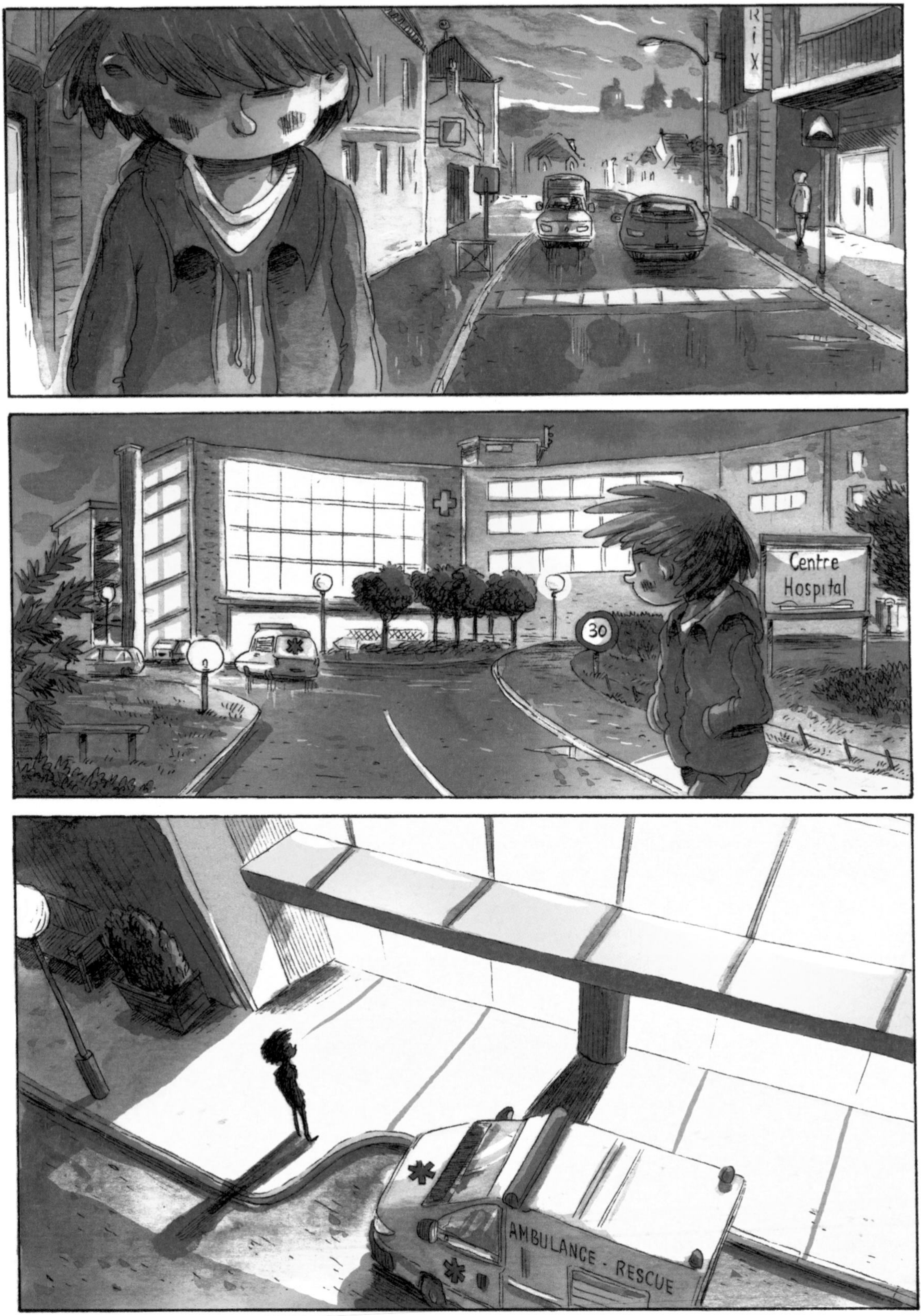
Centre
Hospital
30
AMBULANCE - RESCUE

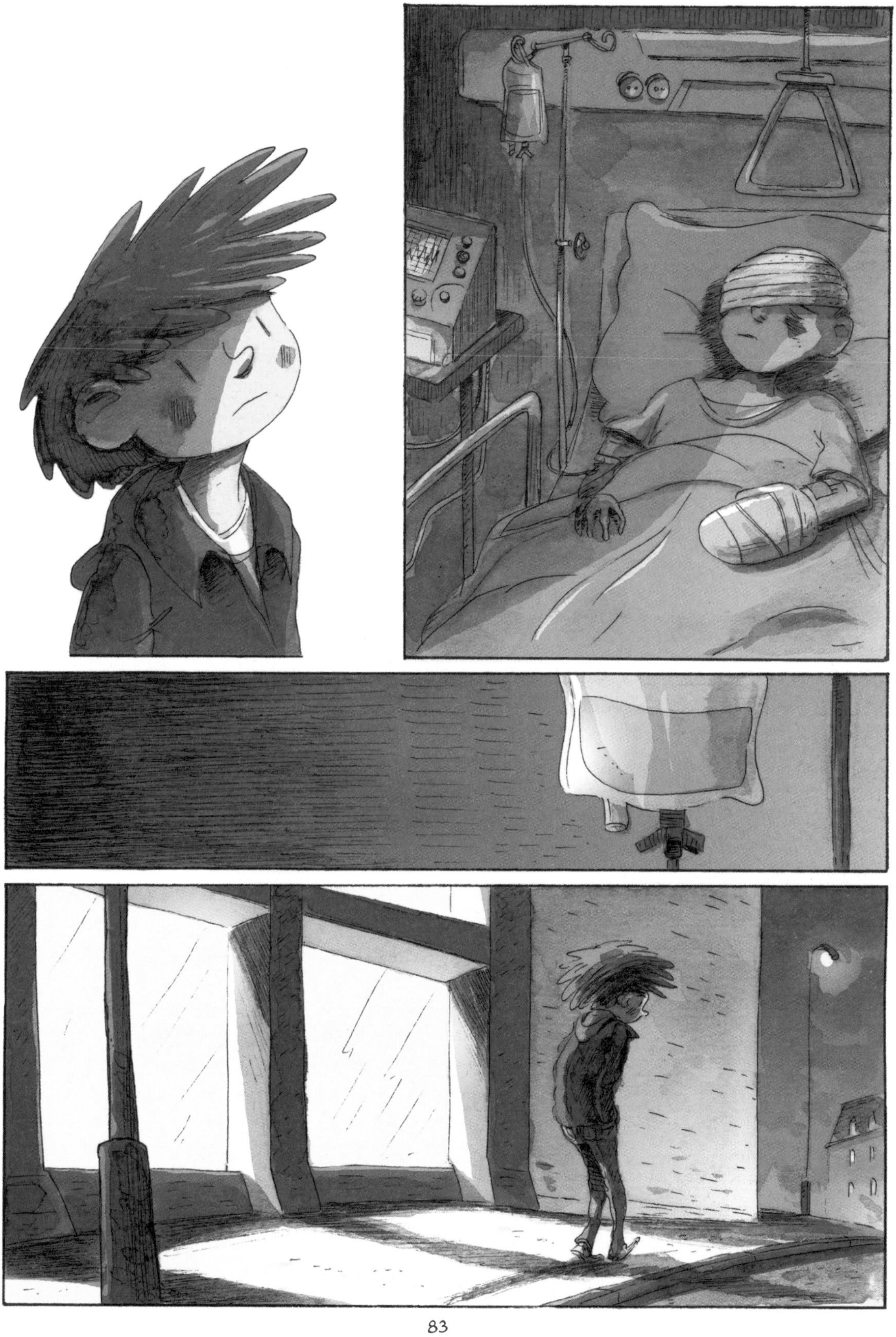

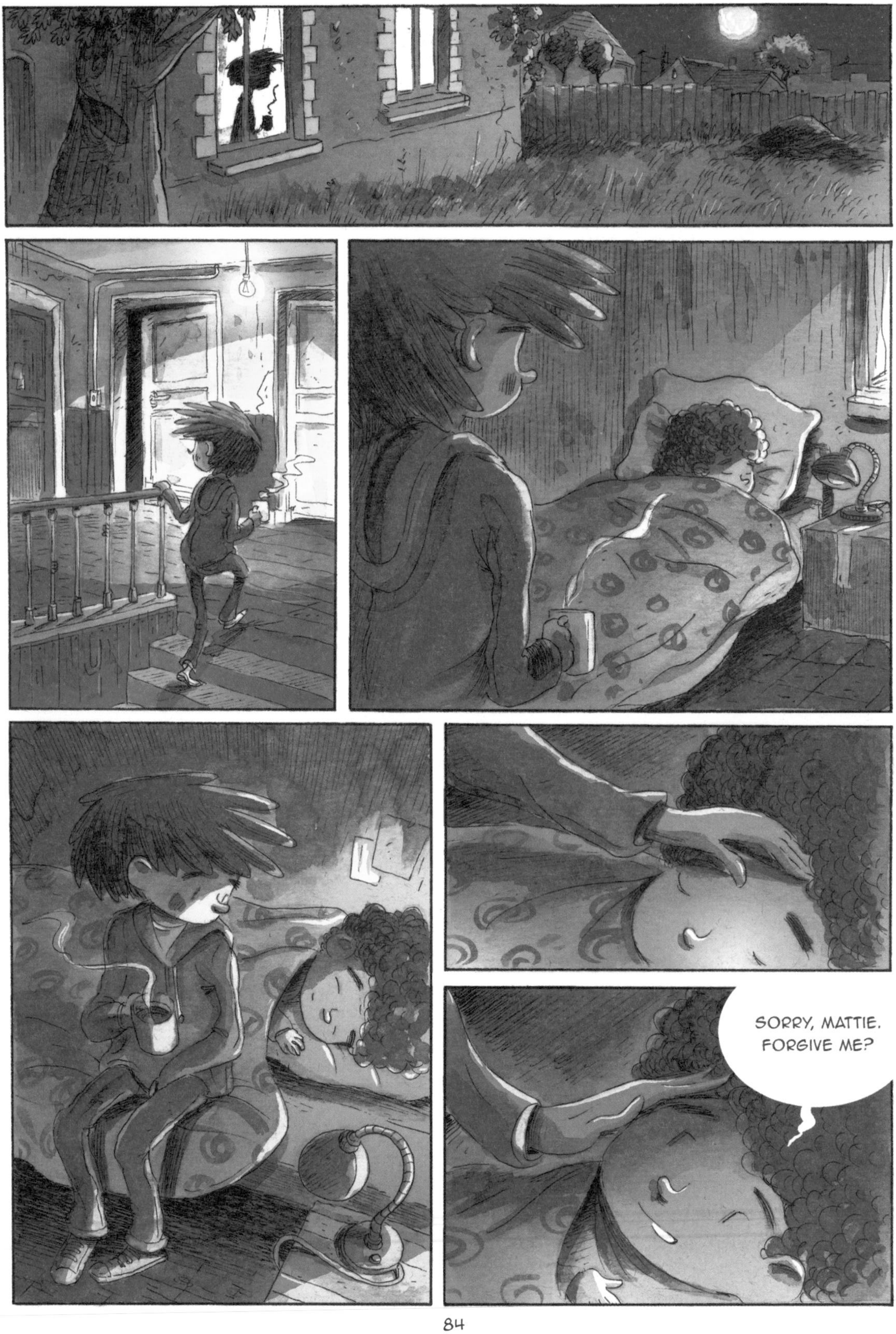
SORRY, MATTIE. FORGIVE ME?

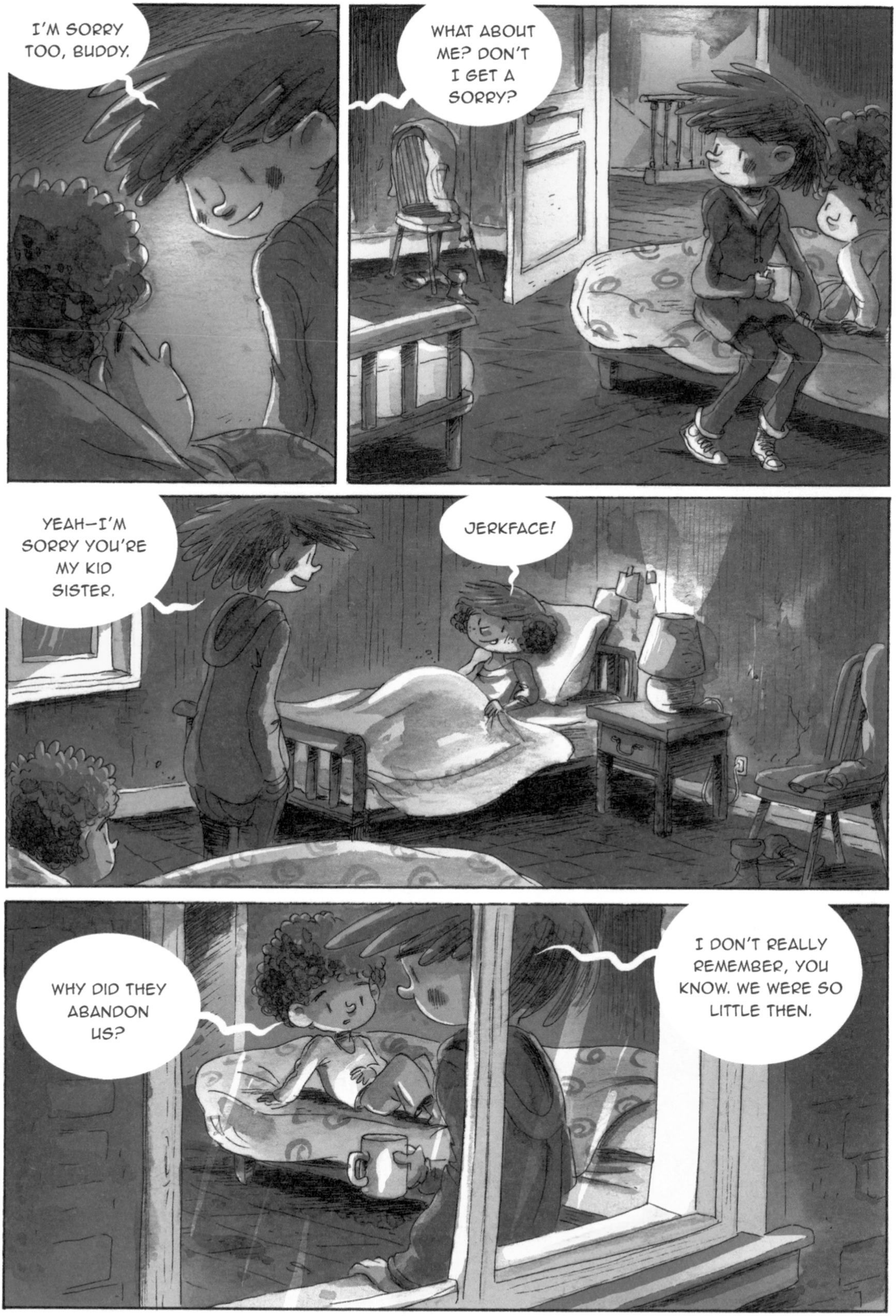
I'M SORRY TOO, BUDDY.
WHAT ABOUT ME? DON'T I GET A SORRY?
YEAH—I'M SORRY YOU'RE MY KID SISTER.
JERKFACE!
WHY DID THEY ABANDON US?
I DON'T REALLY REMEMBER, YOU KNOW. WE WERE SO LITTLE THEN.

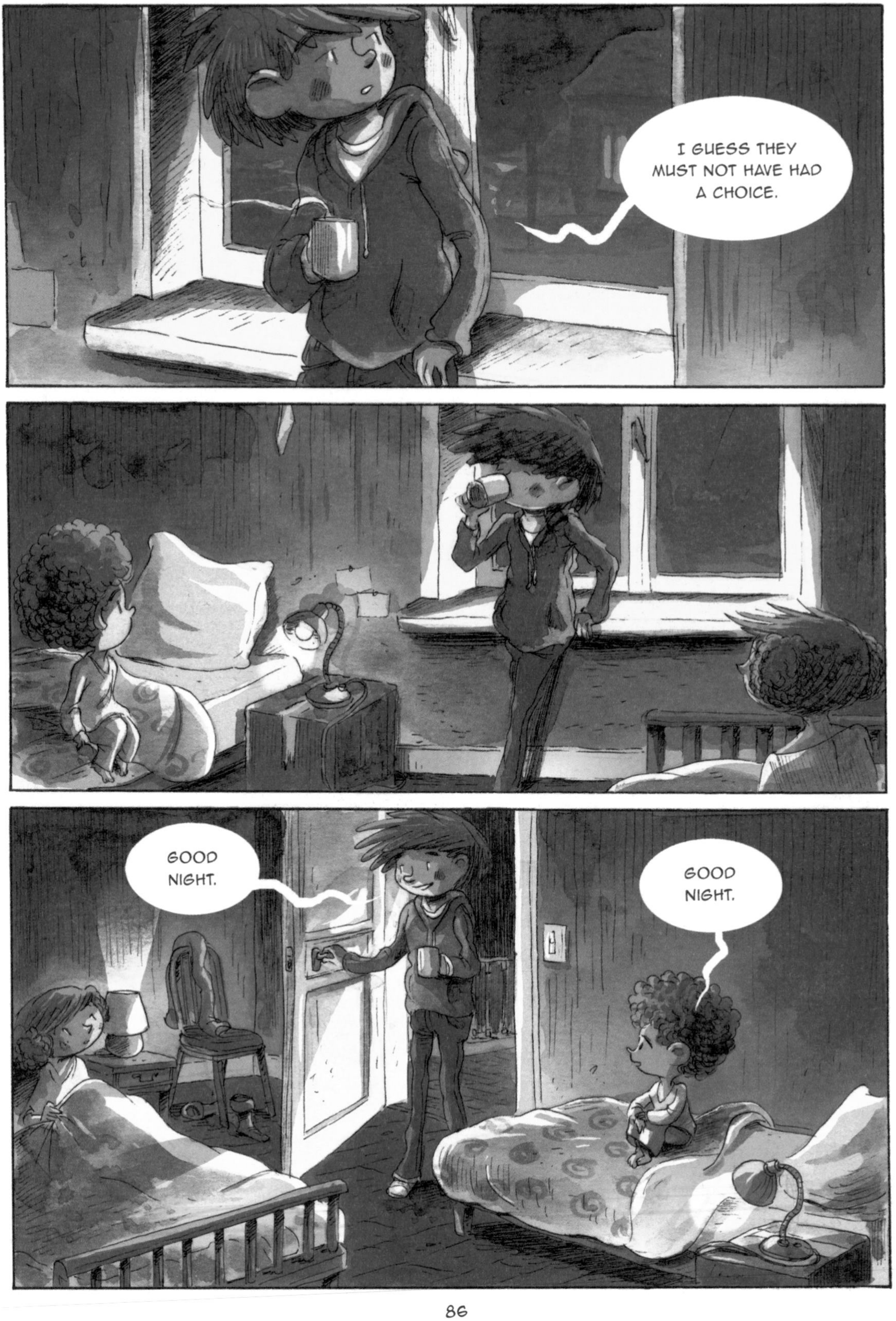
I GUESS THEY MUST NOT HAVE HAD A CHOICE.
GOOD NIGHT.
GOOD NIGHT.

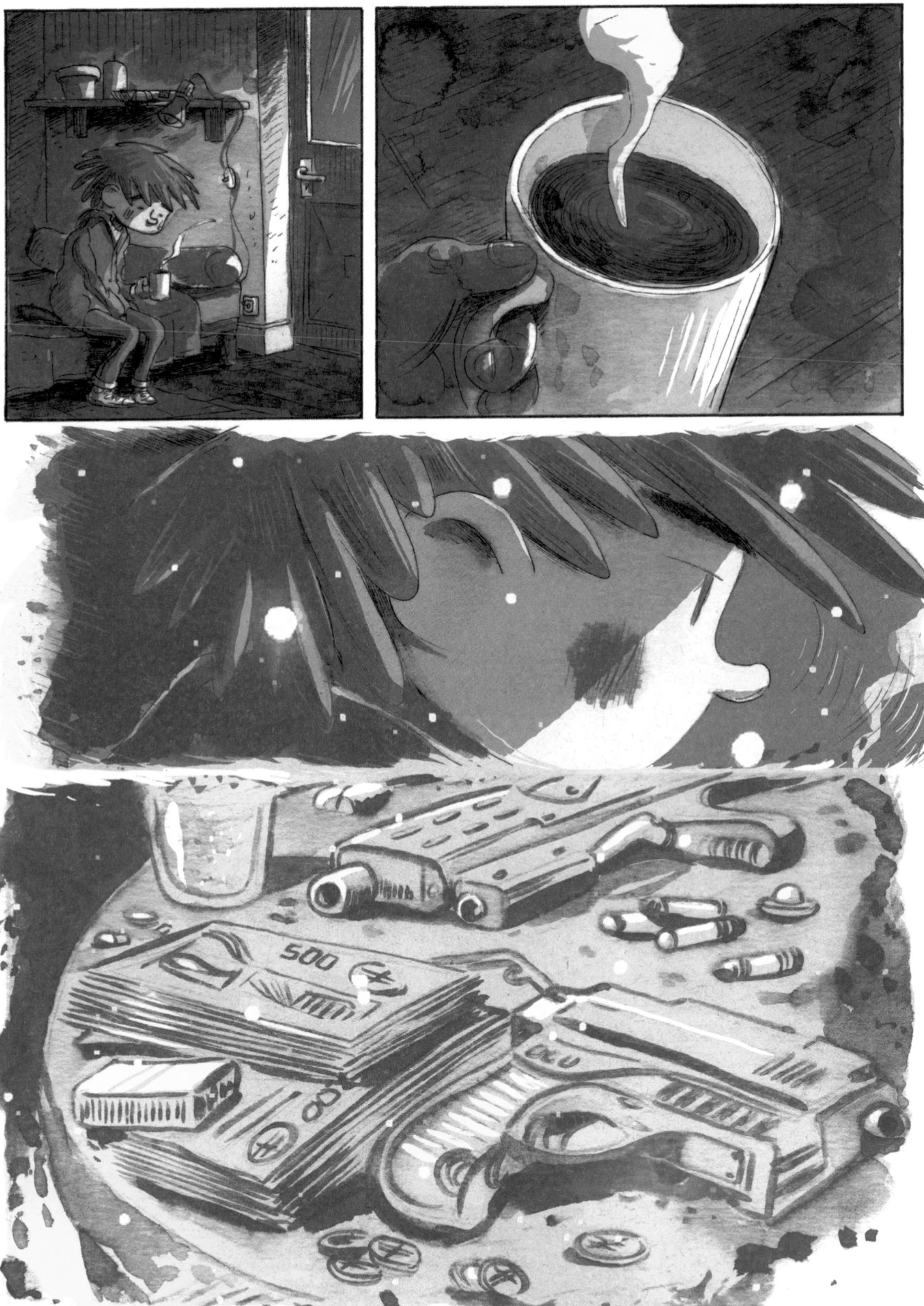
500

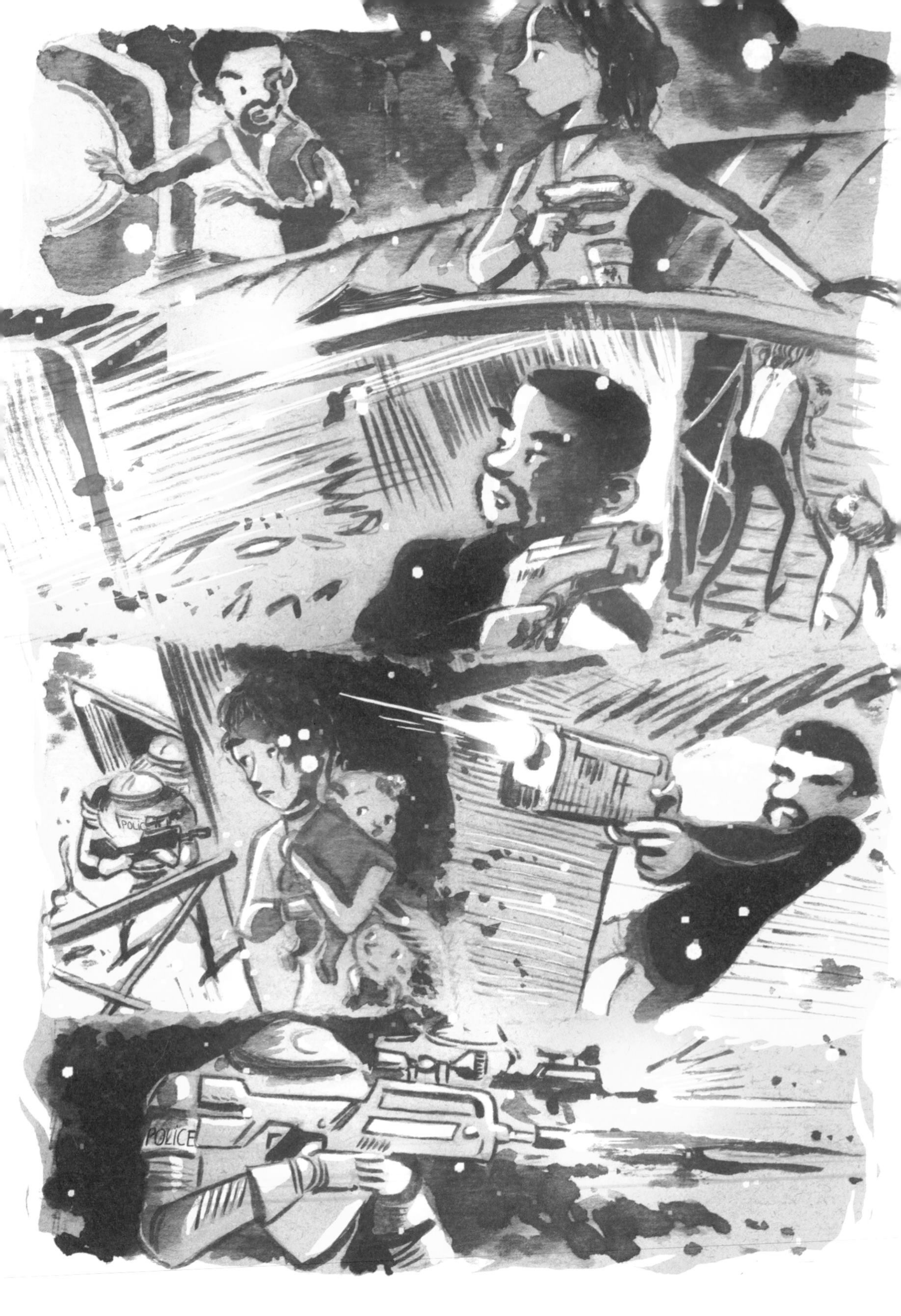
POLICE
POLICE

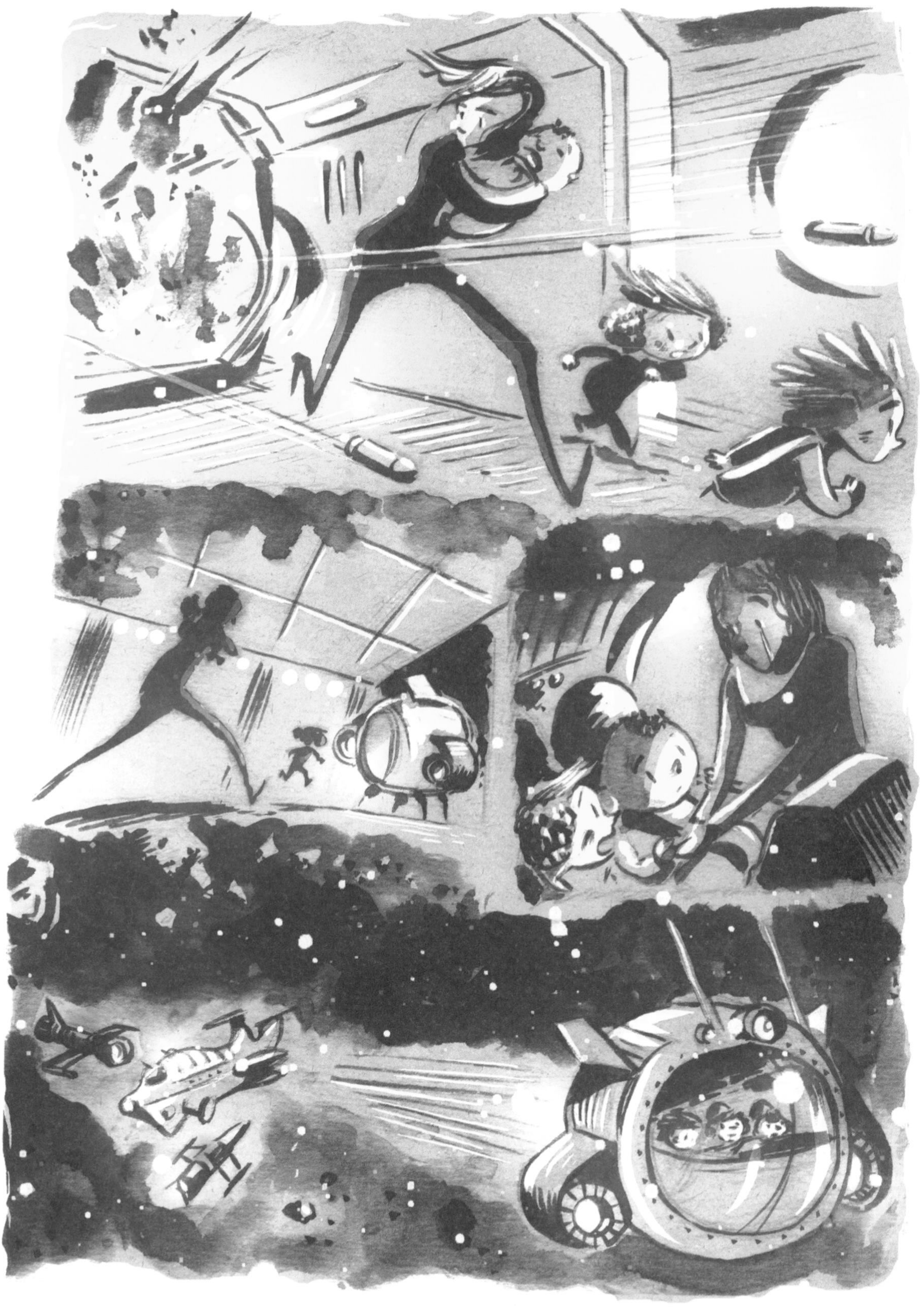

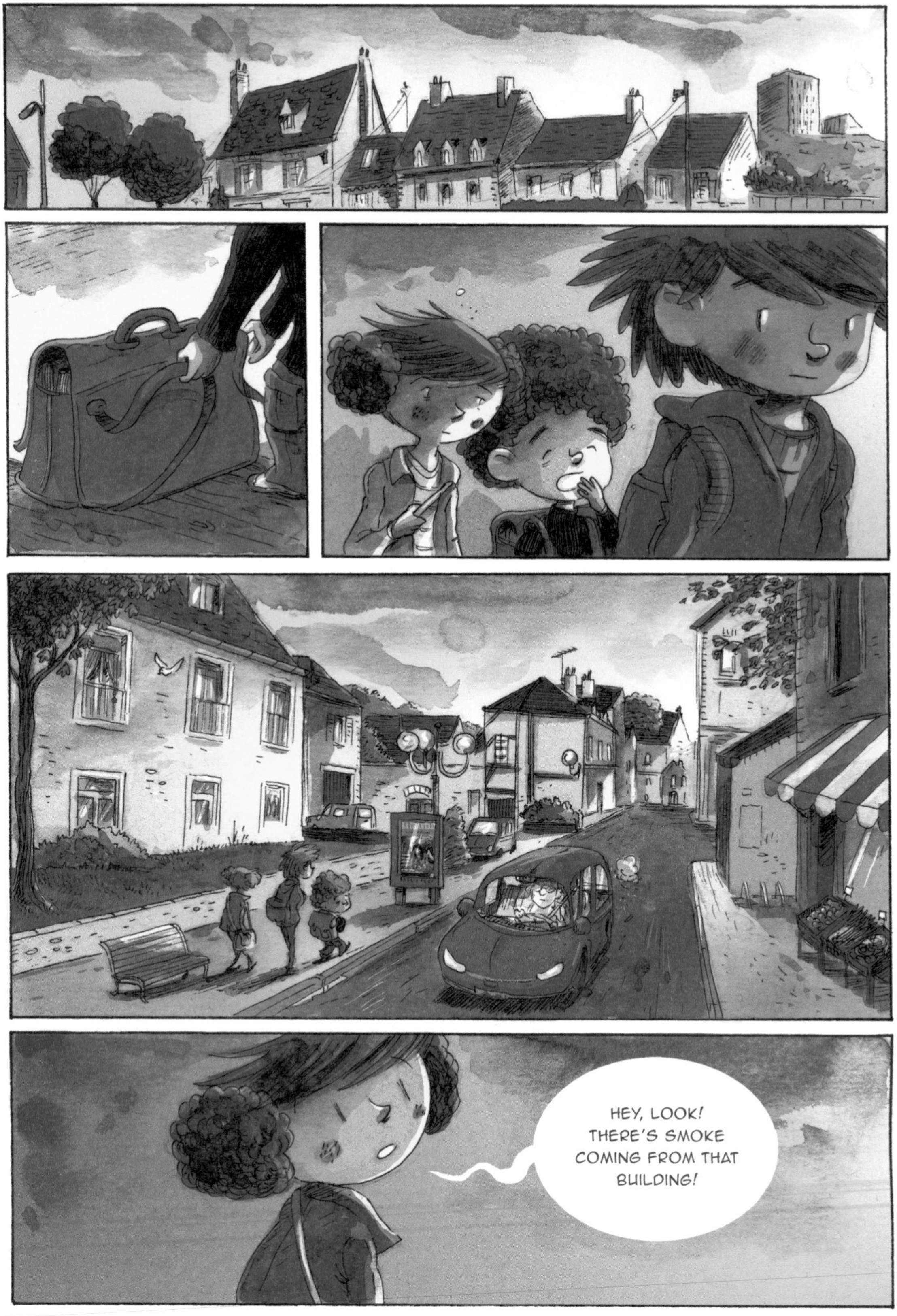
HEY, LOOK! THERE'S SMOKE COMING FROM THAT BUILDING!

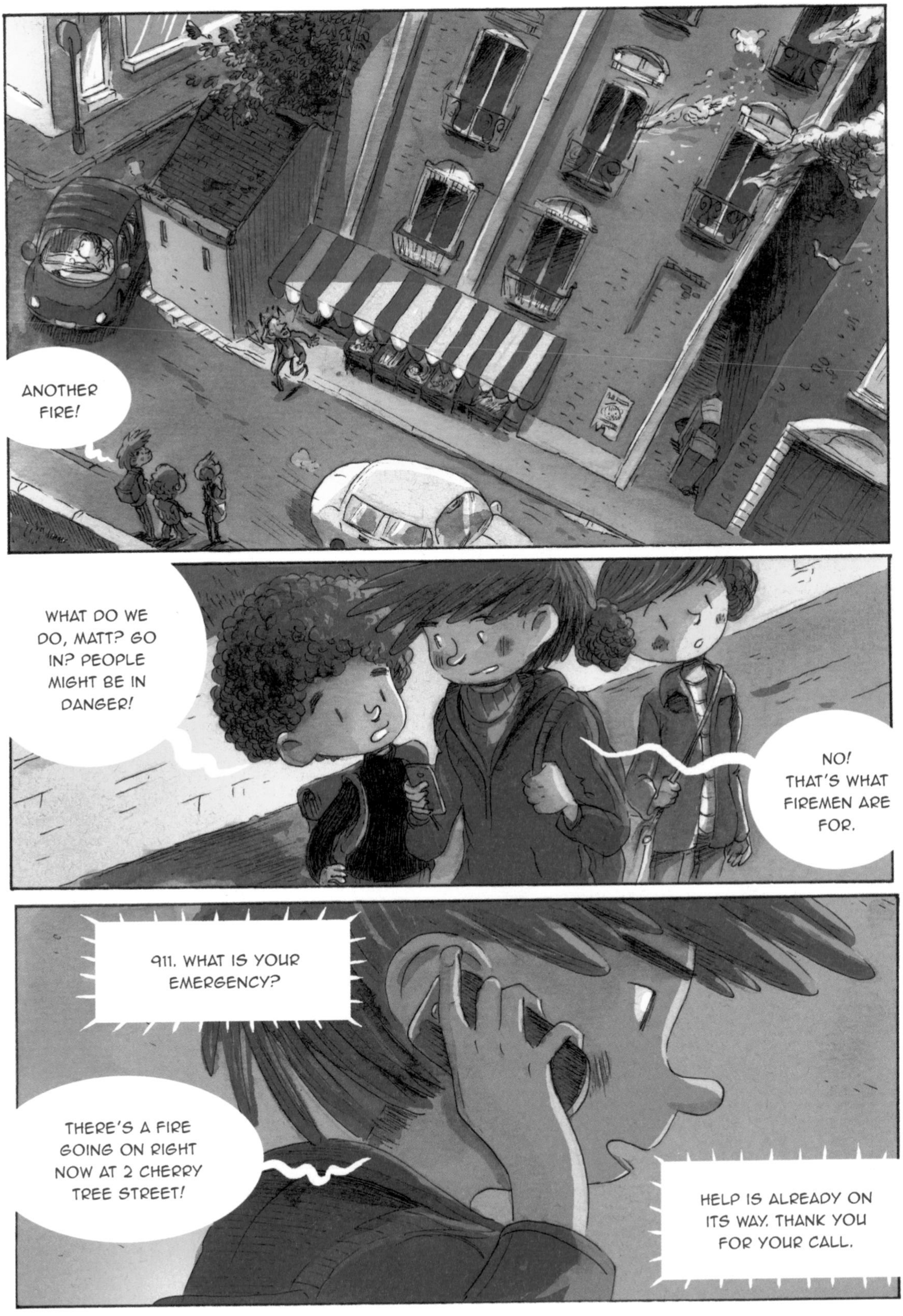
ANOTHER FIRE!
WHAT DO WE DO, MATT? GO IN? PEOPLE MIGHT BE IN DANGER!
NO! THAT'S WHAT FIREMEN ARE FOR.
911. WHAT IS YOUR EMERGENCY?
THERE'S A FIRE GOING ON RIGHT NOW AT 2 CHERRY TREE STREET!
HELP IS ALREADY ON ITS WAY. THANK YOU FOR YOUR CALL.

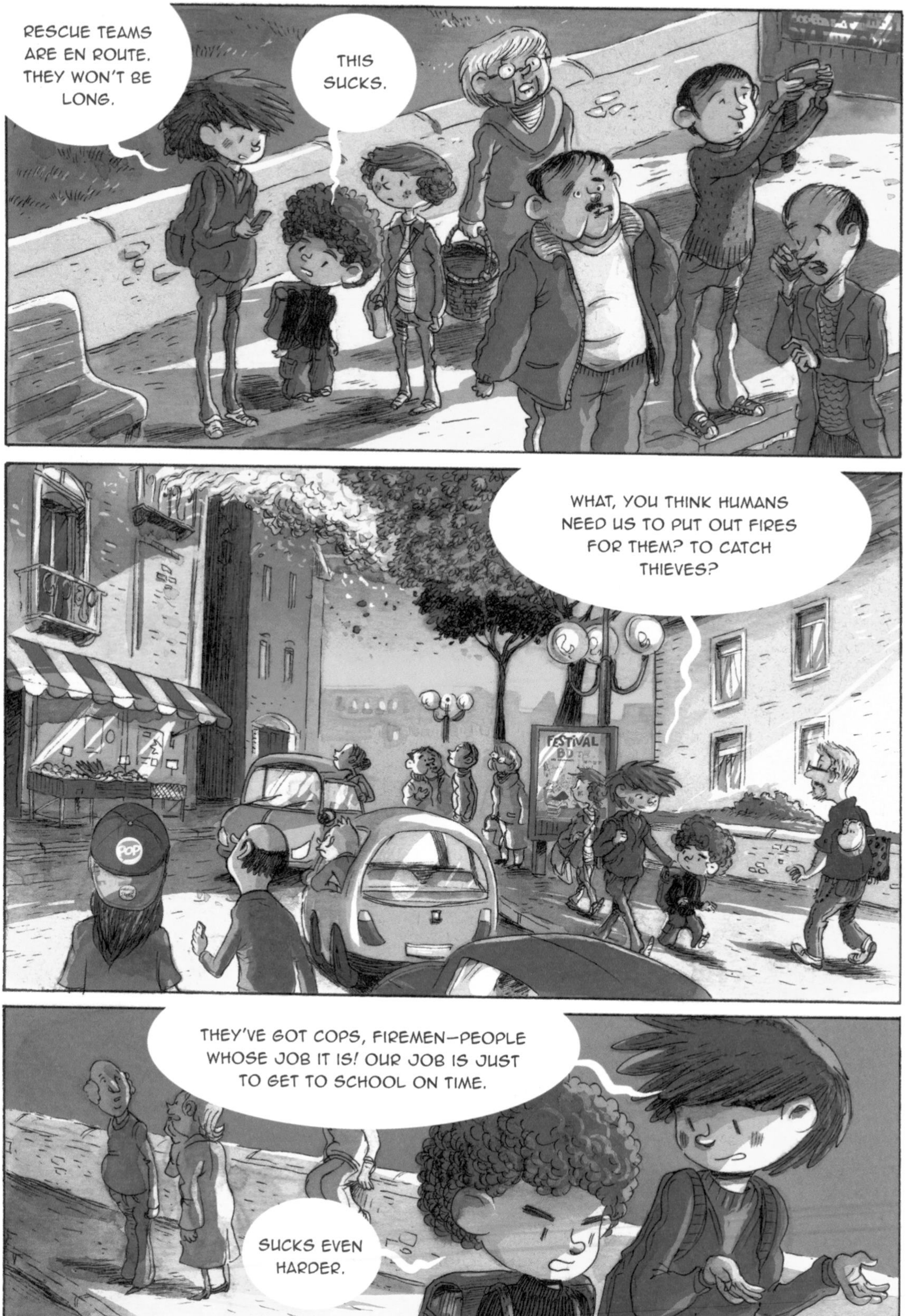
RESCUE TEAMS ARE EN ROUTE. THEY WON'T BE LONG.
THIS SUCKS.
FESTIVAL BD
WHAT, YOU THINK HUMANS NEED US TO PUT OUT FIRES FOR THEM? TO CATCH THIEVES?
THEY'VE GOT COPS, FIREMEN—PEOPLE WHOSE JOB IT IS! OUR JOB IS JUST TO GET TO SCHOOL ON TIME.
SUCKS EVEN HARDER.

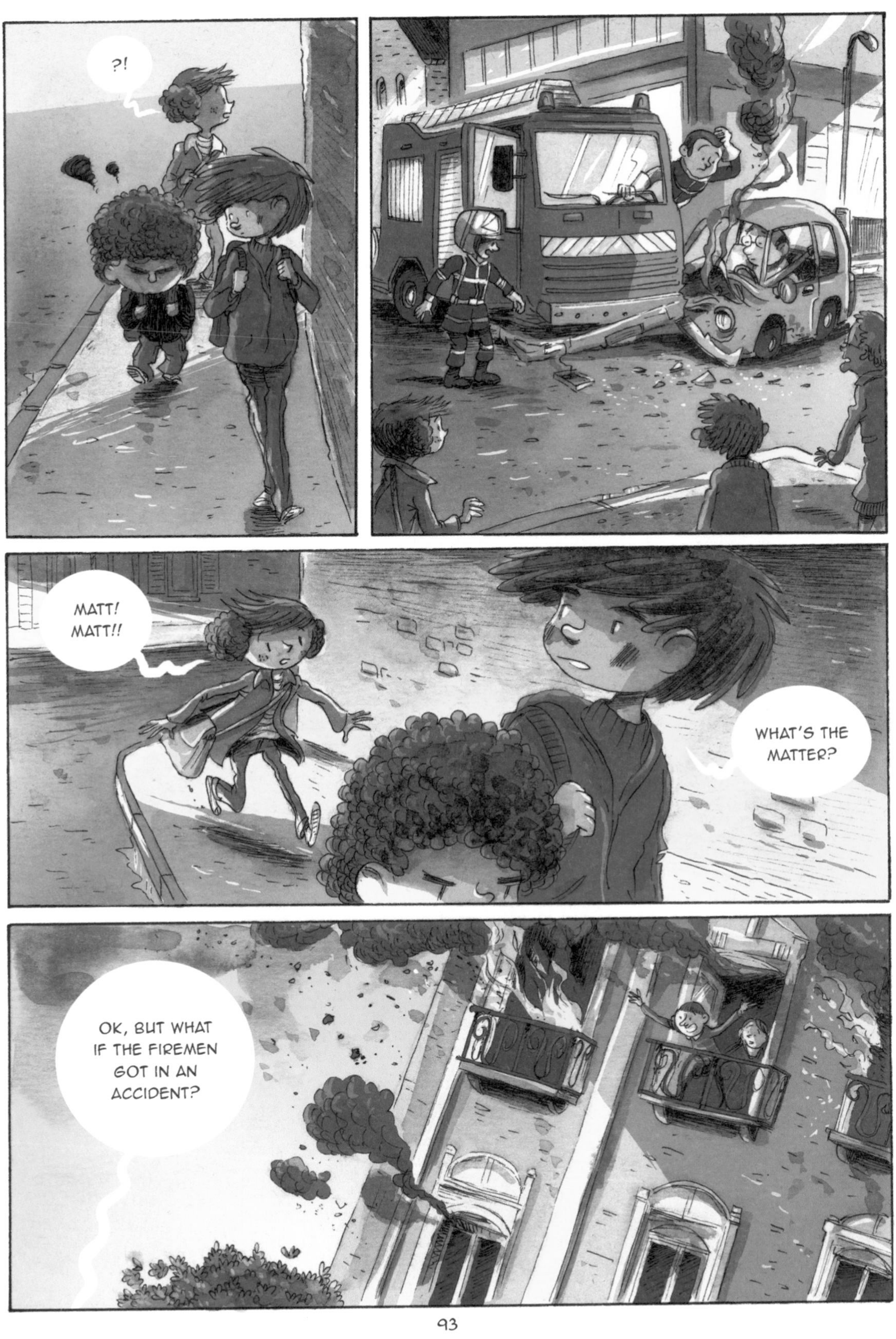
?!
MATT! MATT!!
WHAT'S THE MATTER?
OK, BUT WHAT IF THE FIREMEN GOT IN AN ACCIDENT?

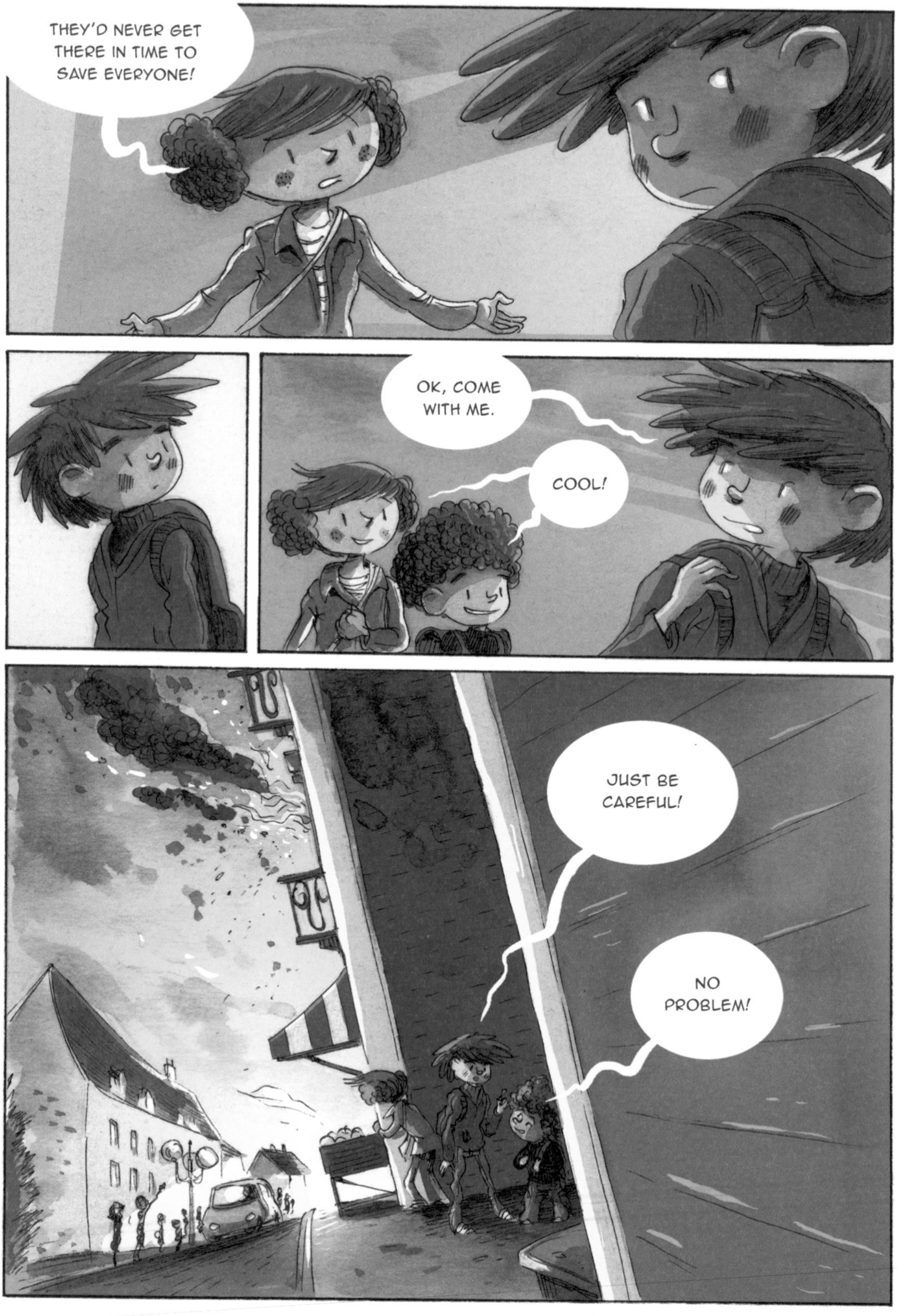
THEY'D NEVER GET THERE IN TIME TO SAVE EVERYONE!
OK, COME WITH ME.
COOL!
JUST BE CAREFUL!
NO PROBLEM!

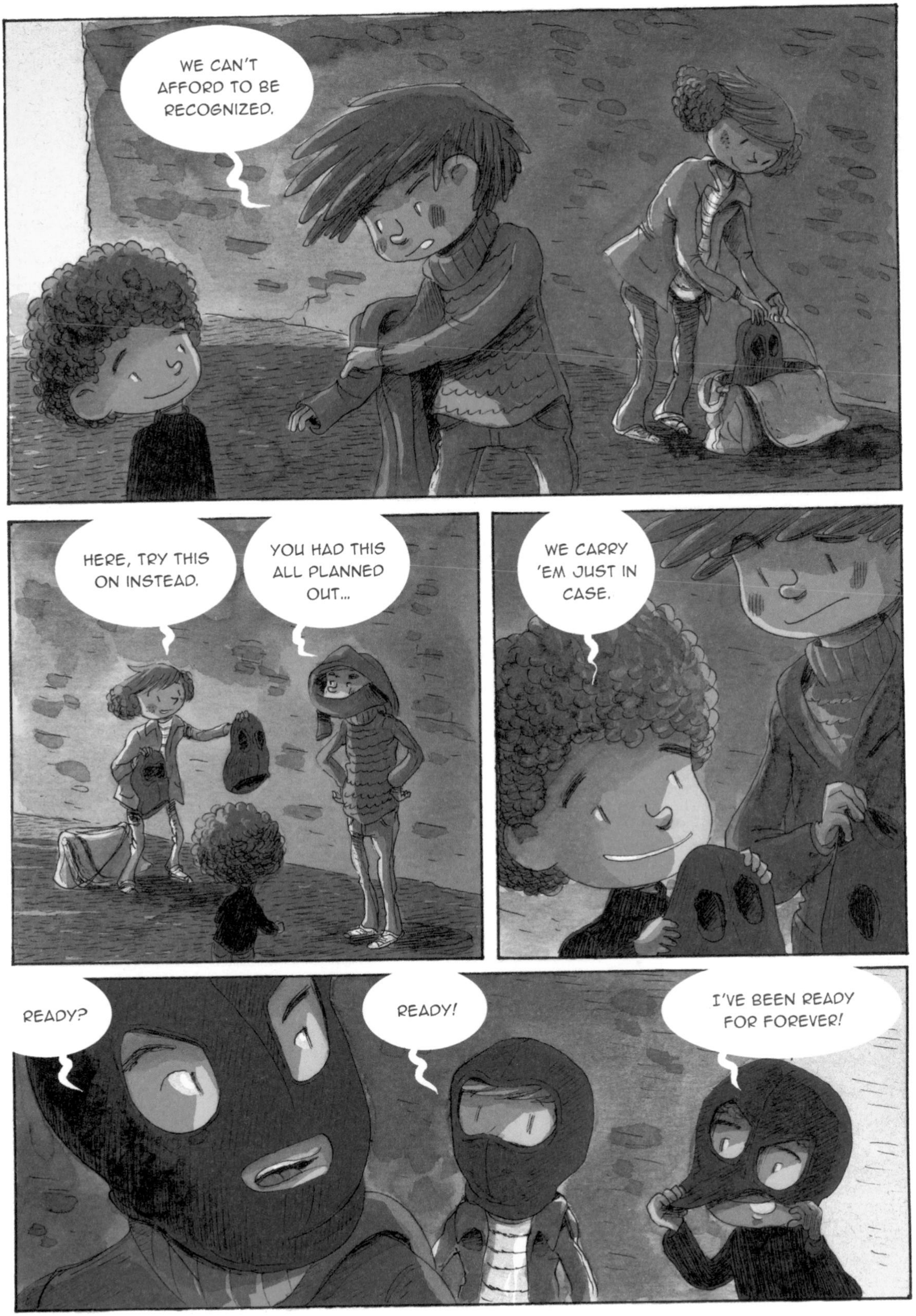
WE CAN'T AFFORD TO BE RECOGNIZED.
HERE, TRY THIS ON INSTEAD.
YOU HAD THIS ALL PLANNED OUT...
WE CARRY 'EM JUST IN CASE.
READY?
READY!
I'VE BEEN READY FOR FOREVER!

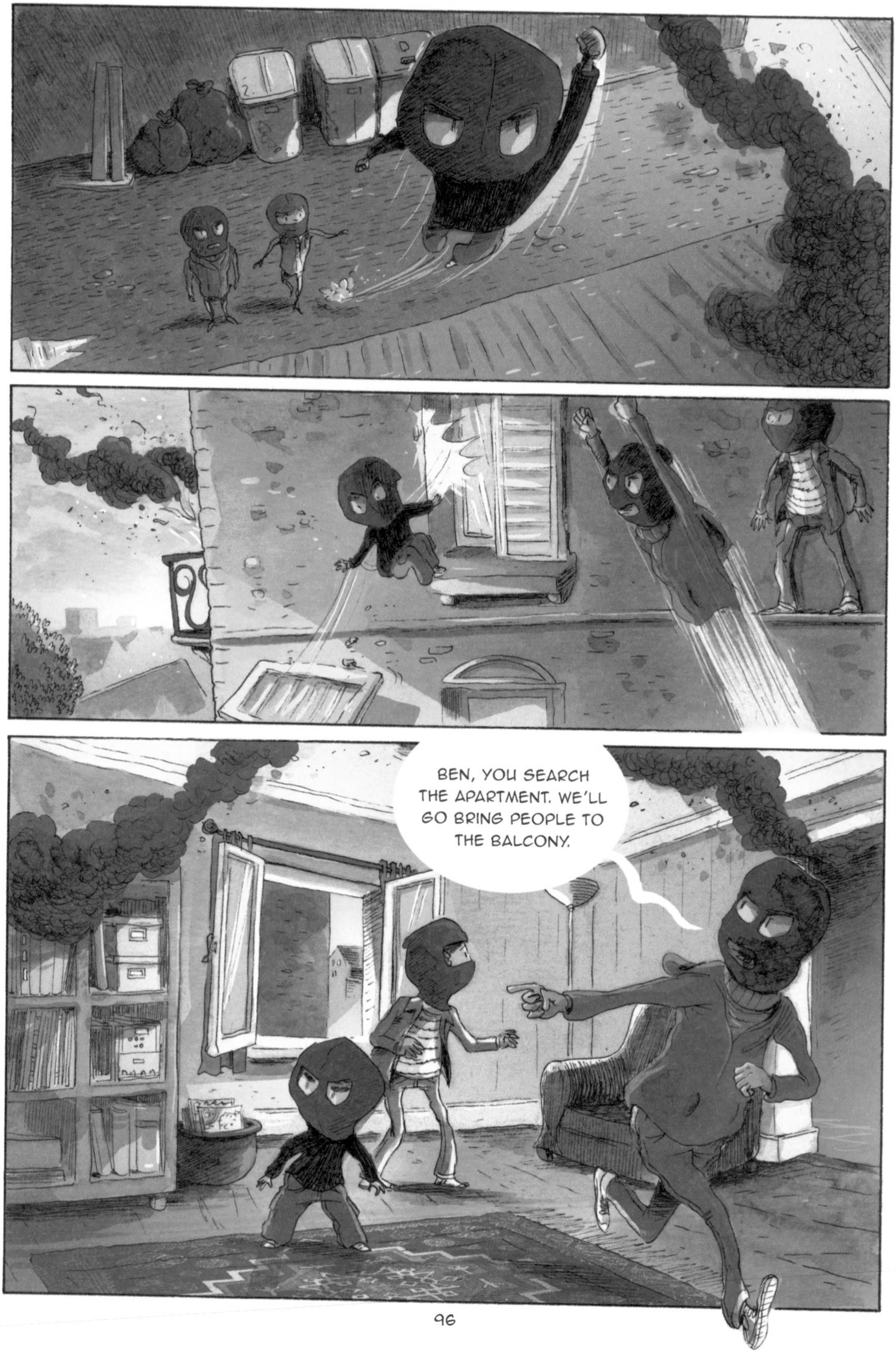
BEN, YOU SEARCH THE APARTMENT. WE'LL GO BRING PEOPLE TO THE BALCONY.

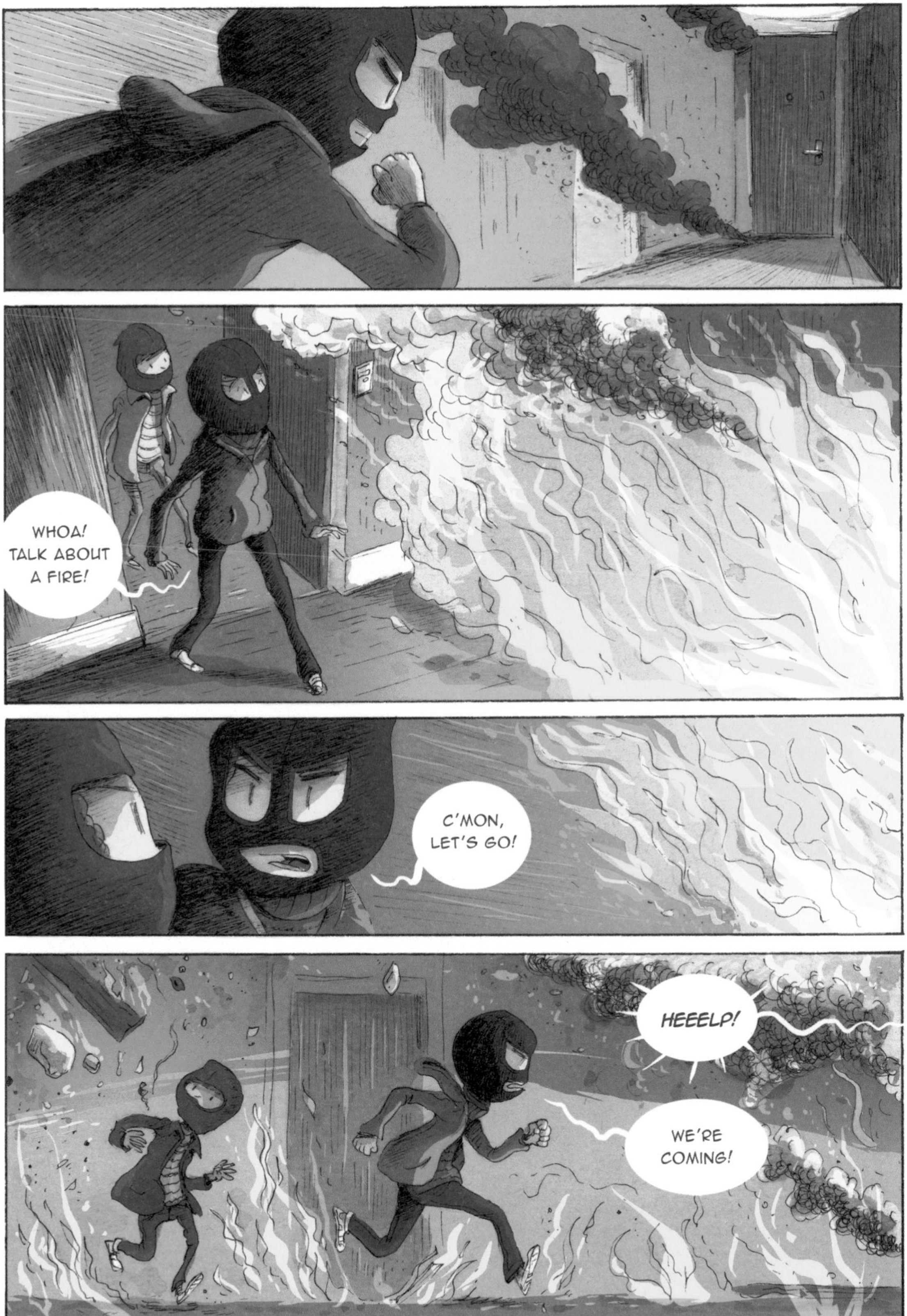
WHOA! TALK ABOUT A FIRE!
C'MON, LET'S GO!
HEEELP!
WE'RE COMING!

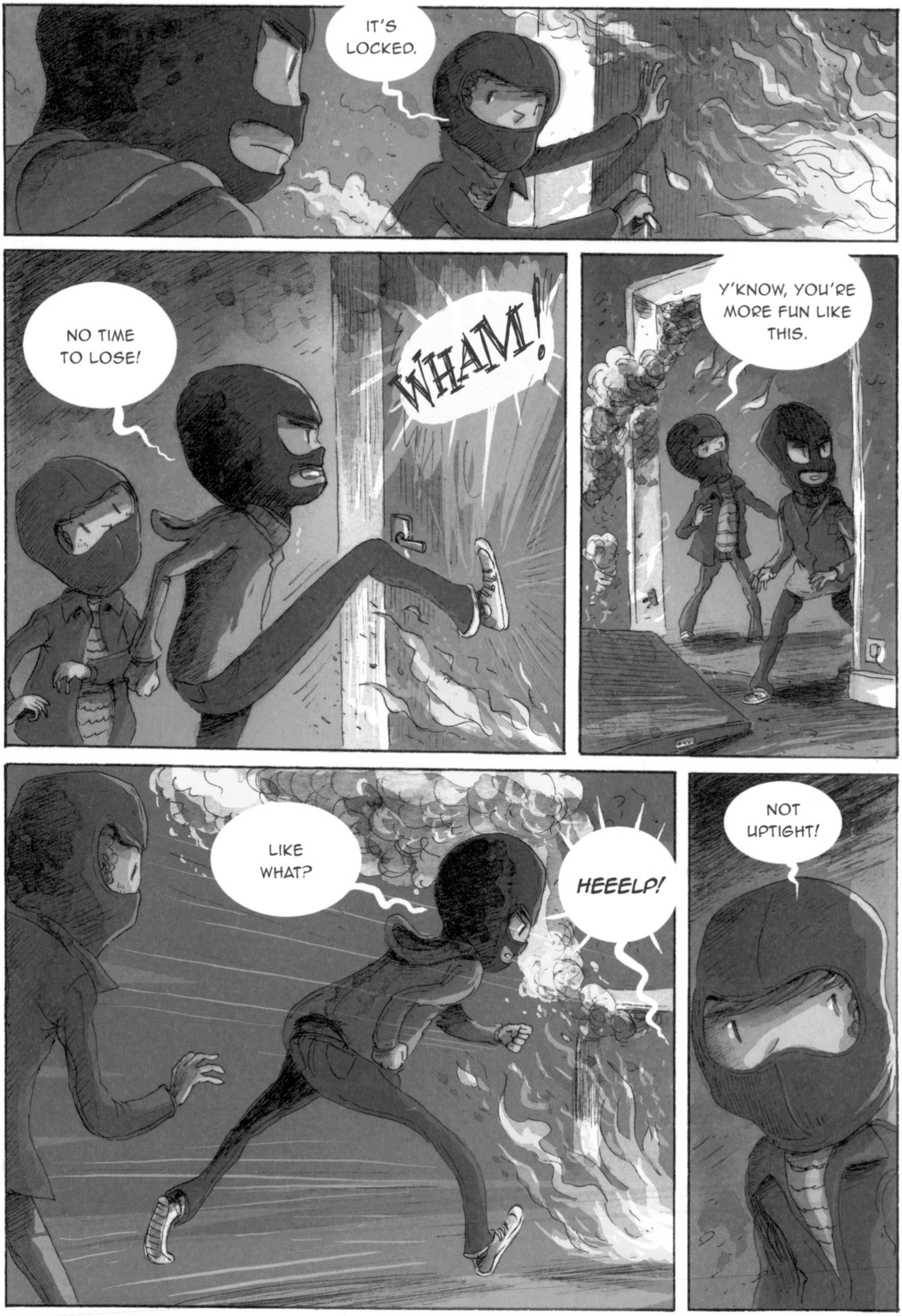
IT'S LOCKED.
NO TIME TO LOSE!
WHAM!
Y'KNOW, YOU'RE MORE FUN LIKE THIS.
LIKE WHAT?
HEEELP!
NOT UPTIGHT!

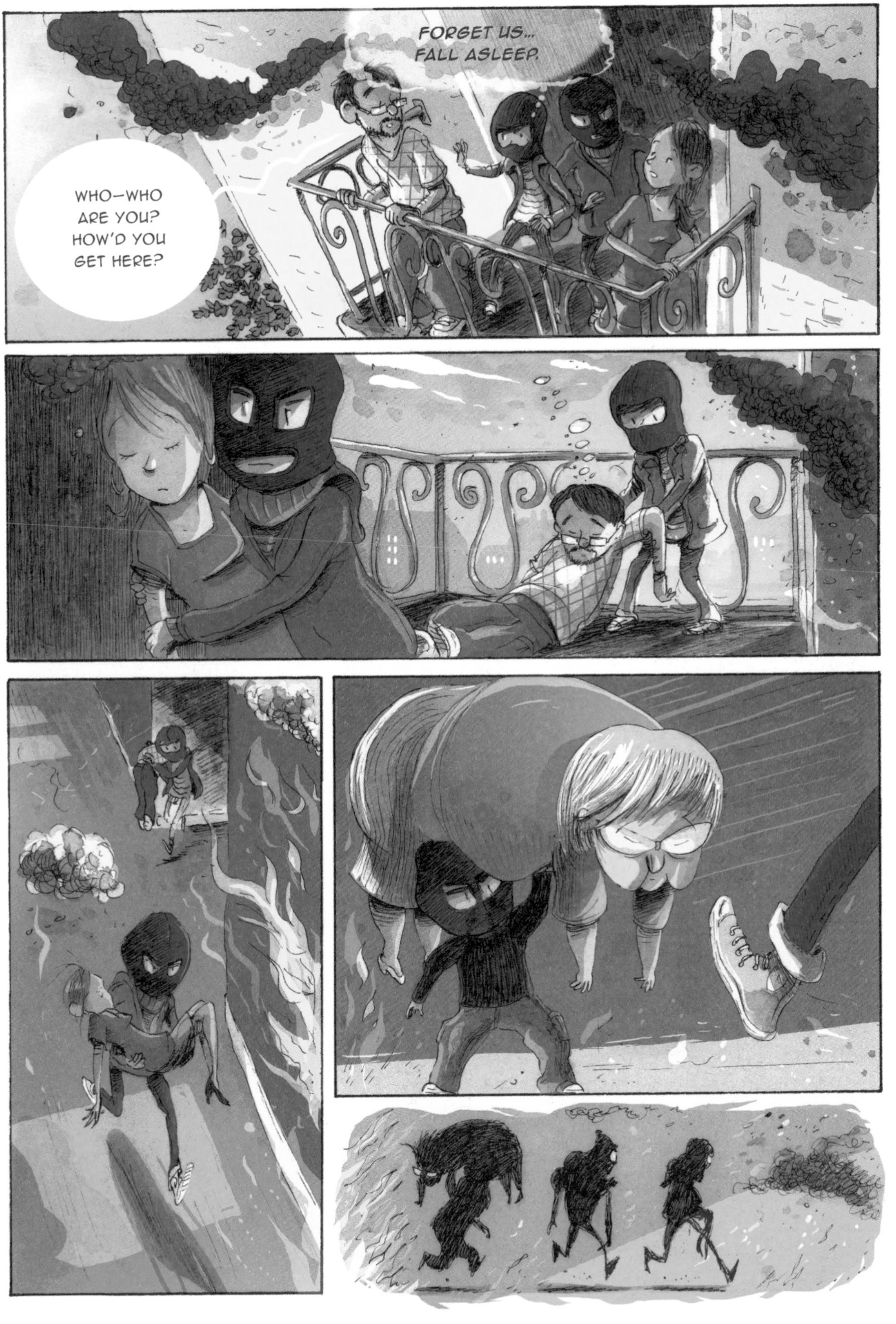
FORGET US... FALL ASLEEP.
WHO—WHO ARE YOU? HOW'D YOU GET HERE?

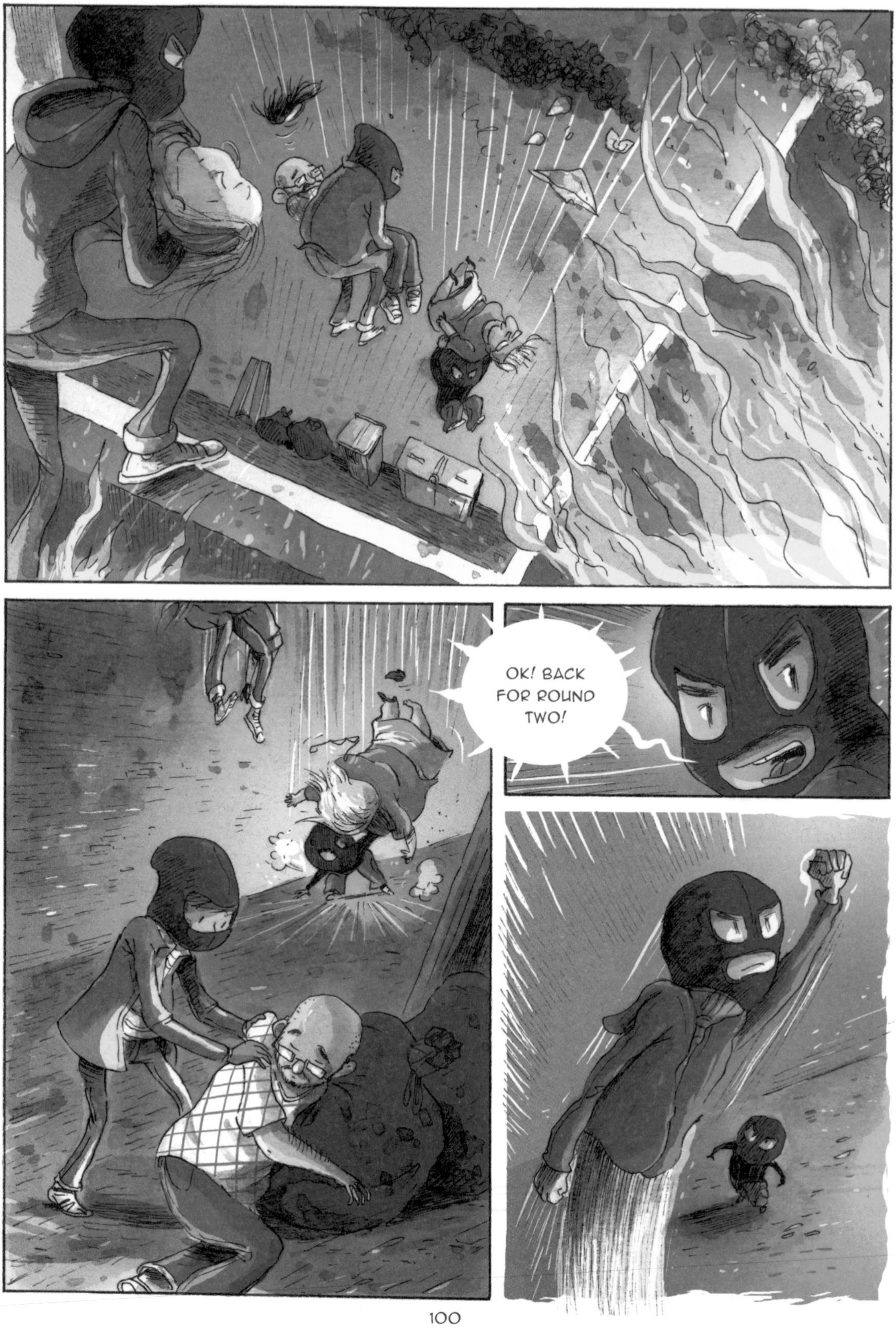
OK! BACK FOR ROUND TWO!

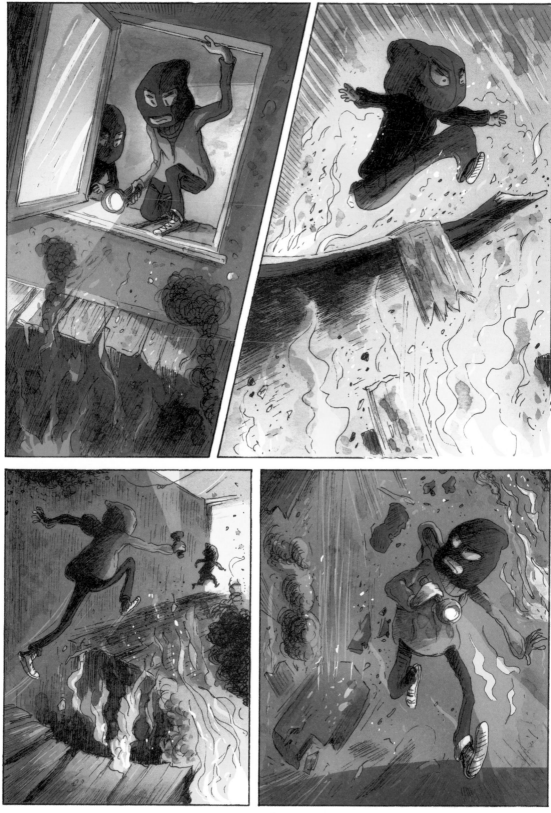

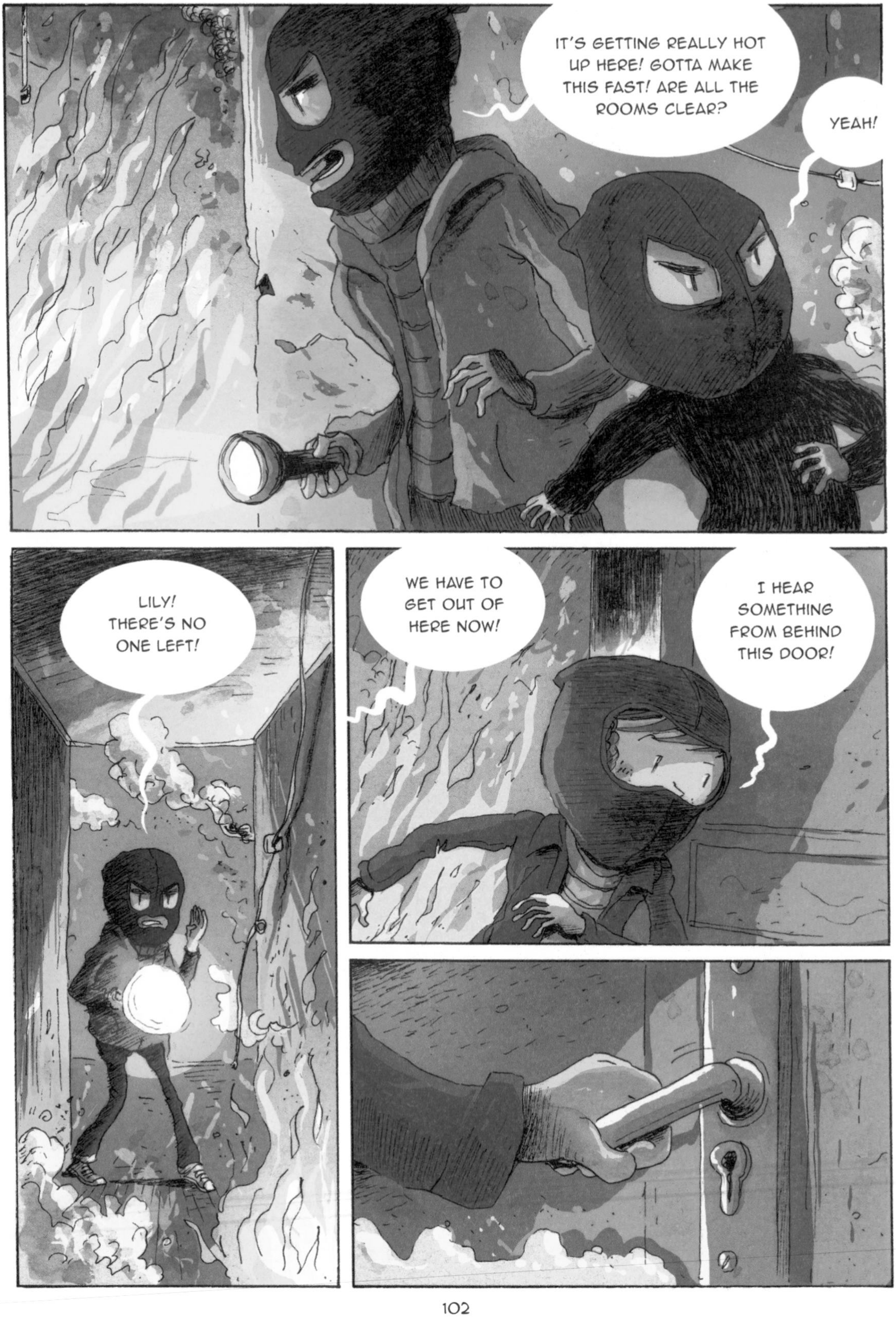
IT'S GETTING REALLY HOT UP HERE! GOTTA MAKE THIS FAST! ARE ALL THE ROOMS CLEAR?
YEAH!
LILY! THERE'S NO ONE LEFT!
WE HAVE TO GET OUT OF HERE NOW!
I HEAR SOMETHING FROM BEHIND THIS DOOR!

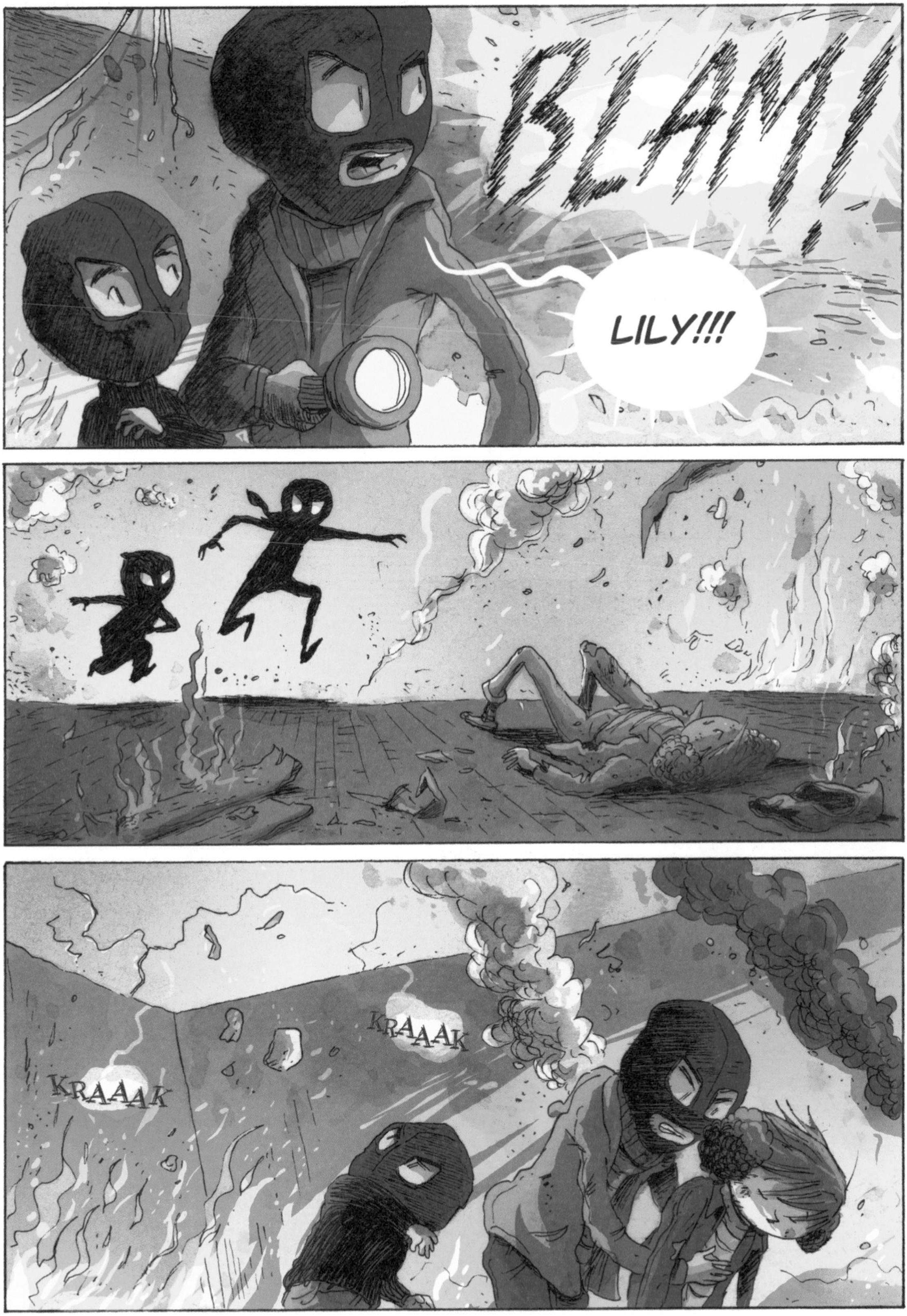
BLAM!
LILY!!!
KRAAAK
KRAAAK

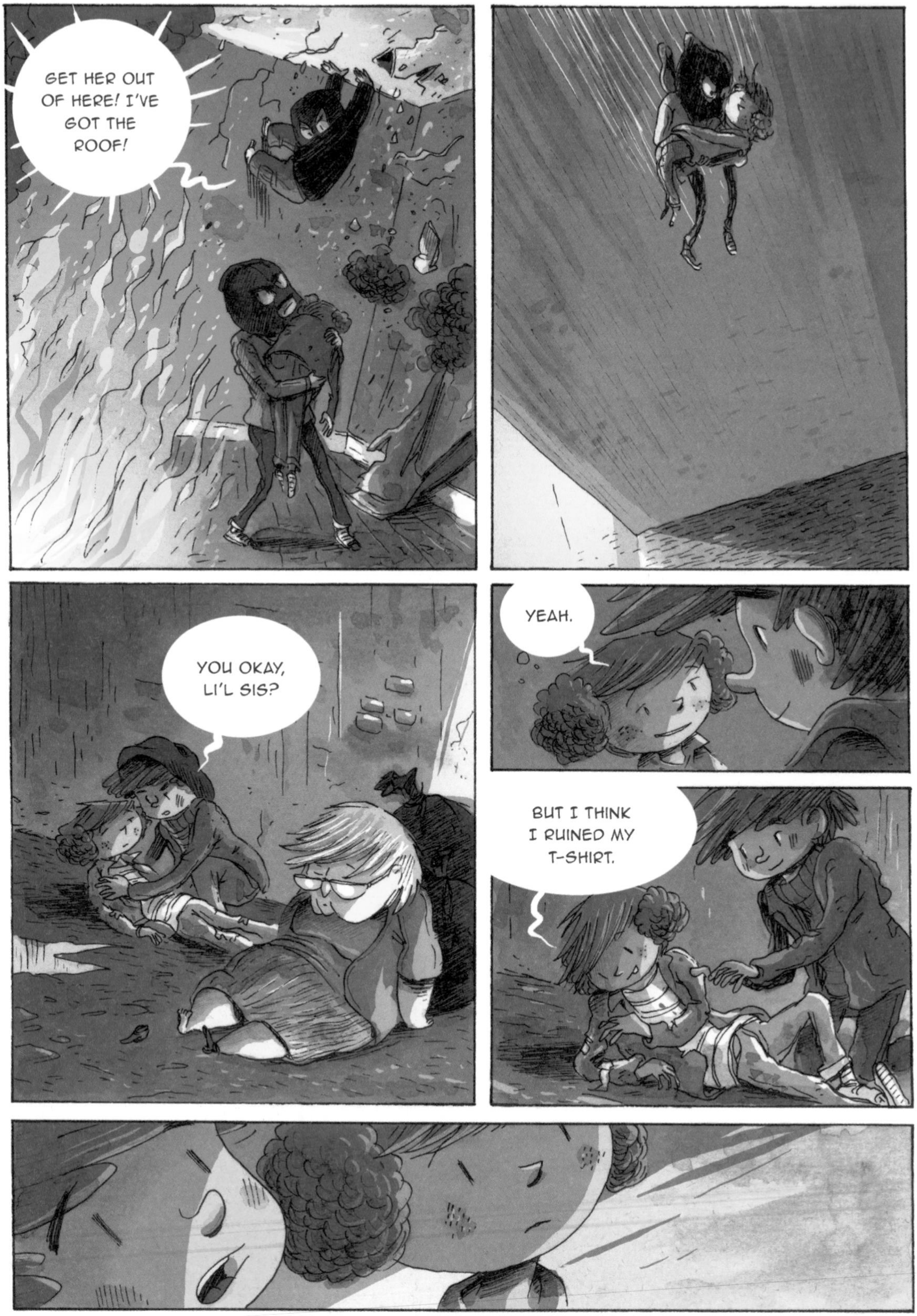
GET HER OUT OF HERE! I'VE GOT THE ROOF!
YOU OKAY, LI'L SIS?
YEAH.
BUT I THINK I RUINED MY T-SHIRT.

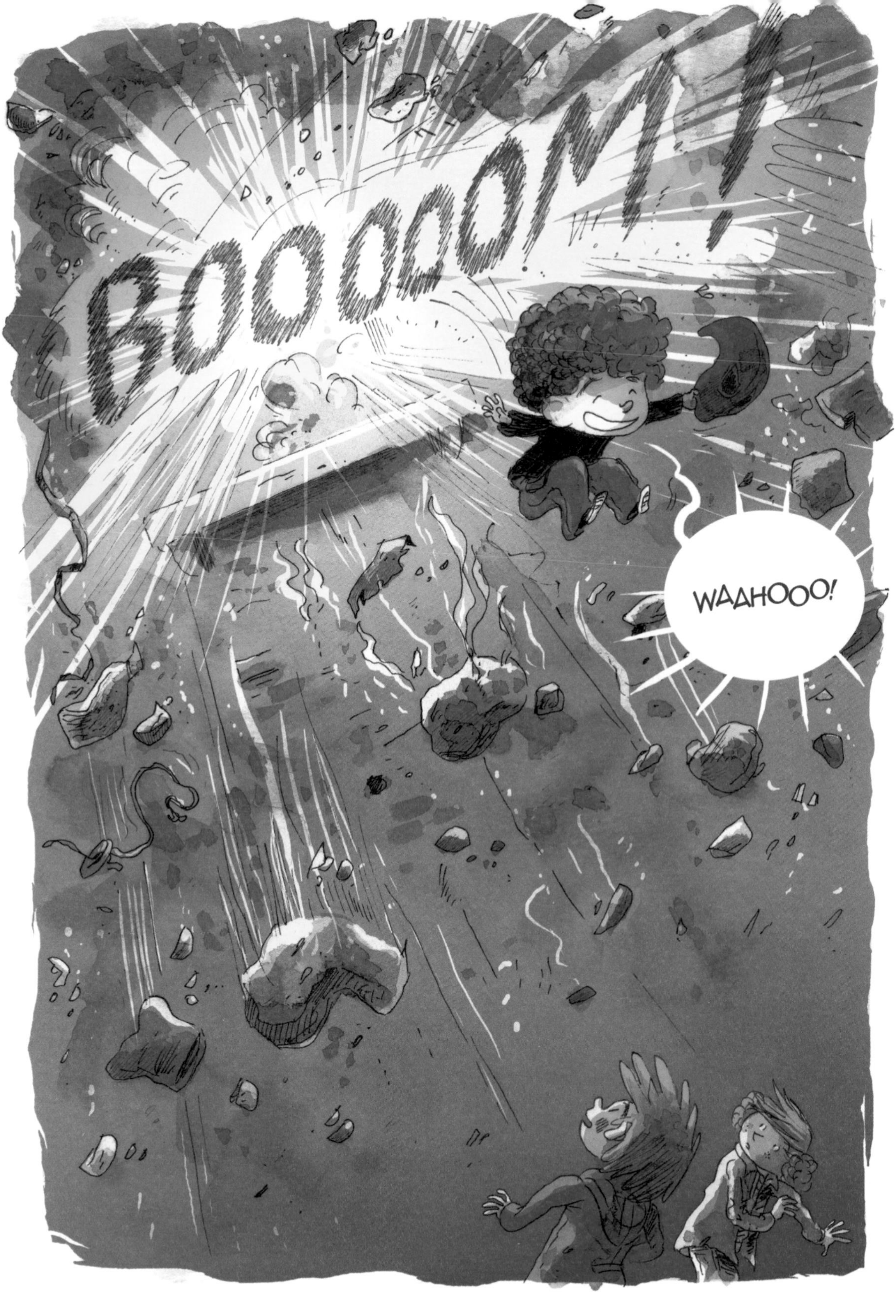
BOOOOOOM!
WAAHOOO!

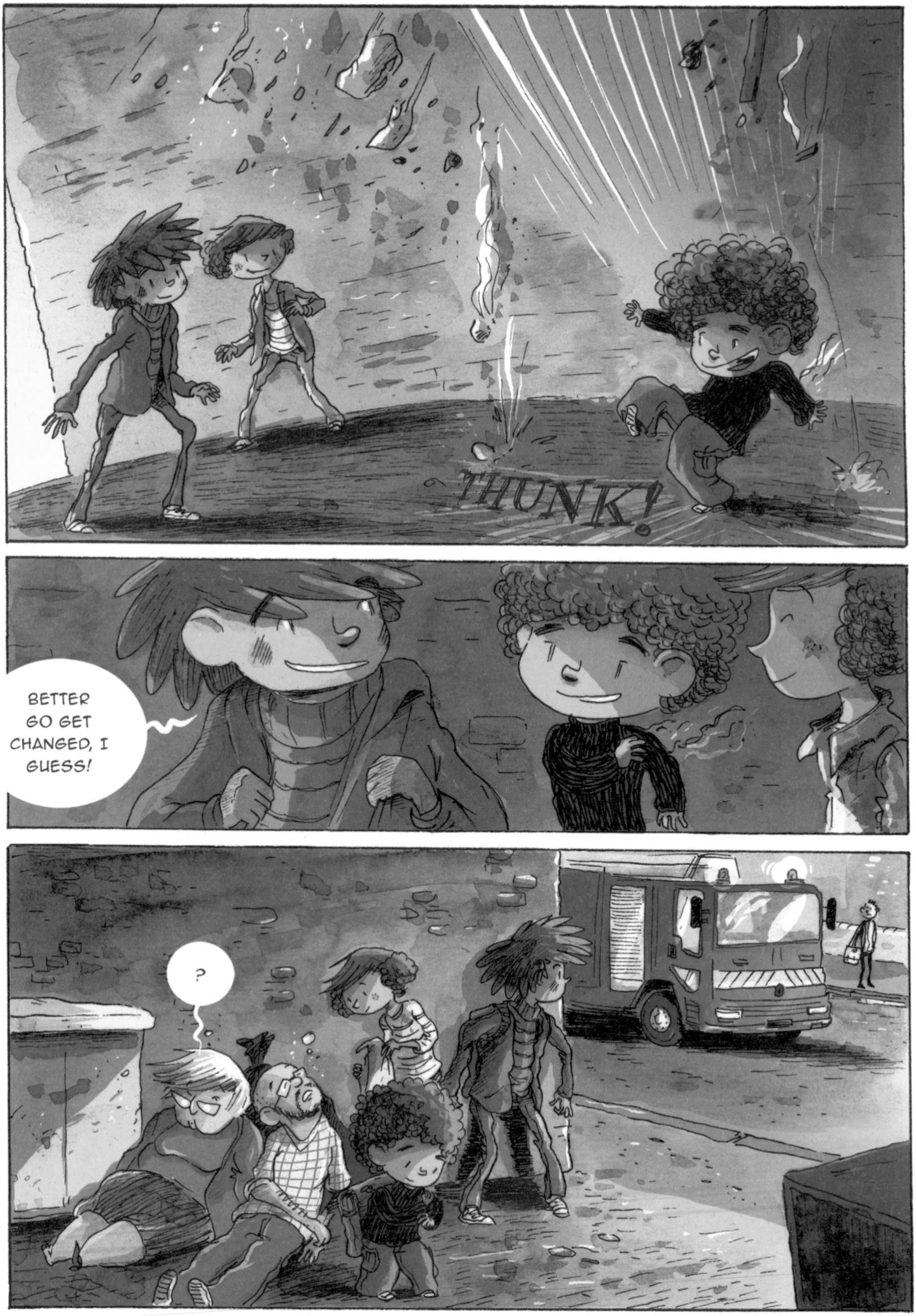
THUNK!
BETTER GO GET CHANGED, I GUESS!
?

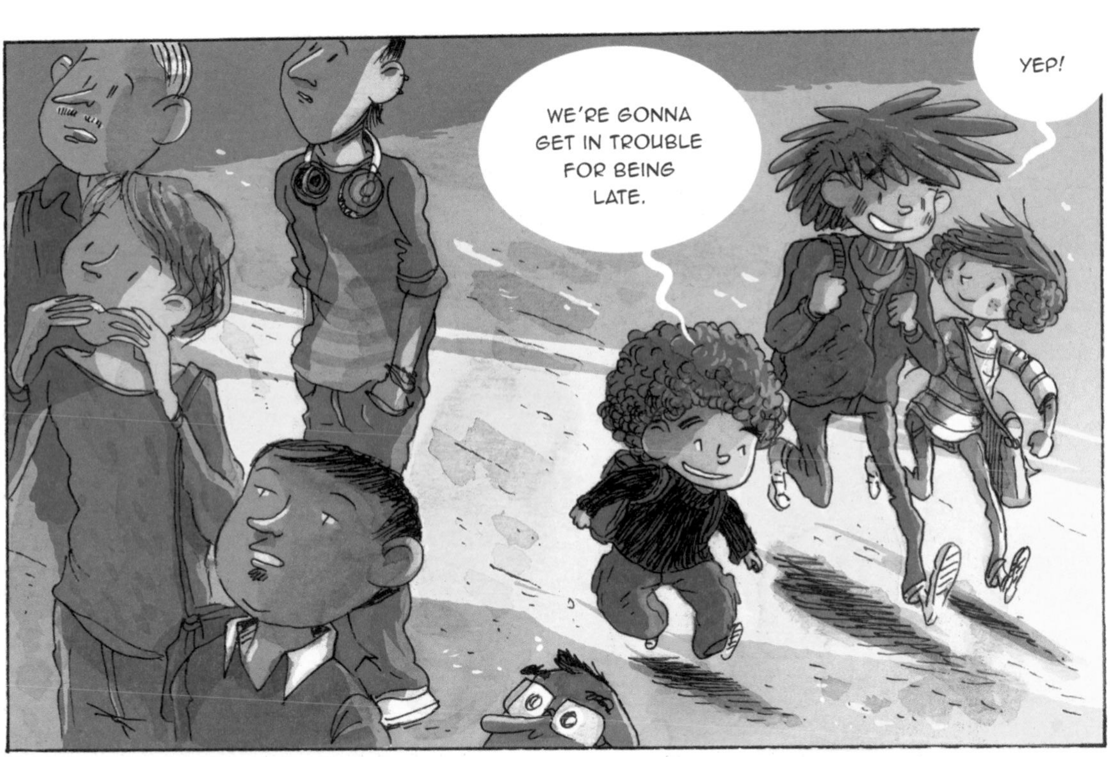
WE'RE GONNA GET IN TROUBLE FOR BEING LATE.
YEP!

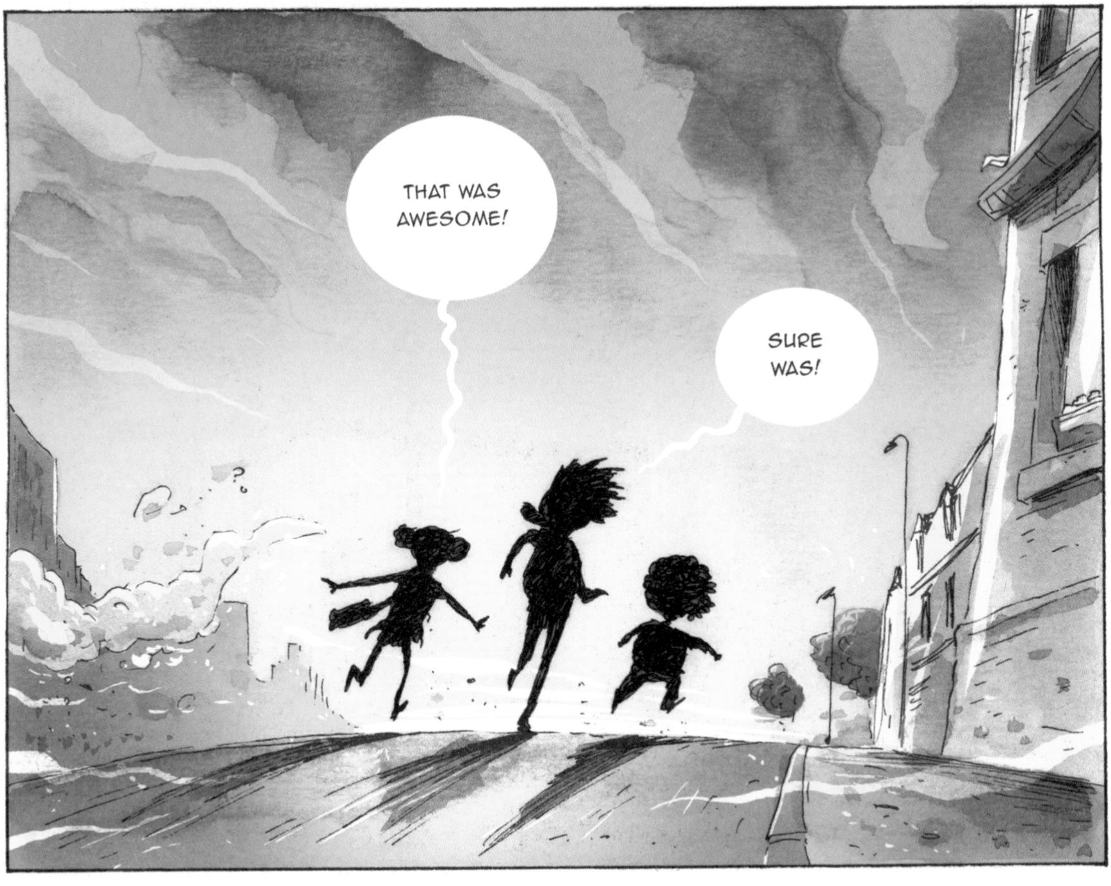
THAT WAS AWESOME!
SURE WAS!

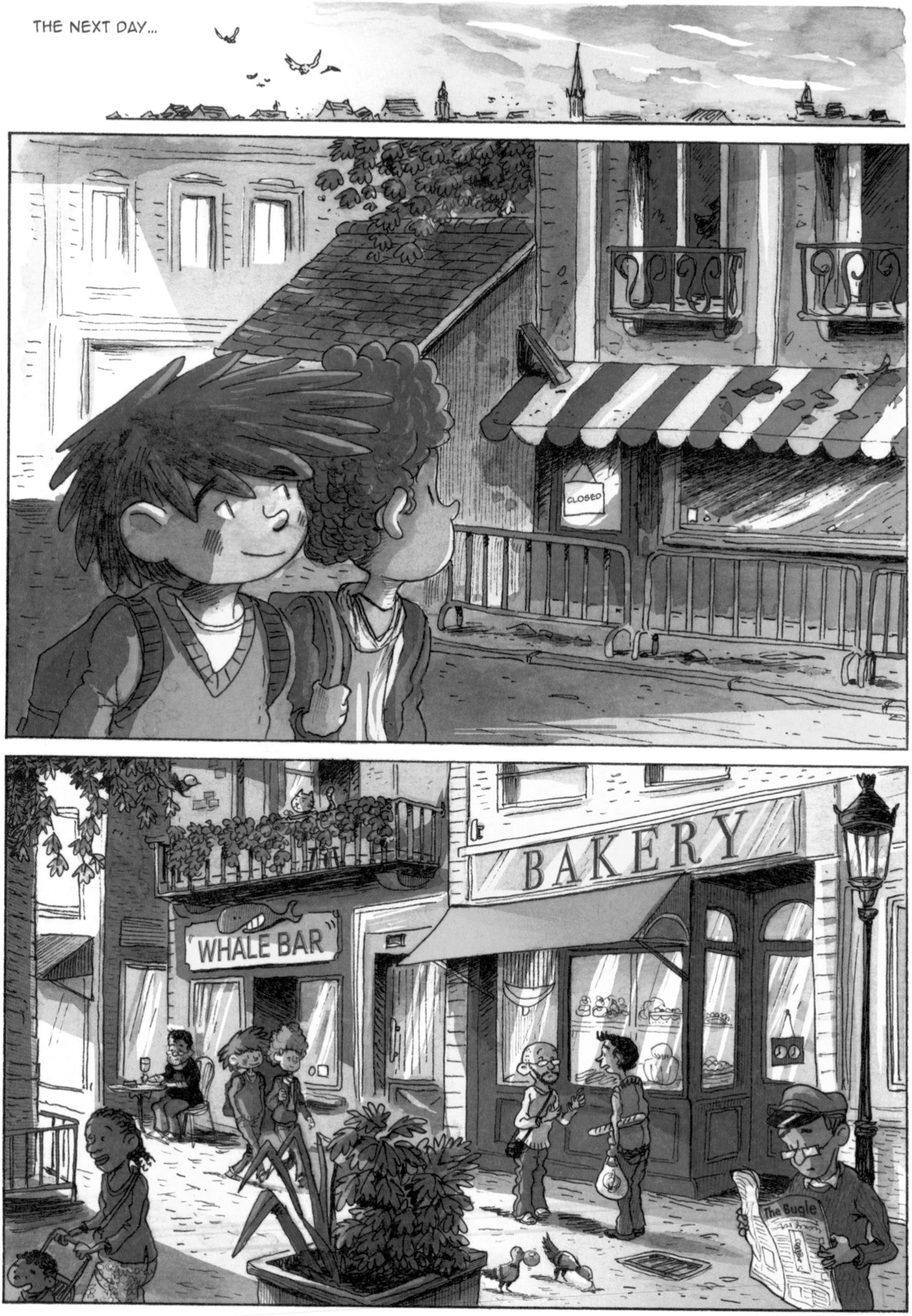
THE NEXT DAY...
CLOSED
WHALE BAR
BAKERY
The Bugle

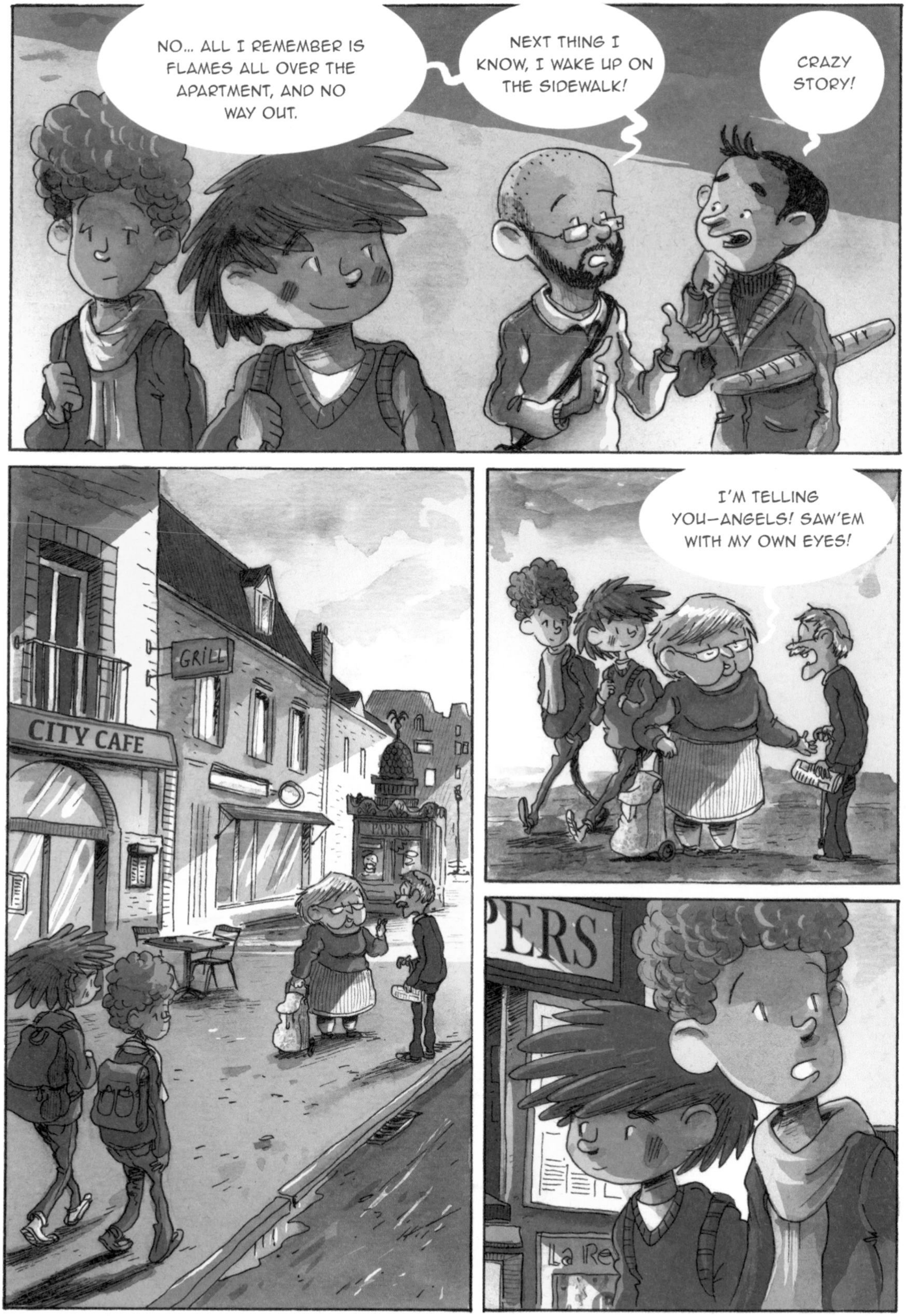
NO... ALL I REMEMBER IS FLAMES ALL OVER THE APARTMENT, AND NO WAY OUT.
NEXT THING I KNOW, I WAKE UP ON THE SIDEWALK!
CRAZY STORY!
CITY CAFE
GRILL
PAPERS
I'M TELLING YOU—ANGELS! SAW'EM WITH MY OWN EYES!
PERS
La Re

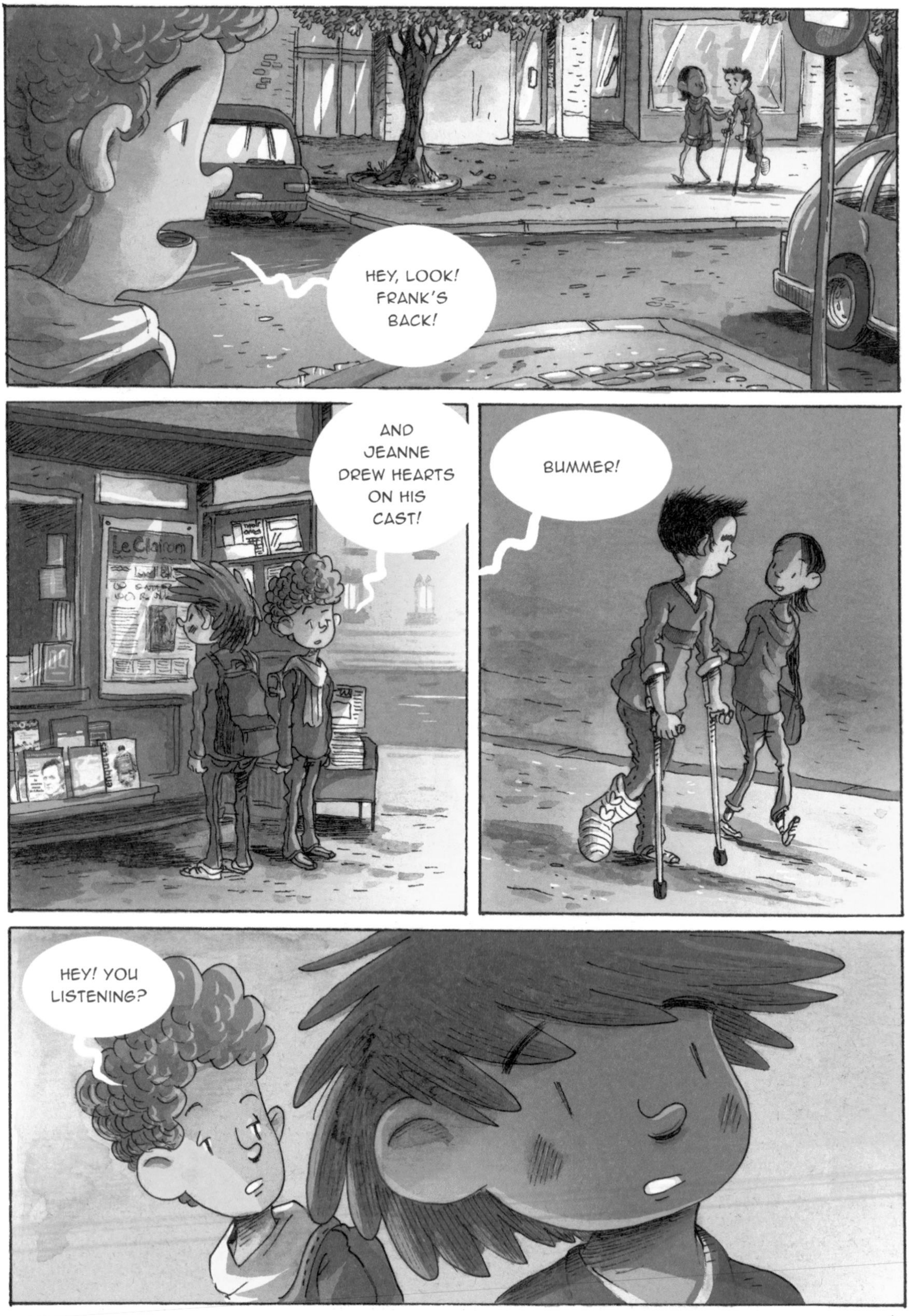
HEY, LOOK! FRANK'S BACK!
AND JEANNE DREW HEARTS ON HIS CAST!
BUMMER!
HEY! YOU LISTENING?

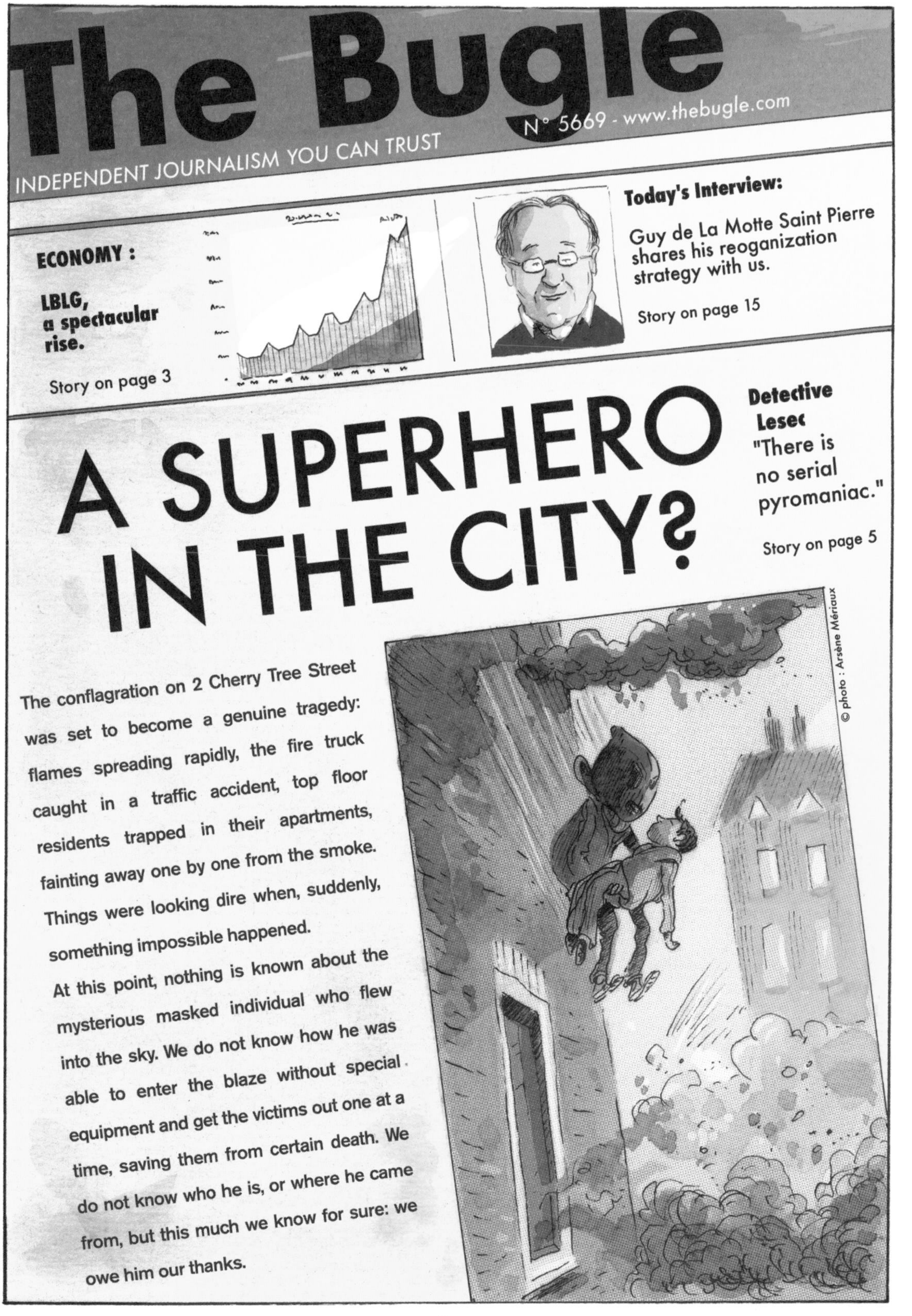

The Bugle

N° 5669 - www.thebugle.com

INDEPENDENT JOURNALISM YOU CAN TRUST

ECONOMY :

LBLG, a spectacular rise.

Story on page 3

Today's Interview:

Guy de La Motte Saint Pierre shares his reoganization strategy with us.

Story on page 15

A SUPERHERO IN THE CITY?

Detective Lesec

"There is no serial pyromaniac."

Story on page 5

© photo : Arsène Mériaux

The conflagration on 2 Cherry Tree Street was set to become a genuine tragedy: flames spreading rapidly, the fire truck caught in a traffic accident, top floor residents trapped in their apartments, fainting away one by one from the smoke. Things were looking dire when, suddenly, something impossible happened.

At this point, nothing is known about the mysterious masked individual who flew into the sky. We do not know how he was able to enter the blaze without special equipment and get the victims out one at a time, saving them from certain death. We do not know who he is, or where he came from, but this much we know for sure: we owe him our thanks.

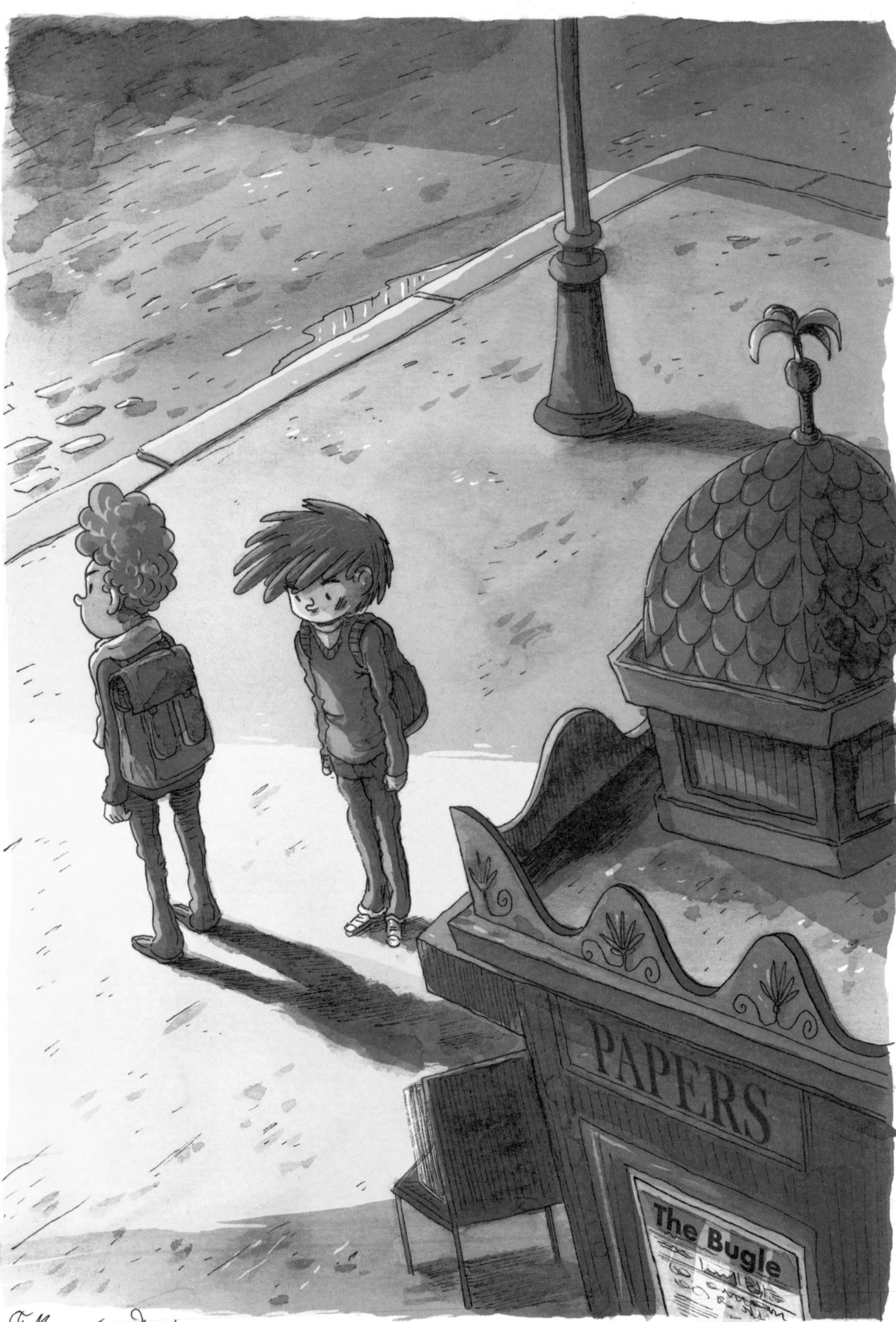
PAPERS
The Bugle

F. Maupomé & Dawid

13 VII 2015